Murder in
Rose Hill

MURDER IN ROSE HILL

A Gaslight Mystery

Victoria Thompson

BERKLEY PRIME CRIME
NEW YORK

BERKLEY PRIME CRIME
Published by Berkley
An imprint of Penguin Random House LLC
penguinrandomhouse.com

Library of Congress Cataloging-in-Publication Data

Names: Thompson, Victoria (Victoria E.), author.
Title: Murder in Rose Hill / Victoria Thompson.
Description: New York : Berkley Prime Crime, 2024. | Series: A Gaslight Mystery
Identifiers: LCCN 2023037123 (print) | LCCN 2023037124 (ebook) |
ISBN 9780593639795 (hardcover) | ISBN 9780593639818 (ebook) |
Subjects: LCGFT: Detective and mystery fiction. | Novels.
Classification: LCC PS3570.H6442 M86553 2024 (print) |
LCC PS3570.H6442 (ebook) | DDC 813/.54—dc23/eng/20230828
LC record available at https://lccn.loc.gov/2023037123
LC ebook record available at https://lccn.loc.gov/2023037124

Printed in the United States of America
1st Printing

*With thanks to the Survivors who gave me
the support I needed in the darkest time
and who make the sunlight on the other side brighter*

Murder in
Rose Hill

I

Iᴛ's ᴀ ɢɪʀʟ!"

Sarah Brandt Malloy held up the squalling infant she had just delivered so the mother could see it.

"Poor mite," the woman said wearily, raising her head from the pillows to see better. "I was hoping for a boy. They have an easier time of it in this world."

Sarah couldn't argue with that. Males had a lot of advantages, and when you started your life as the illegitimate child of a penniless mother, as this baby was, those advantages helped.

"I know you'll do your best for her, Mary," Sarah said.

Mary sank back on the pillows and sighed. "I already been doing my best, and if it wasn't for this clinic, I'd have birthed her in an alley."

Which was why Sarah had founded the clinic in the first

place, to give women like Mary a safe place to have their babies. "Don't lose heart," she said, handing the baby to Miss Kirkwood, one of the other midwives employed at the clinic. "You can stay here until you recover and then we'll help you find a job."

Mary didn't reply, but Sarah didn't notice because she was busy massaging Mary's stomach to encourage the delivery of the afterbirth. Miss Kirkwood had cleaned up the baby and wrapped her in a fresh blanket, but when she tried to hand the child to the mother, Mary turned her head away.

"Don't. I'm not going to keep her. I can't."

"You don't have to decide right now," Sarah said as gently as she could. "As I said, you can stay here until you have your strength back. Then you can decide."

But Mary shook her head. "I already decided. It's best for her. I don't want her growing up in the streets like I did."

Growing up in an orphanage wouldn't be much better for the child, but Sarah knew better than to argue with a woman whose emotions were still running wild from childbirth. "At least nurse her a little," Sarah urged. "It's for your own good. You'll recover faster if you do."

Miss Kirkwood offered the baby again and this time Mary took the tiny bundle, even though she was obviously reluctant.

"I don't know what to do," Mary complained. Miss Kirkwood showed her how to put the baby to her breast, and soon the child was suckling happily.

"She don't have much hair," Mary observed after a few moments.

"It will grow," Miss Kirkwood said, brushing her fingertips over the baby's downy head. "It looks like it will be blond, like yours."

Mary didn't exactly smile but her frown relaxed a bit. Sarah said a little prayer that Mary would fall in love with her baby, as most mothers did no matter what their circumstances. But if she didn't, Sarah would do everything she could to give both Mary and her baby a chance in life.

When Mary and the baby were both cleaned up and comfortable, Sarah bundled up the soiled towels and sheets and was getting ready to leave the new mother and her child to rest when someone knocked on the bedroom door.

It was one of the other women who were currently staying at the clinic. This woman had given birth a few weeks ago and would soon leave. "Mrs. Malloy, there's a lady here, and she asked to see you in particular."

That was odd. Prospective patients didn't usually ask for Sarah since she came to the clinic only occasionally. She had been lucky today to find one of the residents was in labor, so she got to help with a delivery. She had once made her living as a midwife, but rarely had a chance to make a delivery anymore now that she was a rich matron able to sponsor charities.

"She asked for me by name?" Sarah said to clarify.

"Not by name, but she wanted to speak to the lady in charge, and I thought she must mean you."

Sarah smiled and thanked her.

"I'll take care of those," Miss Kirkwood said, taking the bundle of dirty linens from her.

Sarah made her way downstairs and found a young

woman waiting in the parlor of the large house she had pur-
chased and remodeled into the clinic. The parlor was now a
waiting room of sorts with comfortable chairs for the neighborhood women who had a home in which to deliver but
who still came to the clinic for prenatal care. "May I help
you?"

The woman rose. She was probably in her late twenties
with ash brown hair and chocolate-colored eyes. She wore a
dark skirt and jacket with a white shirtwaist, what had come
to be a sort of uniform for women who held paying jobs, and
a rather sensible hat. She didn't look like the type of woman
who needed the services of a charity clinic. "Are you Mrs.
Malloy?"

"Yes."

"The lady who answered the door said you founded this
clinic," the woman said.

"I started it, yes. I was a midwife myself, so I knew there
was a need for it. Are you looking for a place for yourself?"
The young woman was slender as a reed, but she might still
be expecting.

She smiled at that. "Oh no, not at all. I didn't even want
to talk to you about that. It's something else, something to
do with women's health, though, so I thought perhaps you
might be able to help me."

Sarah had to admit this was intriguing, so she invited the
young woman to sit down and asked one of the expectant
mothers who had gathered in the hallway to eavesdrop on
their visitor if she would fetch them something cool to
drink.

While they waited, the young woman said, "I am Louisa Rodgers. I'm a reporter for the *New Century* magazine."

"I see," Sarah said. This was quite impressive since not many reporters were female. "Are you writing an article about women's health? That's what you said, isn't it?"

"Yes, well, I'm writing about something that affects women's health: patent medicines."

Sarah couldn't help wincing. "If you're looking for some sort of endorsement, I'm afraid you've come to the wrong place." Advertisements for these medicines often featured recommendations from various medical professionals even though the preparations seldom contained anything that actually cured or even treated diseases.

"Oh no, Mrs. Malloy. I'm . . . well, just the opposite, in fact. I want to write an article about how dangerous these potions can be."

Sarah needed a moment to absorb this. "And your magazine has assigned you to do this?"

"Well, yes," Miss Rodgers said almost defensively. "I hope you don't think that just because I'm a female that—"

"No, no, nothing like that," Sarah hastily assured her. "I would be the last person to think that. I'm just surprised that a magazine would want to publish something unflattering about these nostrums. Don't magazines usually avoid controversial subjects?"

Miss Rodgers lifted her chin in a show of defiance. She wasn't a beautiful girl, but her confidence and determination made her quite striking. She actually looked as if she relished taking on this monumental task. "The *New Century* wants to make a name for itself as a progressive publication. We want our readers to know they can trust us to tell them the truth and will always be concerned with their well-being."

That was a noble cause, but Sarah had rarely seen any commercial enterprise succeed at it. "I must say, I'm glad they have given this assignment to a woman."

Miss Rodgers shifted uncomfortably in her chair. "Yes, it is an honor, but I must do an excellent job at it or . . ."

She didn't need to explain. If a woman was entrusted with an important job and failed at it, that would make it all the harder for the next woman to be trusted. "Why have you come to me and how can I help?"

Miss Rodgers smiled. "I was in the neighborhood talking to women and trying to find some who regularly use patent medicines. I wanted to know if any of them had been cured or even helped in any way."

"And did you find any?"

"No one who had actually been cured, although most of them swear by whatever concoction they are taking," she said with a sigh.

"People never want to admit they made a mistake, and as you probably know, these medicines often contain alcohol or drugs that actually do ease pain and make one feel a little better, if only temporarily."

"Exactly. Then I thought perhaps a doctor might be willing to tell me the truth. I know some people become . . . well, ill from taking these medicines and end up in a doctor's care as a result."

"Did you think you'd find a doctor at this clinic?" Sarah asked.

"No, but I thought a woman—a nurse or midwife— might be more willing to tell me the truth, and since you deal with only women at this clinic, I hoped some of them might speak freely as well."

Sarah had to admit her logic was sound. Unfortunately, in Sarah's experience, just because *she* thought people should do something didn't mean they actually would. "I'm perfectly willing to ask our ladies if they have ever tried a patent medicine, and it's highly likely that they have."

"So many people use them," Miss Rodgers agreed.

"Yes, well, you have to admit the advertisements are quite impressive, although it's difficult for me to believe that one tonic can cure things as varied as cancer and a toothache."

Miss Rodgers smiled. "And it seems they all cure *catarrh*, whatever that is."

"It simply means *congestion*, although they are never quite clear about what type of congestion they intend to cure."

"Are you aware of anyone here who uses any of these so-called medicines?"

Sarah had no intention of violating anyone's privacy, especially knowing the ladies in the hallway could hear every word, so she was careful with her reply. "I know many women use Lydia Pinkham's Vegetable Compound for female complaints, although the ladies here aren't having their monthly periods, so that isn't a problem for them."

"Indeed it isn't," the woman Sarah had asked to bring them drinks said, carrying in two glasses of lemonade. "Here you are, nice and fresh."

"Thank you so much, Annie," Sarah said.

"I've taken that Lydia Pinkham's myself," Annie said,

handing each of them a glass. "My monthlies were that painful, but Pinkham's helped a lot."

Several women in the hallway murmured their agreement.

"Lydia Pinkham's is twenty percent alcohol," Miss Rodgers said knowledgeably.

"Is it now?" Annie asked. "Is twenty percent a lot?"

Miss Rodgers looked a little startled by the question, but Sarah said, "Enough to get you drunk if you take too much."

"Peruna's is almost fifty percent alcohol," Miss Rodgers added, naming another popular brand.

"I knew a woman took Peruna's, three bottles a day," Annie recalled. "Couldn't hardly walk straight. I guess that explains it. Glad I stuck to Pinkham's."

"Thank you, Annie," Sarah repeated more forcefully. Annie finally took the hint and rejoined her compatriots out in the hallway.

"Isn't Pinkham's also used for change-of-life symptoms?" Miss Rodgers asked.

"Which is also not a problem for our ladies," Sarah replied with a smile to soften her words.

Miss Rodgers seemed a little chagrined. "No, of course not. But . . . older women do use it, don't they?"

"Women of all ages do, I'm sure." Sarah sighed. "Don't misunderstand me, Miss Rodgers. My first husband was a physician, and no one worked harder to cure his patients than he did but . . . Well, we really know very little about how the human body works and how diseases are contracted and how to treat them. Doctors are often guessing when they treat a patient, and a treatment that cured one person might kill another."

"Which is why many people don't trust doctors and refuse to see one even when they are very ill," Miss Rodgers said. "And many others can't afford to visit a doctor even if they would like to."

"Exactly. I'm a nurse and a midwife, and I deal with the same issues. The birthing process should be the same for every woman since all women have the same organs, and yet every birth is unique, and sometimes even years of experience don't help me with a particularly difficult birth. And of course not everyone can afford to hire a midwife and some must give birth alone, which can be dangerous and even fatal for both mother and child. That is why I started this clinic."

To Sarah's surprise, Miss Rodgers was nodding as if she understood completely. If she had been researching this subject, she probably did.

"So naturally, people who are poor or who just don't trust doctors will look for an easier way to cure themselves, and if that comes in a bottle they can buy cheaply, they will do that," Miss Rodgers said, "even if the bottle contains only alcohol and water."

"Or opium or morphine or heroin," Sarah added. "All those things will ease pain, which allows people to feel better or at least think they do for a little while."

"But they will also create a dependence," Miss Rodgers said with a frown that told Sarah she must have seen this herself.

"Yes, an addiction that forces the patient to continue purchasing the so-called medicine, making the manufacturer rich but doing nothing to cure the patient. People who would never dream of going to an opium den or taking drugs of any kind and even people who are morally opposed to liquor in all its forms can become enslaved to these nostrums, believing them to be actual medicines. Miss Rodgers, if you can educate the public about this, you can eliminate a lot of needless suffering."

"That is just what I intend to do," Miss Rodgers said. "I wonder if . . . if you'd allow me to interview the ladies you have staying here and anyone else who would like to speak with me."

"It isn't my place to allow anyone to do anything here. These ladies are free to speak with you or not, as they choose, but I will certainly invite them to do just that." Sarah glanced over her shoulder at the women gathered in the hallway. "I imagine you will have at least a few willing volunteers."

"I'm very grateful, Mrs. Malloy. This is so important." Miss Rodgers's eyes were shining with the fervor Sarah had often seen in would-be reformers.

"Yes, it is. I'm afraid I am going to have to leave soon. I must get home, but you are welcome to stay as long as you like and return if you need to. In the meantime, here is my card." Sarah handed her a calling card with her home address. "Feel free to contact me if I can be of any help."

Miss Rodgers thanked her profusely, and Sarah had to jump out of the way of the women surging into the room to speak with Miss Rodgers. Plainly, they were willing to help her or at least were bored enough to consider speaking with her a novelty.

Sarah hadn't heard of the *New Century* magazine. It might be truly new or perhaps she just hadn't noticed it before. A lot of magazines were being published now that advances in printing had enabled them to have so many pictures, some even in color. The articles were interesting, and the stories entertaining. She remembered reading a wonderful biography of Abraham Lincoln serialized in one of the magazines. If she remembered correctly, it had been written by a woman, too.

Sarah checked on Mary and her baby again, finding them both sleeping. Miss Kirkwood reported that Mary had successfully fed the child and seemed to be softening toward her.

"But if she decides to take her, we must make sure she's really going to keep her," Miss Kirkwood said.

"I know. Selling babies is still much too easy in this city. We'll keep a close eye on her to make sure she really wants to keep the child." Desperate women could sell their babies to unscrupulous people who used them as child prostitutes or even worse. An orphanage would be far better than that, at least.

When she'd gathered her things, Sarah walked past the parlor on her way out. She saw Miss Rodgers in deep conversation with several of the residents. Sarah waved and Miss Rodgers waved back. "Contact me if you need me," Sarah called. Miss Rodgers nodded and went back to her conversation.

Outside, Sarah found her electric motorcar sitting just where she'd left it. Two street urchins had agreed to guard it for a nickel apiece. They had allowed a group of children to examine it closely, but it was still there and unharmed, so Sarah's nickels were well spent. She rewarded the boys and thanked them.

She loved her electric. It was so quiet and easy to drive compared with the gasoline-powered motor her husband drove. Malloy would probably prefer an electric of his own, but they were getting the reputation of being a vehicle for females, so he had resisted. Who could understand men?

Sarah checked the watch pinned to her bodice and realized she was probably going to be late for supper. Mary's labor had taken much longer than anticipated, but she couldn't leave in the middle of a delivery, even though she would have been leaving Mary in very capable hands. Sarah so rarely got a chance to deliver a baby, she wasn't going to miss one.

She was still thinking about Mary and her baby and what would become of them when she noticed a crowd gathered around a newsboy, jostling for a chance to buy a paper.

"Extra! Extra!" the boy was shouting. "President McKinley shot!"

Good heavens. Sarah pulled to a stop, earning the ire of all the vehicles behind her, but she ignored the shouts. "Here, give me a paper!" she cried, leaning out the window and holding up her penny for the single-sheet publication the boy was selling.

"Here, I've read it," a man said, handing her his copy. He wasn't quite as generous as Sarah had thought, though. He took her penny.

She didn't care. She quickly skimmed the short article. The facts were few, since it had apparently just happened this afternoon at the Pan-American Exposition in Buffalo, New York. The president had been greeting people in a receiving line in the Temple of Music and some man had concealed a pistol in a handkerchief and shot him with it. They thought the man was an anarchist. According to the article, the president had survived the shooting, but they had no further information about his condition. The would-be assassin was in custody.

Sarah could no longer ignore the shouts from the wagoners or the horn blasts from the other motorists who were blocked by her vehicle, so she started out again, although her mind was spinning. As awful as it was to hear that the president had been shot, the news had even more significance when she realized what it might mean for her old friend Theodore Roosevelt.

She had known Theodore all her life, and he had been a police commissioner when she had first met Detective Sergeant Frank Malloy. Theodore had learned to respect Malloy's abilities and sought his services more than once in solving crimes that required a special touch.

So much had happened since then. She and Malloy were married now, and they were rich, through no fault of their own. Malloy had left the police force and opened a private investigation office. Theodore had campaigned vigorously for McKinley when he first ran for president and was appointed assistant secretary of the navy for his trouble. Then he had fought in the Spanish-American War and returned a hero, which resulted in his getting elected governor of New York. When McKinley's vice president died in office, he chose Theodore to be his running mate for his second term.

Now McKinley had been shot, and Theodore Roosevelt was next in line to the presidency.

. . .

"Have you heard the news?" Maeve asked Frank the moment he entered the house. She must have been lying in wait.

"About the president?" he asked, hanging his hat on the coat tree beside the front door. "Yes, I picked up an extra on the way home." He held it up for her to see.

Maeve had started her relationship with the Malloy family when Sarah had hired her as a nanny for her ward, Catherine. When Frank and Sarah married, they had added his son, Brian, to her charge. Through the years, she had also begun helping Frank with some of his cases, and now that Catherine and Brian were in school, Maeve worked in his private investigator office when she wasn't busy with the children.

"They weren't out yet when I was walking Catherine home from school," Maeve said, snatching the paper from his hand. "Does this mean your friend Roosevelt will be president now?" she asked, scanning the brief articles.

Frank noticed their maid, Hattie, and their cook, Velvet, had both come out to hear his report. "Only if McKinley dies, and I'm sure he'll be getting the very best medical care. He's the president, after all."

The ladies did not seem as confident.

"But he was shot, Mr. Frank," Hattie said.

"In the stomach, they say," Velvet added.

"Twice," Maeve added. "That's what Mrs. Decker said. She telephoned as soon as she heard."

"Trust Mother Decker to be the first to know," Frank said about his mother-in-law. "Where are the children?"

"Playing in the nursery," Maeve said. "I didn't say anything to them."

"They shouldn't be too upset since they don't actually know the president," Frank said, "although I suppose we need to tell them, so they don't get frightened when they hear other children talking about it at school."

"Tomorrow is Saturday, so we have plenty of time. Mrs. Frank will know what to say to them," Maeve said.

Frank was glad she thought so because Frank was pretty sure he'd make a botch of it. Explaining it to his deaf son, Brian, would be a challenge since they would have to use American Sign Language, and their rudimentary skills might not be up to the task.

"Miss Catherine will be able to sign it for him," Hattie said with a twinkle, as if she'd read Frank's mind. She probably had. "She does those signs even better than Mr. Brian."

Frank grinned. "That might be true. At any rate, it's a good idea to wait for my wife. Do we have any idea when she'll be home?"

"She telephoned. She had a delivery, so she'll be late for supper," Hattie said.

"Does my mother know about the president?" Frank asked. Mrs. Malloy lived with them, but she had her own quarters in their large house. Frank was surprised she hadn't come out when she heard him arrive home.

"Yes. She's in her rooms, saying a rosary for the president," Maeve said. "Do you think it would be a good thing if Mr. Roosevelt becomes president?"

"Let's not wish President McKinley dead just yet," Frank said.

"I'm not," Maeve said. "I was just asking."

Frank sighed. "He'd be an interesting president, I'm sure. Now, let's not talk about this until we've had a chance to speak with the children. I don't want them to get frightened."

Hattie and Velvet returned to the kitchen with the extra to read the details for themselves, and Maeve went upstairs to check on the children. Frank didn't want to interrupt his mother's devotions, so he also went upstairs, to the private parlor he and Sarah had created for themselves, to wait for Sarah.

SARAH WAS GLAD THEY HAD LEFT IT TO HER TO INFORM the children about McKinley being shot. Telling the children the news proved easier than anyone had expected, though. Since they didn't know the president personally, they weren't terribly upset. They asked a few questions but then promptly lost interest.

Malloy went out to see if any of the newspapers had published a later edition with more details, but all they learned was that McKinley had been taken to a private home in Buffalo and his doctors expected him to recover, which was a great relief.

Sarah put the children to bed herself that night, in case they had more questions, but they wanted to talk only about what they would do the next day since they didn't have school. When they had finally settled down, Sarah joined Malloy, Maeve, and Mother Malloy in the downstairs parlor.

"Theodore must be getting nervous," Sarah said.

"Roosevelt?" Malloy scoffed. "He's probably practicing his inaugural speech."

"That's a mean thing to say," Maeve chastened him gleefully.

"We all know how he likes the limelight," Malloy said. "Being vice president must gall him."

"The newspapers all say the president is going to make a full recovery," Sarah reminded them, "so Theodore will just have to continue being galled."

"Can't you talk about something else?" Mother Malloy said from where she was sitting and knitting in the glow from the electric lamp.

"Yes, we can," Sarah said, pretending not to see Maeve's and Malloy's amusement. "I had an interesting caller today at the clinic."

"A caller?" Maeve echoed. "Since when do you get social visits at the clinic?"

"This wasn't a social visit. A young woman came by and asked to speak to whoever is in charge, so I met with her. She turned out to be a reporter for the *New Century* magazine."

"*New Century*? I don't think I've ever heard of it," Maeve said.

"I have," Mother Malloy said. "It just started this year, I think. Because the new century began and all that." Although some people disagreed, the official consensus was that the twentieth century had begun on the first of January 1901.

"Have you read it?" Sarah asked, knowing she most likely had. Mother Malloy and their neighbor Mrs. Ellsworth were always exchanging magazines.

"Oh yes. It's not as good as *McClure's* and *Collier's*, but I expect it will get better if this girl is as good as the girl reporter they have at *McClure's*," Mother Malloy said.

"Ida Tarbell," Maeve said knowledgeably. "She's the best."

"She wrote that series on Lincoln, didn't she?" Sarah asked.

Maeve just gave her a blank look, making Sarah realize she would have been too young to care about such things when those articles had come out a few years ago. Mother Malloy had been reading magazines for years, though.

"She's a pistol, all right," Mother Malloy said. "Is this girl you met today anything like her?"

"I don't know, but she is certainly writing about an interesting topic: patent medicines."

That got even Malloy's attention. "Don't tell me she's going to recommend them."

"Oh no, just the opposite. She was giving me facts and figures to prove they are nothing more than liquor and dangerous drugs that cause more harm than good. She wants to expose the people who make them as charlatans."

"That seems like an enormous job," Maeve remarked. "Think about how many patent medicines there are."

"And how many people use them," Sarah said.

"Why do they call them *patent* medicine?" Maeve asked.

"Miss Rodgers will probably explain it in her article," Sarah told her with a grin.

"I remember when Francis was a babe," Mother Malloy said, not even looking up from her knitting. "We had a neighbor whose baby had the colic. Cried and cried, he did.

Then his ma started giving him Soothing Syrup. All the neighbors were that glad. But then the poor babe got so he had to have it. He would cry for it if his ma didn't give it."

A chill went down Sarah's spine. "Those concoctions that soothe babies usually have laudanum in them. Or just plain opium."

"No wonder he cried for it," Maeve said. "How awful."

"Don't tell me you gave me those drops, too, Ma," Malloy said only half in jest.

"You were a good baby, Francis," his mother said. "Too bad you grew out of it."

That made everyone laugh, even Malloy.

When they had settled down again, Sarah said, "Miss Rodgers assured me that her magazine would publish her article although I realized after we spoke that they probably also publish ads for patent medicines. Mother Malloy, you said you had read the *New Century*. I assume it has those ads just like all the other magazines."

"I never paid much attention to that," Mother Malloy admitted. "I don't read those ads. They're all full of lies."

"Then you think the magazines would be afraid to write unflattering things about the medicines for fear of losing the advertisements?" Maeve asked.

"Yes. Most people don't realize that the price of the magazine itself doesn't come close to covering the cost to print it," Sarah said.

"Which is why magazines and newspapers have so many advertisements," Malloy added. "That's where they make most of their money."

"Ah," Maeve said, nodding. "So, if they published an article saying that patent medicines not only didn't really work but that they were also dangerous, the companies would stop buying advertising."

"Exactly," Sarah said. "Miss Rodgers said some noble-sounding platitudes about how her magazine wouldn't care about such things as profits, but it's difficult to believe she's right."

"Didn't she say she had been assigned to write the article?" Maeve asked.

"I got that impression, but . . . Well, it isn't really our business, is it?"

"Why did she want to talk to you in particular?" Malloy asked.

"She thought the person in charge of the clinic would be a nurse or a doctor, and she wanted an expert's opinion. She also wanted to interview the women at the clinic to see if any of them had used patent medicines and what their experience had been. I told her to contact me if she needed any more help, although I don't know how I could actually help her."

"You'll probably never hear from her again," Malloy said.

"But we might see her article in the magazine," Maeve said. "That would be exciting."

AS THE DAYS WENT BY, THE NEWSPAPERS WERE FULL OF updates on the president's condition. His surgeon kept reassuring the public that President McKinley was doing well and was expected to make a full recovery. Sarah couldn't figure out what made him so optimistic since wounds like the president's were extremely dangerous and easily became infected. Once that happened, nothing short of a miracle could save the patient.

However, the papers also reported that Vice President Roosevelt had taken his family on a camping trip in the Adirondacks, which must mean he was confident the president would recover. Since Theodore was certainly privy to information Sarah did not have, she hoped she was wrong about her concerns.

That morning she had borrowed several magazines from Mother Malloy while the children were at school, Maeve and Malloy were at the office, and Mother Malloy was at school with Brian. Sarah used this quiet time to flip through the publications, growing more and more appalled by the number of patent medicine advertisements and the outlandish claims they made. One tonic promised to cure all diseases known to man. How could anyone in their right mind believe such a thing? And if it were true, why weren't doctors handing out bottles of it to all their patients?

She was fuming when someone rang their doorbell. Happy for an interruption to such an upsetting task, Sarah got up to answer it, calling to Hattie so she wouldn't bother coming from wherever she happened to be in the house.

She opened the door to a rather dignified, middle-aged man. Seeing she was the lady of the house and not a maid, he removed his hat to reveal light brown hair touched with gray. He wore a tailor-made suit and a shirt striped in blue to match it. Everything about him said *prosperous businessman* except his expression. He was obviously experiencing a great deal of strain or worry.

"Are you Mrs. Malloy?" he asked in a husky voice that might have been holding back tears.

"Yes, I am," Sarah said.

"I'm Bernard Rodgers."

She blinked at the name, wondering . . .

"I believe you met my daughter, Louisa," he said before she could respond.

"Yes, I did. She's a delightful young lady."

Some painful emotion flickered across his face. "I . . . We found your card in her purse. We thought perhaps you had seen her recently."

"I saw her last Friday, I believe. I remember because it was the day the president was shot."

He winced at that. "Yes, of course," he said, apropos of nothing.

"How may I help you?" Sarah asked when he didn't continue.

"My daughter . . . Louisa . . . She . . . Someone murdered her."

II

I'M SO SORRY, MR. RODGERS," SARAH EXCLAIMED. "HOW awful. Please, come in."

Sarah ushered the poor man into the house and on into the parlor, where she encouraged him to be seated since he looked as if he might fall down if he didn't sit. She called for Hattie and asked her to bring some coffee.

"Or would you like something stronger, Mr. Rodgers?"

"I don't use spirits, Mrs. Malloy," he said. "We're temperance."

"Of course," she said, although she wasn't sure why. "We'll have some coffee for you in a moment. I'm so sorry to hear about Louisa." She had a dozen questions but wasn't sure which ones were appropriate to ask this stranger who had just lost his daughter.

"Thank you," he said as if by habit. He was plainly still in shock.

"I hope you haven't come here because you think I knew Louisa well," Sarah said as gently as she could. "I only met her once. She stopped by a clinic where I do volunteer work to ask me some questions about an article she was writing. I gave her my card in case she had more questions."

He frowned at that, but before he could reply, Hattie arrived with his coffee. Sarah poured it and stirred in several spoonfuls of sugar for the shock.

When she handed him the cup, he said, "Did you say she was writing an article?"

"Yes, for the magazine where she works . . . worked, I mean. The *New Century*. She consulted with me about . . . about women's health," Sarah said to avoid any questions he might have about the topic.

He gave his head a little shake as if to rearrange his thoughts. "Louisa didn't write articles for the magazine. She was just a secretary."

"I thought that's what she said, but perhaps I'm mistaken." Sarah wasn't mistaken, but she was more than willing to ease the poor man's mind. What did it matter now in any case? "Did you say she was murdered?"

He took a sip of his coffee with shaking hands before answering. "She . . . Yes. She was strangled."

Which was a terrible way to die. The killer's face would be just inches away as he—or she—choked the life out of you, and it took far longer than one might imagine to actually kill a person that way. Sarah often regretted how very much she knew about murder.

"Did they catch the person who did it?"

He took another swallow of his coffee. It would have been left from breakfast and was probably very strong. She hoped it would do him some good. "The police think . . . They say it was random, and they'll never find out who did it."

Sarah also knew far more about the New York City Police Department than she liked. "You may not be aware that the police are much more interested in solving a case if there is a reward."

He smiled wanly. "I know that, Mrs. Malloy, and I did offer, but I could see they had made up their minds. She was . . . It happened at night in the lobby of the building where the magazine offices are. She was coming out from working late. They said . . ." His voice broke, and his cup began to rattle in its saucer.

Sarah could imagine what they had said about a young woman out alone late at night. She jumped up and took the cup and saucer from his unresisting fingers to set them on a nearby table.

"The police can be unthinking," Sarah said.

"Oh, they were thinking. They were thinking Louisa wasn't any better than she should be, but she was a good girl."

"I know she was. She was intelligent as well. We had quite an interesting discussion."

"But they never knew her, so they . . . they made assumptions. They aren't even going to *try* to find her killer. That is why I'm here. It's up to me now. I won't rest until I find out who stole my little girl from me."

He pulled a handkerchief from his pocket and wiped the tears from his eyes.

"Do you have investigative experience, Mr. Rodgers?" Sarah asked.

"What? Well, no, not exactly," he admitted in surprise.

"What kind of business are you in?"

"Insurance," he said, still surprised by her questions.

"I'm sure you're very good at what you do, but do you have any idea how to find a killer?"

Now he was angry. "Don't try to discourage me, Mrs. Malloy. Nothing can stop me."

"I wouldn't dream of it, Mr. Rodgers, but I would also like to see Louisa's killer brought to justice. How would you do that if you do, indeed, identify the killer?"

He frowned. "I . . . I suppose . . . I . . ."

"Would you kill that person in revenge?"

"Of course not! I could never take someone's life!" he insisted, outraged.

"Then what *would* you do?"

He took a few ragged breaths. "Turn him over to the police, I guess."

"With enough evidence to convince them to try him for murder?"

He opened his mouth to speak but nothing came out. He closed it with a snap. "Why are you asking me these things, Mrs. Malloy?" he asked furiously.

"To convince you that your chances of finding Louisa's killer are very small, and even if you succeed, what is to stop that person from simply killing you in order to remain free?"

What little color he had left drained from his face. "I hadn't thought of that."

"Mr. Rodgers, I can't imagine the pain you must feel over

losing your daughter in such an awful way, but I do under-stand that you want to see her killer punished. I know a little about this kind of thing because my husband was a detective with the New York City Police Department."

Mr. Rodgers glanced around the well-appointed parlor of the rather large house. Plainly, he was wondering how a police detective could afford such a home. Sarah had no intention of explaining it to him.

"But the police said they couldn't find Louisa's killer," he said.

"I thought you said they weren't going to *try* to find her killer."

He rubbed his head as if it ached. It probably did. "I see what you mean."

"Mr. Rodgers, I should tell you that my husband owns a private investigation agency, and he has solved many mur-ders that the police had given up on. I am not in the habit of procuring clients for him, and I certainly don't want you to feel I am pressuring you or even suggesting you hire him, but he could at least advise *you* in how best to proceed." Sarah could have as well. In fact, she already had, but she knew he would be more likely to listen to another man.

"I think I could use some advice. This has all been such a shock. I know I haven't been thinking straight."

"That is perfectly understandable. I will get one of my husband's cards for you, and if you would like to seek his services, you may feel free to do so. There are also many other private investigators in the city you can hire if that makes you more comfortable."

She didn't even notice that he failed to rise when she got

up and left the room to fetch the card. When she returned, he did make the attempt, but he was noticeably unsteady on his feet.

"I'm sorry," he said when she grabbed his elbow to steady him. "This has taken a lot out of me, I'm afraid."

"How did you travel here?"

He looked up at her in surprise. "By the El. We live in Morningside Heights, and coming by carriage would have been very slow."

Morningside Heights was a very pleasant neighborhood. "Would you object if I offered to drive you home in my electric motorcar?"

Now he really was surprised. "That's kind of you, but I . . . I wasn't planning on going home just yet. I thought I would speak with your husband first."

"If that's true, then allow me to drive you to his office. You really shouldn't be walking around the city in your current condition."

To Sarah's amazement, he agreed without any more coaxing. Not many men would willingly ride with a female driver, especially a woman he did not know. Perhaps he really wasn't thinking straight. In any case, she would deliver Malloy's next client right to his doorstep.

FRANK LOOKED UP FROM HIS DESK WHEN HE HEARD someone enter the receptionist's office, and he rose when he recognized his wife's voice. What would Sarah be doing here? He went out to Maeve's office to greet her and found her with a rather distraught-looking man.

"Mrs. Frank has brought you a client, Mr. Malloy," Maeve told him gleefully.

She had definitely brought someone. He gave Sarah a questioning look.

"You remember the young woman reporter I told you about the other day?" Sarah said. "This is her father, Mr. Bernard Rodgers. He would like to consult with you on a very important matter."

Frank introduced himself and shook Mr. Rodgers's rather cold hand. The man looked like he'd been poleaxed.

"Did you by any chance drive Mr. Rodgers here, Sarah?" he asked with a sly grin.

Sarah gave him a sharp glare and said, "He isn't upset from my driving. Shall we go into your office?"

"Maeve, would you bring our guests some water?" Frank asked, suitably chastened.

When Sarah and Mr. Rodgers had settled into the two client chairs in front of his desk, Frank sat down and said, "How may I help you, Mr. Rodgers?"

"I . . . My daughter . . ." His voice broke and he gave Sarah a pleading look.

"Would you like for me to explain, Mr. Rodgers?" she asked him very gently.

He nodded gratefully.

"As I told you," she began, letting Frank know with her eyes that she hadn't forgotten his remark about her driving, "I met Mr. Rodgers's daughter, Louisa, last week at the clinic."

"The reporter. Yes, I remember."

"I gave her my card in case she wanted to speak with me again. Sadly, Miss Rodgers was murdered a few days later."

She gave Frank a moment to absorb this shocking information before continuing.

"It was Monday night, I believe. Is that right, Mr. Rodgers?"

He nodded again, swallowing down his grief.

Now Frank understood Sarah's annoyance with him. This was serious. "I'm very sorry, Mr. Rodgers."

"Thank you," he said by rote, his gaze fixed on his hands, which were clenched in his lap.

"Louisa was working late at the magazine," Sarah continued, "and someone attacked her in the lobby of the building, presumably as she was leaving for the night, and strangled her."

Mr. Rodgers made a small sound of distress but squared his shoulders as if determined to bear this unbearable loss. He looked up, and Frank saw that determination in his eyes. "The police gave us Louisa's belongings, and we found Mrs. Malloy's card in her purse. I thought she must be a friend of Louisa's and might know something, so I went to your home to speak with her."

Frank was glad the police hadn't gone to question Sarah. He knew from having been a police officer himself that they could be very rude. Sarah could handle them, but she shouldn't have to. "Aren't the police investigating your daughter's death, Mr. Rodgers?"

"No, they . . ." His voice broke again, and he pulled out a handkerchief to wipe his eyes.

"The police," Sarah explained for him, "have decided that it was a random attack and will never be solved."

Frank nodded his understanding. "She was strangled, you say?"

Mr. Rodgers was still blowing his nose.

"Yes," Sarah said.

"Was she . . . ?" Frank glanced at Mr. Rodgers, knowing this question would upset him even more. ". . . interfered with?"

Sarah looked surprised at the question. Had she not considered this possibility?

"Oh, my little girl," Mr. Rodgers said brokenly. "Please God, say she was spared that."

"I guess we don't know," Sarah said quickly. Frank nodded to let her know he understood they needed to drop this subject for the time being.

"Mr. Rodgers, why have you come to see me?" Frank asked.

He looked up in surprise. "Your wife, Mrs. Malloy, she said you could help me, that you could find Louisa's killer."

Sarah gave him a little apologetic smile. "I said you had solved other murders the police had given up on."

"I can certainly try to find your daughter's killer, Mr. Rodgers, although I can't promise that I will. If the police are right about it being a random attack, the killer could be anyone, but I can look into it and at least try to find out what happened and, hopefully, who is responsible."

"That's all I can ask, Mr. Malloy. Louisa was a remarkable young woman. She was everything a man could want in a child. I know I can't bring her back, but I can at least avenge her death in some way. Some *legal* way," he added to Sarah.

Had she persuaded Frank not to take matters into his own hands? She hoped so.

"May I ask you some questions about your daughter, Mr. Rodgers? The more I know about her, the better."

"I . . . I suppose that would be all right," he said, glancing at Sarah for her approval. She nodded.

At that moment, Maeve came in with some glasses of water.

"Maeve, would you stay and take notes?" Frank asked, which would also mean he wouldn't need to explain everything to her later. "Mr. Rodgers has just lost his daughter and he would like us to find out who is responsible for her death."

Maeve nodded and went to fetch a tablet. Then she took a chair in the corner of the room, out of Mr. Rodgers's line of sight so he would forget she was there.

"Tell me about yourself and your family, Mr. Rodgers. Do you live here in the city?" Frank began.

Rodgers gave them his address in Morningside Heights and said that he was in insurance. Judging by the cut of his suit, he did well. The family consisted of himself, his wife, and his children, Louisa, who was the elder, and her brother, Oscar.

"And do your children still live at home?" Frank asked.

Plainly, this was a topic of contention, judging from Mr. Rodgers's expression. "My son does. He's . . . uh . . . still trying to find his way in life, I'm afraid. Louisa wants . . ." He swallowed hard and continued. "She *wanted* to have some freedom, she said. When she started working at the magazine, she moved into a rooming house in Rose Hill, near the offices. She claimed it would be so much better than riding to our home late on the El every day."

The elevated train was fast, since it traveled on tracks a story above the street and didn't have to stop for traffic, but it was often tightly packed with passengers, giving mashers the opportunity to grope defenseless ladies. A woman alone late in the evening would be an especially attractive victim.

"So, she was concerned about her own safety," Sarah said gently.

"For all the good it did," Mr. Rodgers said bitterly.

"How long had she worked at the magazine?" Frank asked.

"Since shortly after it began publication last January. She was hired to answer the telephone and do various clerical tasks." So, over eight months.

Frank frowned. "I thought she was a reporter." He glanced at Sarah for confirmation.

"I thought so, too," Sarah said, "but—"

"She could not have been a reporter," Mr. Rodgers insisted. "If she had been promoted, she would have told us, and I can't believe she would lie about such a thing."

"I probably just misunderstood her, Mr. Rodgers," Sarah said, diplomatic as usual, "although she did ask me for information, which led me to believe she was doing research for an article."

"She must have been helping one of the reporters, then," Rodgers said. "At any rate, she shouldn't have been working so late that night. No one needs to answer the telephones after the offices are closed."

"I'll look into it," Frank said. "I'm sure there's an explanation. Did your daughter have any enemies, Mr. Rodgers?"

"Enemies? What do you mean by that?" he asked, affronted.

"Anyone who was angry with her or jealous or who might want to do her harm?" Sarah clarified for him.

Rodgers frowned at this, and Frank thought he must have someone in mind, but he said, "Everyone loved Louisa. She was a fine girl."

"Did she have any suitors?" Frank asked.

Mr. Rodgers's frown deepened. Perhaps this was another area of contention. "Absolutely not. I told you, Louisa was a good girl. She had no time for men."

"I'm sorry to upset you, Mr. Rodgers, but as I said, the more I know about Louisa, the better chance I have of finding her killer. Would it be all right if I also met with your wife and son? They may know something that would help."

Plainly, Mr. Rodgers did not like this request. "I'm sure my son won't know anything. He and Louisa . . . Well, they weren't close, and he took very little interest in her life."

"Your wife, then?" Frank prodded.

"My wife is, as you can imagine, prostrate with grief. She has been confined to her bed since we heard the news."

"Perhaps she would see me," Sarah said, still speaking to Rodgers as if afraid he might shatter. He did look pretty fragile. "I'm a nurse and I might be able to help her."

Rodgers still looked wary. "I . . . We'll have to wait until she is more herself, I'm afraid. I don't want her to be upset any more than she already has been."

"Of course. I would be very careful with her."

Frank noticed Rodgers still had not actually given them permission to speak with his wife. Just how fragile was Mrs. Rodgers? "If Louisa has just been at the magazine since January, was she employed somewhere else previously?" Frank asked. He remembered Sarah had guessed Louisa's age as close to thirty.

"Yes, she taught school, but she never cared much for it."

"Where did she teach?"

Rodgers gave him the name of a primary school near their home.

"Was your daughter a writer, Mr. Rodgers?" Sarah asked as if merely interested.

"A writer? What do you mean?"

"I mean did she write poetry or perhaps stories to amuse herself. A lot of young women do."

"She was always scribbling something, if that's what you mean. She said it was her diary, but I could never understand what she had to write in a diary. She led a very ordinary life."

"Young women can be very imaginative, Mr. Rodgers," Sarah said.

"Not Louisa. She was a very sensible girl. Not one to get her head turned by boys or fripperies. Always the smartest one in her class. That's why I sent her to college. Her mother didn't see the need, but how could we let a mind like hers go uneducated?"

"That's very generous of you, Mr. Rodgers," Sarah said. "Many men would have agreed with your wife."

When Rodgers didn't reply, Frank said, "Did your son attend college as well?"

"Oscar?" he said in surprise. "No. Oh, I sent him, but he left after a month. Too much studying for his taste, he said. He wanted to get some real experience."

Plainly, Mr. Rodgers did not approve of his son's choices.

He didn't seem to approve of his son either, which may or may not be important to the case. They'd have to figure out a way to speak with young Oscar and find out.

Frank asked Rodgers for the names of the police detective he had spoken with and then Maeve escorted Mr. Rodgers out to her office to discuss their fees.

Frank motioned for Sarah to remain behind.

"If you're going to chide me for convincing Mr. Rodgers to give you the case, I didn't. I only convinced him he couldn't find his daughter's killer on his own."

"What was he planning to do if he did find him?" Frank asked.

"He wasn't sure, but I'm glad to say that when I asked if he was going to kill the perpetrator, he was horrified."

"That's a relief. But I wasn't going to chide you about anything. I was going to warn you that we're probably going to need you to question Mrs. Rodgers."

"That was obvious. You know I'll always help in any way I can, but we really should discuss putting me on the payroll."

The twinkle in her eye made him want to kiss her, but that would be very unprofessional. "If I do, you'd have to limit your spending to what I pay you in salary," he countered.

"Then you'll have to pay me a lot, won't you?" she asked with a grin before sashaying out to join Maeve and Mr. Rodgers in the outer office. Frank followed, stopping in the doorway.

Mr. Rodgers was just handing Maeve a check.

"Would you like me to drive you home, Mr. Rodgers?" Sarah asked.

He looked a little sheepish. "I must thank you again for your help, Mrs. Malloy, but I'm feeling much better now, and I think I'd like to make the trip alone. It will give me a chance to clear my head, and don't worry, I'll hire a cab this time. I also need to decide how I am going to tell my wife that I have hired a private investigator."

"Do you think she would object?" Sarah asked in surprise.

Mr. Rodgers didn't quite meet her eye. "Everything concerning Louisa's death upsets her, so I'm sure this will as well. But I don't regret it, Mrs. Malloy. I really do want to see Louisa's killer caught."

"We'll do our best for you, Mr. Rodgers," Maeve said.

He seemed a little alarmed that Maeve had addressed him or maybe he was just amazed that the secretary felt she would be involved, but he managed a small smile and bid them good day.

When he was gone, Sarah turned to Frank. "May I offer you a ride, then?"

"Yes, you may," he replied, "but only if I drive."

WHEN THEY WERE IN THE MOTORCAR AND HEADING TO-ward Police Headquarters, where Malloy would find out what he could about the case, he glanced over at Sarah, who was, in spite of his joking, driving. "Are you all right?"

"I'm very sad, of course," she admitted, and she was, so very sad. "It's upsetting to find out someone you know has been murdered."

"You didn't know her long," he said by way of comfort.

"But I knew her very well, even though I only met her once. She is like so many young women who want to make a life for themselves in this world, who don't want to always depend on a man to take care of them. Now some man has taken away any chances she had."

"We'll do everything we can to find her killer," he said, which she knew was the only real comfort he could offer.

"But we can't bring her back," Sarah said with a sigh.

SARAH LET FRANK OFF ON MULBERRY STREET, IN FRONT of Police Headquarters. She was going to visit the Daughters of Hope Mission, which was just up the street. Sarah used to volunteer at this shelter for homeless young women before she opened the clinic. It was where she had found Maeve and their daughter, Catherine, in fact. They would always have a place in their hearts for the Mission.

Meanwhile, Frank would track down the detectives who had investigated Louisa Rodgers's death and see what he could learn. Tom, the doorman, greeted him warmly.

"Are you here to turn yourself in, Mr. Malloy?" he joked.

"Yes, I've been nabbed for loitering, Tom. It's about all I do now that the police won't have me."

Tom was still laughing when he closed the door behind him. Inside was the usual chaos of a police station, with drunks objecting to anything that was happening and ordinary criminals resisting whatever the cops were doing with them. Frank walked in, inhaling the familiar scents of alcohol and sweat emanating from the men sitting on the benches lined up against the wall awaiting their dispositions.

Just like old times.

The desk sergeant greeted him gruffly. The men who worked here would always resent Frank for having struck it rich. Frank just pretended not to notice. He greeted the sergeant by name and asked about his family. The man replied and after a few minutes of chatting, he let his resentment slip away. Frank had been one of them, after all.

"Is Gilbride upstairs by any chance?" Frank asked finally.

"Gilbride, is it? I'd be surprised if he wasn't. We don't let him out of the house much."

Frank knew this. As soon as Mr. Rodgers had given him the name, he had understood why "the police" didn't think Louisa's murder could be solved. It was because Gilbride liked cases where the police walked in and found the killer standing over the dead body with a weapon still in his hands and shouting about how he didn't mean to do it. Those cases didn't require him to work very hard.

Frank thanked the sergeant and took the stairs up to the detectives' room.

He found Gilbride at a desk in the far corner of a room full of desks, mostly empty. The other detectives would be out working. He had his feet propped up and was leaning his chair back as far as he could without falling. If he wasn't asleep, he was doing a good imitation of it.

Frank shouted his name, and he came up sputtering. "What the . . . ?" he demanded, looking around. Then he saw Frank.

"Malloy, what are doing here? I thought you quit the force when you came into money."

"I'm a private investigator now," Frank said. "I need to ask you—"

"Did you lose all your money that quick? I thought you was a millionaire."

"Easy come, easy go," Frank said, playing along. "I wanted to speak to you about a case."

Gilbride scrubbed both hands over his face and looked up again with bloodshot eyes. "A case, you say?" Frank nodded, noticing Gilbride's enlarged nose and the broken blood vessels on his cheeks that betrayed his heavy drinking. Gilbride patted his rounded belly as if to make sure it was still there and leaned back in his chair again. "Ask away."

"Louisa Rodgers. What do you know about it?"

"Oh, the poor wee lass," Gilbride said, shaking his head. "Shoulda been at home with her babies instead of taking some man's job at that magazine, shouldn't she? But that's what this world is coming to. If women want to have jobs like men, they have to take their chances just like men do."

Frank chose not to comment on that. He pulled over a chair from an empty desk and sat down. "What can you tell me about the murder?"

"Not much to tell. Some bum must've seen her and decided to kill her. The outside doors of the building weren't locked."

"Was she raped?"

Rodgers shook his head. "No sign of it, and the coroner said no. Untouched, she was. A regular spinster."

"Do you know what time it happened?"

"Don't know exactly when it happened. The beat cop saw her laying in the lobby around dawn. Thought she was a drunk who had slipped inside the building to sleep it off. He went in and saw she was dead and had been for a while."

"Didn't the building have a night watchman?"

Gilbride shrugged. "Seems like he wasn't watching."

"What about the other people in her office? Could they tell you what time she left the night before?"

"They swore they had no idea. Said she actually left early that day, and they didn't even know she'd come back."

Now, that was strange. "What about the other offices? Did anyone else see her?"

Gilbride blinked at him stupidly. "How would I know? Besides, I know what happened. It was some drunk. He'd snuck in to sleep it off in a nice, safe place, and then the girl comes down and scares him. He panics and kills her, then hightails it out of there."

"Why would he kill her? She wasn't any threat to him."

"I don't know. He was drunk, not thinking straight. He was afraid she'd call the cops or something."

"So, you didn't question anyone in the other offices?"

"They were closed for the day when it happened," he said defensively. "Nobody saw a thing, I tell you." He jerked open one of the lower drawers of the desk and pulled out a flask. He took a long pull from it, then offered it to Frank.

Frank shook his head. "No thanks. But she was strangled, I take it."

"Yes. Bare-handed, too. The killer didn't plan it," he added, lest Frank think he hadn't given the matter his full consideration. "Crime of passion, as they say."

But crimes of passion aren't committed by total strangers.

If her killer had raped her, he might have killed her so she could never identify him. But would some stranger have seen her there and suddenly decide to murder her for no reason? Would someone have gotten satisfaction out of just that unprovoked act?

"I don't suppose she was robbed," Frank said, thinking that was one thing they hadn't considered.

Gilbride winced at that. "We did find her purse."

"I see, and you helped yourself to the money that was in it," Frank guessed. Relieving the dead of their cash was an unwritten perk of being a cop.

"Let's just say her killer didn't take it."

Frank crossed his arms and sighed in disgust. "So, she wasn't robbed or raped. None of this indicates she was killed by some stranger."

Gilbride straightened his shoulders as if trying for a bit of dignity. "But why would anybody who knew her want to kill some poor secretary? That doesn't make sense either."

Not unless you did some investigating, but Frank didn't say that. He needed Gilbride's cooperation.

"Could anyone explain why Miss Rodgers was at the office so late?"

"Everybody said she shouldn't've been there at all. Nobody was working late that night. Her family said they didn't know where she went or why because she didn't live at home, and the women at her rooming house didn't know anything either."

It looked like they weren't going to learn anything useful from the police.

"Wait a minute," Gilbride said suddenly, narrowing his eyes in suspicion. "What do you care about all this?"

"Her father hired me to find out who killed her."

"Hired you?" he echoed in confusion, but then he obviously remembered. "Oh yeah, you're a private investigator now, you said. The old man did offer a reward, but I didn't see the point. You'll never solve this case."

But he would at least try, unlike Gilbride. "If I do, I'll let you know," Frank said, rising from his chair.

"You do that. Then I'll collect the reward."

Frank sighed again. Not if he could help it.

F RANK KNEW SARAH WOULD WANT TO SPEND SOME TIME at the Mission, talking to the girls, so he decided he would go on his own to the building where Louisa had worked to see what he could find out. Coworkers often knew more about a person than family did. They would at least know the truth about what Louisa's role at the magazine was.

The building was fairly new. Made of brick with attractive arches over the doors and windows and terra-cotta accents, it stood seven stories tall. Frank could see immediately why Gilbride had decided a vagrant had been sleeping in the lobby. The first floor of the building was an open space designed to support the streetcar substation on the second floor. Sandwiched between the machines upstairs and the boilers in the basement, the ground floor housed no businesses.

With no offices and no one around, it would have been a good place to find some solitude, but Frank couldn't believe they would leave an area like this unguarded since the engines above were so vital to the running of the streetcars.

Indeed, a man in a guard's uniform strolled over and asked him his business.

"I have an appointment with the editor of the *New Century* magazine," he lied.

"That will be the fourth floor. The elevator is just there." He pointed.

"Were you here when the young woman was killed the other night?" Frank asked.

The man's expression immediately went from official professionalism to frightened citizen. "Are you from the police?"

When Frank really had been a cop, people always could tell. He must still look or act like a cop, even in his very expensive suit. "Answer my question," he said so he wouldn't have to tell another lie.

"I don't work nights. That's Billy. Or it was. They fired him after . . . Well, he isn't here anymore."

"What is Billy's last name?"

"Funhouser. We already told the police all this. Billy was . . . Well, he wasn't at his post when the young lady come down. Nobody saw what happened."

"Where did they find her?"

The guard swallowed nervously. "Over there." He pointed to a spot near the outer door. Which meant that Billy had been gone from his post most of the night, since he couldn't have missed Louisa's body lying in plain sight. "I didn't see her, mind you, but they told me later. There wasn't no blood or anything. Nothing to clean up. They just took her away."

Frank looked around, trying to imagine the place after dark. He'd have to come back to see for himself, but he figured if the building was empty and the guard wasn't at his post, anyone could do anything here without being seen.

"Did you say the magazine is on the fourth floor?"

"Yes, sir," the guard said quickly, obviously anxious for Frank to get on the elevator and disappear.

The elevator was enormous, making Frank wonder what they used it for besides carrying the workers up and down. It could probably hold a carriage.

He found the offices without any trouble. The magazine's name was painted on the door's glass window in gold leaf.

He entered to find a large oblong room where more than a dozen people were hard at work. Most of them were seated in two rows beside the large windows, obviously to take advantage of the natural light, because they were all drawing something, using what looked like music stands to hold their pads of paper. A small, low table sat beside each artist holding his—or her, because he saw two of them were women—art supplies. The men, he noticed, were in their shirtsleeves, which was unusual for an office. Artwork must be rather messy.

A long table lined the side of the room opposite the windows, and a woman was arranging finished drawings on it. She noticed him and came forward. "May I help you?"

"I'd like to speak to whoever is in charge here," Frank said. "It's about Miss Rodgers."

She blanched, but to her credit, she said, "We aren't commenting to the newspapers."

"I'm not from the newspapers. I'm investigating her death."

"Oh, I see. Well, you should probably see Mr. Tibbot, then. This way, please."

She led him down the long aisle between the artists and the display table to where a portion of the room had been divided into small offices. She stepped into one, motioning for Frank to wait. "This gentleman would like to speak with you about Miss Rodgers," she said to the man inside.

Mr. Tibbot made what could be described only as a growling noise. "If he's a reporter, I'll throw him out. He's not a reporter, is he?"

"No, he's not," Frank said for himself, stepping up so Tibbot could see him. "I'm investigating Miss Rodgers's murder."

The woman made a hasty retreat, leaving Frank to fend for himself.

Tibbot was a tough-looking man of middle age with a full beard and bushy hair, both coal black. His scowl would probably curdle milk, but Frank was used to tough men. He scowled right back. "I just need to know what Louisa Rodgers was doing here on Monday night."

"You're wasting your time, then, because Louisa Rodgers didn't even work here."

III

W**HAT DO YOU MEAN, SHE DIDN'T WORK HERE?**" F**RANK** demanded, not bothering to hide his fury. "Her parents were under the impression she has been working here since January."

In spite of his bluster, Tibbot looked a little chagrinned. "I should've said she didn't work here *any longer*. She quit on Monday afternoon."

Which made it even more odd that she had returned to the building on Monday night. But he would get to that in a minute. "Why did she quit?"

Tibbot sighed. "I guess you'd better sit down, Mr. . . ."

"Malloy," Frank supplied. Tibbot's office was a mess, with stacks of pictures and typewritten pages, and file folders on every possible surface. Frank had to move a pile of papers off the one and only visitor chair in the room. Tibbot took a seat behind his desk and sighed like a man who was being generous against his better judgment.

"Louisa was a good worker. She was polite to people when they called on the telephone, even when they were rude to her. She did everything we asked. She used to be a teacher, so we even let her do some editing."

"Then what was the problem?"

"She comes to me on Monday. She had this idea. She told me *McClure's*—you know *McClure's Magazine*?"

"I think my wife reads it," Frank hedged.

Tibbot made a face but continued. "Louisa said she found out *McClure's* is going to do a series about John D. Rockefeller and Standard Oil. Now, this isn't really news. *McClure's* does this kind of thing all the time. They did a series on Lincoln a few years back. A girl reporter did it, Ida Tarbell. She's pretty good for a woman. Anyway, she did one on Napoleon, too. It was very popular although I never would've thought Americans would be interested in some little Frenchman."

"This is all very interesting, but why did Louisa tell you about the Rockefeller piece?"

"Because this one was going to be different. See, they made Lincoln look like this big hero and even Napoleon looked pretty smart, but they weren't going to be nice to Rockefeller. Oh no. Turns out Tarbell grew up in the oil business. Father owned a refinery or something. Rockefeller put him out of business. This series is going to expose all of Rockefeller's shenanigans and make him look like the devil himself, breaking poor, honest men just to make a buck."

"Now, that sounds like something I would like to read," Frank said.

"Yeah, well, me, too, but that's *McClure's* for you. Louisa, though, she thought *New Century* should do something like that, too."

"She wanted to write about Standard Oil, too?"

"No, that would be a waste of time. *McClure's* already got a head start on that one, but she had another idea. She wanted to do a series on patent medicines," he said in disgust.

So far, this matched what Louisa had told Sarah, although Frank was pretty sure Louisa had claimed she had been assigned to write the story. "And you didn't want to do it?" Frank guessed.

"Look, Malloy, I don't know how much you know about publishing, but we rely on advertising to pay our bills and make a profit. That twenty-five cents you pay for a magazine doesn't come close to paying the bills. It's advertising that does, which is why we have a whole room full of artists drawing those ads."

"And pages and pages of them in the magazine," Frank said.

"Exactly. Most of those ads are for patent medicines, too, so if we insult those people, they'll pull their ads, and we'll be out of business in a week."

"I guess that's what you explained to Miss Rodgers," Frank said.

"I didn't have to. She already knew it, so I only had to remind her. But that wasn't the half of it. She also wanted to write the articles herself."

"Didn't you say she was an editor?"

"Editors edit, Malloy. They check spelling and punctuation, but they don't write. I didn't even hire her to edit really! She was supposed to be a secretary."

"I suppose you reminded her of that, too," Frank said.

"Of course I did. Can't have every Tom, Dick, and Harry thinking they can be a writer, can I?"

"Weren't you willing to give her a chance, though? She could have been the next Ida Tarbell."

"I wasn't going to let *anybody* write about patent medicines, Malloy. This is a family magazine. Can't have stories that upset people or get them stirred up. We try to uplift them. Be inspirational and all that garbage."

"A very noble endeavor," Frank said with only a hint of sarcasm, which Tibbot apparently didn't catch.

"Now, I did tell Louisa I'd give her a try as a writer if she was so set on it. She could write about women's things. As a trial, you understand. If she was any good, I'd give her more assignments."

"And that was when she got angry, I guess," Frank said, certain he was right.

"She is an ungrateful brat. Anybody else would've kissed my feet for an offer like that, but not Louisa. She just called me a name—some big word I can't remember—and told me she quit and marched out of here without another word to anybody."

"She said she was quitting?"

"She did. Said she was going to take her idea to another magazine, although she didn't clean out her desk. That's why I figured she'd be back the next day with her tail between her legs, begging for her job back. I'd have given it to her, too. She's a very good secretary. Or she was," he added sadly.

"Do you have any idea why she would have been in the building later that night?"

"No. Everyone had gone home, and the place was all locked up. They even have a guard on the ground floor in case anybody tries to get in."

"Your staff doesn't work late, then?"

"Sometimes we do, but only in emergencies. We left at the usual time on Monday."

Frank thought this over and realized Tibbot had given him a valuable piece of information. "You said Miss Rodgers didn't clean out her desk. May I look through her things? There might be something there that would give us a clue about who might have wanted to harm her."

"Help yourself. I doubt you'll find anything useful, though. Like I said, she was just a secretary."

A secretary who was doing research on patent medicines on the side, but Frank wasn't going to remind him of that.

Tibbot pushed a button on his desk and the woman who had shown Frank in appeared in the doorway, looking exasperated.

"I'm not your secretary, Mr. Tibbot, and if you don't stop pulling me away from my work, the magazine won't be laid out in time for the printer."

"We're all pulling together to get over losing poor Louisa," Tibbot said a little sheepishly. "Would you show Mr. Malloy here where Louisa's desk was? I told him he could look through it."

She made an impatient noise, glared at Frank, and said, "This way."

He followed her to a desk tucked away in an alcove created by the row of cubicle offices. A box sat on top of it, and when Frank glanced inside, he saw it was full of neatly stacked papers and folders.

"Have you already gathered up her things?" he asked, pulling a drawer open to find it empty.

"Not me. That box was there exactly like that when they finally let us back into the building on Tuesday morning. I thought maybe the police had packed up her things, but they didn't want the box, so I just left it here. I figured her family might come for it."

He quickly checked the other desk drawers. All empty. "And no one in the office cleaned out her desk?"

"None of us women, and I know the men wouldn't have touched it," she said with a hint of bitterness.

That left only one person, the person who probably needed these papers if she hoped to take her patent medicine article idea to another magazine. But why hadn't she taken them with her when she left on Monday night?

"Misogynist," the woman said.

Frank looked up in surprise. "I beg your pardon?"

"Misogynist," she repeated. "That's the name Louisa called him. It means a man who hates women."

Frank nodded. He knew that, but he just said, "I see."

"It's accurate, too." She fairly vibrated with suppressed fury.

"Were you and Louisa close?"

"Not many women work here. We stick together."

"I'm sure Louisa appreciated that. Would it be all right if

I took this box? I'm sure her family would love to have her things as a remembrance," Frank added, thinking that sounded like a plausible story.

"I thought the police didn't need anything from her desk," the woman said, suddenly suspicious.

"But I'm not the police." He pulled a business card out of his pocket and handed it to her.

"You're a private investigator," she said as if it were an accusation.

"And I'm investigating Louisa's murder. Her family hired me."

"But the police . . ." she tried to object.

"Aren't interested."

She sighed in resignation. "Of course they aren't. She's just a woman. And yes, you can take her things. No one here wants to know anything about her secret story idea, especially if it got her killed."

GINO DONATELLI SMILED AS HE ENTERED THE OFFICES of *Frank Malloy, Confidential Inquiries*, where he served as Frank Malloy's partner. He smiled because he was pretty sure Maeve would be sitting at her desk and he wanted her to know he was happy to see her.

He knew she tried very hard not to look like she was as pleased to see him, too. She couldn't hide the way her eyes lit up in that certain way, though.

"Did you find the missing Mrs. Dobbins so quickly?" she asked, referring to the case Gino had been working on.

"Yes, she was at her sister's house."

"I thought that was the first place Mr. Dobbins looked when he realized she was gone."

"It was, but of course the sister told him Mrs. Dobbins wasn't there and she had no idea where her sister might be."

She did smile at that, a teasing little grin. "But you got the sister to admit it."

He shrugged modestly and pulled one of the client chairs closer to her desk. "I explained who I was and asked if we couldn't try to work things out. The sister was tired of listening to Mrs. Dobbins weep and wail about her dastardly husband, so the sister made her sit down and tell me what Mr. Dobbins had done that was so dastardly. Then I advised Mr. Dobbins to apologize and promise to never do it again, which he did, so now they are reconciled."

"You are a wonder, Mr. Donatelli," she said without much sincerity. "Now, what was it that Mr. Dobbins did that was so awful?"

"That is not for your delicate ears I'm afraid, Miss Smith," he assured her.

She feigned offense. "My ears aren't all that delicate."

"But mine are and I don't want to have to hear it ever again." She pouted but he ignored her. "Where is the boss?" He nodded toward Mr. Malloy's office.

"Out on a case."

"A new one?" Gino asked, perking right up.

"Yes, and it's a *murder*," Maeve said provocatively.

Gino managed not to rub his hands together in anticipation. "I don't suppose you can tell me about it?"

"I can tell you all about it, and I'll start with the most

important fact: Mrs. Frank personally escorted this new client to our offices."

Gino whistled at this amazing information. "I'm sure you'll explain how that came to be, too."

"Of course I will."

And she did.

FRANK WAS STRUGGLING WITH THE BOX FROM LOUISA Rodgers's desk as he made his way toward the huge elevator when a man stepped out of the shadows to block his way.

"Excuse me," Frank said a little impatiently. The box was very heavy.

"I need to speak to you. In private," the man said. "It's about Miss Rodgers."

Frank noticed the man was in his shirtsleeves. He must be one of the artists he had seen working in the office. "All right, but I'll need to set this box down first."

"Over here," the man said, opening a door that led to the stairwell.

Frank stepped in and set the box down on a step. "You work for the magazine?"

"Yes, I'm Clyde Hoffman. I . . . I wanted you to know that Louisa and I were engaged."

So much for her father's belief that Louisa had no time for men. "Her family don't seem to be aware of this," Frank said, being diplomatic.

"It was a secret. It had to be because her family didn't approve. They wanted Louisa to have a career and do something important with her life."

Frank took a moment to study Clyde Hoffman. He was a rather plain-looking man in his thirties with a large nose and light brown hair that was thinning on top. He wore a thick mustache and long sideburns. His shirt was poorly pressed, as if he did his own laundry, and his pants and vest were a little worn. Plainly, the artists weren't overpaid at the magazine, and he certainly wasn't a young woman's idea of a Prince Charming. But love was blind.

Thank heaven or he wouldn't be married to Sarah.

"Does anyone else know about your relationship?" Frank asked.

"No, we knew that, well, Mr. Tibbot doesn't allow fraternization between the employees."

A very good rule, Frank thought, although he knew his own employees were fraternizing to beat the band.

"Were you aware that Miss Rodgers wanted to be a reporter?"

Clyde blinked a few times, as if fighting tears. "She . . . She was an amazing young woman."

"So I understand. Did you speak with her after she resigned on Monday?"

Clyde took a moment to pinch the bridge of his nose. Then he said, "I couldn't leave the office until the end of the day. It would have looked suspicious. And when I called on her at her rooming house after leaving here, she wasn't there, so no, I never had an opportunity to speak with her before . . ." His voice broke and he turned his head away.

"I'm sorry for your loss," Frank said quite sincerely. "It must be doubly hard because you can't mourn her in public."

He nodded and swiped his hand over his eyes before

turning back to Frank. "Although I don't suppose it matters if people find out now, does it?"

Frank wasn't sure so he didn't answer. "And you didn't know she was planning to come back to the office that night?"

"Oh no, not at all. The neighborhood isn't particularly dangerous, but it still isn't a good idea for a woman to be out alone after dark. If she had just sent for me . . ." He choked again.

"Do you have any idea who might have wished her harm?" Frank asked. He'd learned to ask it of everyone.

"None at all. Everyone loved Louisa. She was the perfect woman."

Frank doubted everyone would agree on that, but he nodded sympathetically. "If you think of anyone, though, let me know, please." He handed Hoffman his card.

"And you must let me know what you find out, Mr. Malloy," he said, looking down at the card. "I'm entitled to know who killed her, since I'm her fiancé."

"The only person entitled to information from me is my client," Frank said firmly.

"Client?" Hoffman glanced down at the card he still held, reading it for the first time. "You're not with the police."

"No, I'm not. I'm just trying to find out who killed Louisa. You're welcome to investigate on your own, of course, but if you do it just so you can get revenge, you'll only end up in trouble yourself, Mr. Hoffman," Frank warned, thinking of Mr. Rodgers.

"I only want to be kept informed," Hoffman insisted, "and her family isn't likely to do that, are they?"

"No, since they don't even know you exist. Why don't

you make yourself known to them? They might be willing to tell you what I find out."

Hoffman didn't look too happy at the prospect. "Do you happen to know when her funeral will be?"

Frank debated whether or not to tell him, but he would probably see it in the newspapers anyway. "I believe it will be on Saturday."

Hoffman nodded his thanks. "I need to get back. Thank you for your help, Mr. Malloy. I know Louisa would bless you for it."

With that, he left Frank in the stairwell with his box and a whole new suspect to consider.

AFTER MR. RODGERS LEFT, MRS. FRANK DROVE MR. MAL-loy to Police Headquarters to see if he could find out what the police know," Maeve explained to Gino when she was finished telling him the whole story about Louisa Rodgers.

"Did he leave any instructions for me?" Gino asked hopefully.

"No, but I'm sure he thought you'd have your hands full with the Dobbins case."

"And since I don't, I'm free to help."

"I'm glad to hear it," Mr. Malloy said, coming through the door. "You can start with this."

He plopped an obviously heavy box down onto Maeve's desk. Then he pulled out a handkerchief and mopped the perspiration from his face.

"What is that?" Gino asked as Maeve cautiously lifted a flap to peer inside.

"That is the contents of Louisa Rodgers's desk at the magazine," Mr. Malloy said.

"That was fast work," Maeve marveled.

"Did Maeve tell you about this case?" Mr. Malloy asked Gino.

"Yes, she just finished. Did you find out anything useful at Police Headquarters?" Gino asked.

"Not much. The office building has a guard in the lobby, but he was not at his post on Monday night, so no one saw what happened."

"Where was the guard?" asked Gino. He could be an important witness.

"That's something we'll need to ask him, but he was fired, so we'll have to track him down."

"I can do that," Gino said. "I should probably go by and talk to the new night watchman, too, and see if he knows where the guard was."

"What about the Dobbins case?"

"Mrs. Dobbins is back with her loving husband, so I'm at our disposal."

"As you were saying," Maeve said to get them back on track.

"Yes, well, Louisa told her boss on Monday that she wanted to do an article on patent medicine, and he told her she couldn't, so she quit."

"She quit?" Maeve repeated in amazement.

"She just walked out. Looks like she went back to the office that evening to collect the stuff from her desk, though. She must have packed this up then because we know she didn't do it before she walked out. The box was sitting on her desk, just like this, when the rest of the staff came in on Tuesday morning."

Gino reached into the box, pulled out a handful of papers, and began flipping through them.

"If she went back to pack up her things, why didn't she take them with her that night?" Maeve asked, craning her neck to see what Gino was looking at.

"Try to lift this box," he said.

Maeve looked up in surprise. "Me?"

"Yes, try to lift it."

She exchanged a confused glance with Gino but then wrapped her arms around the box to lift it. She got it a few inches off the desktop, then let it drop again with a thump. "That's heavy."

"I know. I had to get a cab back to the office because I wasn't going to try to carry it all the way here. I think Louisa must have realized she couldn't carry it either, which would explain why she left without it that night."

"And why she was at the office so late," Maeve said. "She wouldn't want to face the people in the office after her dramatic exit, so that would explain why she went after hours to collect her things."

"But how did she get in?" Gino asked.

"She probably had a key to the office," Maeve said. "I have to have one to this office so I can get in here when you men are out."

"And I don't think her boss would have thought to get it from her after their argument," Mr. Malloy said.

"They had an argument?" Maeve said, delighted. "This is really getting interesting."

Gino gave her a disapproving look, which she ignored.

"I believe their discussion was rather heated, yes," Mr. Malloy said.

"Good for her, God rest her soul," Maeve said.

"Do you think her boss might've killed her?" Gino asked. "If he was mad enough, I mean."

"It's possible, I guess, but he didn't strike me as that type. He was more likely to complain about her leaving than to seek blood vengeance or something."

"Still, it's something to consider," Gino said.

"Don't worry, I won't forget about him. I did meet someone else who was interesting, though. Turns out, Louisa was engaged to a man who also works for the magazine, one of the artists."

"Engaged?" Maeve said with approval. "Still waters run deep. I'll bet a week's pay her parents don't know about him."

"He said it was a secret engagement, so no, they don't know."

"And your salary is safe," Gino said, not even looking up from the papers.

"I would have won the bet," she pointed out.

Gino just smiled.

"At any rate," Mr. Malloy went on doggedly, "we are now fairly certain why Louisa returned to the office that evening."

"Do we think she was alone?" Maeve asked. "Wouldn't it be spooky going into an empty office building after dark?"

"It would," Mr. Malloy said. "Her fiancé, whose name is Clyde Hoffman by the way, didn't accompany her because he wasn't asked to. Or so he says. He said he went to her rooming house after he got off work in order to check on her, but she wasn't there."

"Who else could have gone with her, then? That might be the person who killed her," Gino said.

"Or maybe she was alone, and her killer simply saw a chance to kill a defenseless female," Maeve countered.

"Do men just roam the city looking for young women to murder?" Gino asked.

He instantly regretted his question when he saw the withering look Maeve gave him. "Look at how many young women are murdered in this city, and you realize that just might be the case."

"We don't know that's what happened to Miss Rodgers yet," Mr. Malloy pointed out in the same tone he used on his children when they were arguing. "But it would be a good idea to find out if anyone saw her that night and if she was alone."

"I'll need to go to the building to find out where the guard lives, and I can also note who is around there late at night and find out if they saw anything," Gino hastily offered.

"Do we know where Louisa went when she left the office that afternoon? Knowing who she saw might help us find out if anyone went back to the office with her," Maeve said.

"I would expect she went to her rooming house, even though Hoffman said she wasn't there later," Mr. Malloy said. "It's supposed to be just a few blocks from the magazine."

"I could check on that," Maeve said. "The other women who live there would be more inclined to talk to me than to a man."

"She's right," Gino said, earning him an approving smile from Maeve.

Mr. Malloy consulted his pocket watch. "It's almost time for you to get Catherine at school, so you can wait until this evening to go to the rooming house. The other residents are probably still at work now anyway. Then the funeral is Saturday, so I'll want to attend that and see what we can find out."

"Should Maeve and I plan to attend as well?" Gino asked.

Mr. Malloy hesitated for a long moment as he considered. "No, I don't think so. I may want to use one or the other of you in different ways, so I don't want anyone to know you work for me."

Maeve looked pleased at this news, as well she might. She was usually confined to the office.

"So, after supper, Maeve, you go to the rooming house and talk to the landlord and anyone else you can find. Gino, you'll have to locate the guard they fired. His name is Billy Funhouser. Your idea of asking about him at the building is a good one, too. Someone there should know where this Billy lives."

"What will you do?" Maeve asked Mr. Malloy.

"I think Sarah and I will pay a condolence visit to the Rodgers family and see what else we can find out. In the meantime, we need to go through all these papers and see what we can learn from them."

WHEN MR. MALLOY LEFT, MAEVE COULDN'T HELP GIVING a little squeal of joy at getting an actual assignment. She did prefer being a detective to being a nanny.

"I can walk you to the rooming house later. It's just a few blocks from the magazine office and I'm going there anyway," Gino said a little too casually. He was, she knew, just looking for an excuse to be with her.

"You don't have to be at the magazine building until much later, and I certainly don't need an escort," she said.

He pulled a face. "A woman was murdered in that neighborhood just a few days ago."

"Yes, but—"

"But nothing. What if she was killed by a man who is just wandering the streets looking for a lone female to murder?"

She glared at him for echoing her own theory, but she couldn't argue back since she had suggested it herself. Instead, she said, "We'll see. Besides, you have to stay here and go through these papers from Louisa's desk."

"That won't take long," he said.

"It will if you read them," she countered, reaching into the box and pulling out a batch. She handed it to him and pulled out one for herself. She flipped through a few pages and realized a lot of them were notes about patent medicines.

"We should probably sort these before we try reading them," she said. "This pile is for information about patent medicines and this pile is for everything else."

He frowned but he laid a few sheets on the everything else pile and started going through his stack again.

"What do you think about this secret engagement?" Gino asked after a few minutes. The stacks were getting higher, and sorting was easier than he'd thought it would be.

Maeve had to think about his question. "I was surprised when Mr. Malloy mentioned it. Somehow, I didn't see Louisa as being the type for romantic nonsense like secret engagements."

"We never knew her, though. Maybe she was a romantic at heart."

"But don't romantic girls who are set on getting married dedicate their lives to that instead of getting a job at a magazine and trying to get promoted?"

"I'm not a girl, so it's hard for me to judge, but I know that all some girls think about is getting married."

Maeve smiled. He also knew she wasn't one of them, although thoughts of marriage had been cropping up a lot lately, now that Gino had made his feelings for her obvious. "Louisa seems to have worked pretty hard at having a career instead of getting married, though. I can't quite make myself believe she was engaged, although why would that fellow lie about it?"

"Maybe he wants sympathy," Gino said.

"Lying about a dead woman seems like an odd way to get it."

"There are a lot of odd people in the world, though."

Maeve sighed as she added to the patent medicine pile. "You're right, there are. I just hope Louisa had a friend at this rooming house. Maybe a friend could tell us for sure what was going on between Louisa and this fellow since her family obviously didn't know."

"Chances are good she did have one. Girls tend to confide in one another, don't they?"

"Sometimes," Maeve said, thinking how rarely she had

done so. She'd had so much to hide when she was growing up. As the last in a long line of grifters, she had known she could trust no one. Now she had a new family, and she was sure she could trust all of them. The problem was, she still couldn't bring herself to do it. "How is little Roberto doing?" she asked to change the subject.

Gino grinned proudly. "He's sitting up now, which I'm told is a great accomplishment for a baby." Gino was quite taken with his nephew, the first grandchild in the Donatelli family. "And don't let Teo hear you calling him *Roberto*. She wants him to be completely American, so she decided we have to call him Robert."

"Is *Robbie* all right? I don't think I can call a baby Robert," Maeve said.

"You'll have to ask Teo. My sister-in-law has turned into a real firebrand when it comes to her baby. Even Rinaldo is afraid of her."

Maeve laughed. "If the baby's father is afraid of her, I guess I should be careful, but you can't blame her for wanting the best for her child."

"No, you can't," Gino said. "We should go visit them on Saturday. You haven't seen Robert for weeks. Teo was asking about you at dinner last Sunday. Or maybe you could come to Sunday dinner with the whole family," he added with a sly smirk.

She frowned. He knew she was terrified of his mother. "I have to watch Catherine and Brian on Saturday since the Malloys will be at Louisa's funeral."

"Then Sunday dinner it is. I'll let Ma know," he said with a grin.

IV

AFTER SUPPER, SARAH ALLOWED MALLOY TO DRIVE HER electric motorcar up to Morningside Heights where the Rodgers lived. Maeve had brought Catherine home from school, eaten a hasty meal, and left to visit Louisa's rooming house. She hoped to catch some of the lodgers as they arrived home from their jobs. Gino had stayed at the office to look through Louisa's papers until it was late enough to visit the office building.

"I feel guilty leaving your mother with the children," Sarah told Malloy as they made their way through the early-evening traffic.

"She loves it, and you know it," Malloy said.

"They can be a handful, and Maeve is supposed to have the care of them in the evening. I know your mother is tired after volunteering at the school all day."

"I don't think they work her too hard. She mostly sits with the children and practices the signs with them."

"Which explains why she is so much better at signing than we are," Sarah said with a sigh.

"At least we're trying to learn," Malloy reminded her. "Not all the parents do."

"I know," Sarah said sadly. "I can't understand how a parent of a deaf child could refuse to learn to sign. How would you communicate with your child? How would the child let the parents know what she needs?"

"Let's talk about something more cheerful," Malloy suggested.

"Like murder?" Sarah guessed.

"Yes, like murder," he confirmed with a grin. "I see you brought your medical bag."

"Just in case Mrs. Rodgers will let me examine her. That's a good way to start a conversation, since you're all alone with the person with no one to hear or interrupt."

"And if she won't let you examine her?"

"I'll still try to have a conversation with her while you're talking to her husband, and hopefully her son."

"I wonder if there's any point in trying to search Louisa's room there, too. She might have brought something home with her when she visited."

"I can't imagine I'll get a chance to do that, but I'll try," Sarah said.

They found the Rodgerses' house with no difficulty. Located on a tree-lined side street, it was a five-story town house with a white marble facade. Quite impressive, Sarah had to admit, except for the black mourning wreath on the door.

They parked the motor in front, and Sarah left her medical bag in the vehicle, so she didn't look too pushy. A maid answered the doorbell, and Malloy gave her his card and told her they were there to see Mr. Rodgers if he was available.

"The house is in mourning, sir," the girl said with a frown. "They aren't receiving visitors."

"This concerns Miss Rodgers's death. Mr. Rodgers has hired me to investigate, and I need to speak with him about it."

The maid didn't look too convinced, but she showed them into the parlor and asked them to wait while she checked to see if her master was "at home." If a person didn't want to see a visitor, they would simply instruct the servant to tell the visitor they were not at home.

The parlor was a pleasant room with a large window overlooking the small garden behind the house. The last of the summer flowers were just visible in the twilight shadows. The room was luxuriously furnished with velvet-covered sofas and chairs grouped around an elaborately carved fireplace. Velvet drapes adorned the window.

The girl returned a few minutes later to say that Mr. Rodgers would join them soon.

They waited about five minutes and Mr. Rodgers came in. He looked much steadier than he had that morning when he first showed up on Sarah's doorstep, but his face was still haggard with grief. Sarah couldn't even imagine the pain he must be feeling at the loss of his child.

"Mrs. Malloy, I didn't expect to see you here, too," Mr. Rodgers said.

Sarah couldn't tell if he was annoyed by her presence or just the visit in general. She smiled and said, "I thought I would come along and offer Mrs. Rodgers some support, if I may."

He frowned at that, then turned to Malloy. "I hope you have some news for me."

"I have found out some things, but it's only been a few hours since you hired me, so I don't know very much just yet. I wanted to ask you about the things I've discovered before I go any further, though."

"Very well, but I believe I already told you everything I know. Please, sit down. Can I get you some coffee? I'm afraid I can't offer anything stronger, since we are temperance."

Malloy glanced at Sarah, who nodded. "We'd appreciate some coffee," he said.

Rodgers instructed the maid, who was still loitering in the hallway, to bring the refreshments. Sarah and Malloy sat down on the sofa and Mr. Rodgers took one of the chairs facing them. "Now, what do you want to ask me?" he asked with resignation.

"We learned that you were correct about Louisa being a secretary for the magazine, but it seems she was also working on writing an article for them. She wanted to become a reporter."

"As I told you, that was how I met her," Sarah said quickly, before Mr. Rodgers could challenge Malloy. "She was doing research for this article she was writing."

Mr. Rodgers frowned. "I don't suppose I should be surprised. Louisa always excelled at everything she turned her hand to. She wouldn't have been satisfied with being a secretary for very long."

"We also discovered that Louisa told Mr. Tibbot about her plan to write the article and he told her he wouldn't publish it," Malloy said.

"Tibbot? He's the one who owns the magazine, isn't he?" Mr. Rodgers said.

"Yes. He isn't a very tactful man, I'm afraid," Malloy said, "and I'm sure he wasn't very kind when he turned down Louisa's idea, which is probably why she resigned from the magazine."

"Resigned?" Mr. Rodgers echoed in outrage. "Who told you such a thing?"

"Mr. Tibbot did, and others on the staff confirmed it. She walked out of the office in the middle of the afternoon on Monday."

"And you think this had something to do with her death?" Mr. Rodgers asked.

"We aren't sure, but knowing where she went after she left the office and who she saw and spoke with might help us figure out what happened."

A middle-aged woman dressed in mourning black appeared in the parlor doorway. "Who are these people and what are they doing in my house?" she demanded.

MAEVE HAD FINALLY CONVINCED GINO THAT SHE DIDN'T need a bodyguard to visit Louisa's rooming house. She had set off early enough that it would still be light when she arrived, at least. She found the Rose Hill neighborhood to be very civilized, though, with nary a plug-ugly lurking and ready to pounce on a victim.

Louisa Rodgers's rooming house was a five-story brownstone in a long row of town houses. It looked a little shabby next to its neatly kept neighbors. But then, prosperous people didn't rent out rooms, did they?

Like its neighbors, the house was less than twenty feet wide, but she knew it would probably stretch back more than fifty feet on the oblong lot. It would have plenty of rooms to rent. The sign in the window said there was a room available, too. They weren't wasting any time replacing Louisa.

Maeve climbed the front steps and rang the bell. A pleasant-looking young woman opened the door. Her brown hair was gathered in a knot on top of her head in a poor imitation of the classic Gibson girl style. She wore a black skirt and white shirtwaist, the basic uniform of every working woman in the city. The only variations were the quality of the materials and the splash of color in the tie or bow the woman wore at her throat. This woman wore a colorful scarf to brighten up a rather threadbare ensemble.

"You here about the room?" she asked.

"Yes," Maeve said, thinking that would get her in the door faster than admitting her true purpose. "Are you the landlady?"

The woman laughed at that. "Not hardly. That's Mrs. Baker. Come in and I'll get her."

Maeve did as directed. She had dressed carefully in her own dark skirt and white shirtwaist with a jacket to look a little more formal. She had chosen a modest hat. She wanted to look like someone who needed to rent a room but who could afford it.

"I'm Nellie. Nellie Potter," the woman who had answered the door said. "Wait here. I'll get Mrs. Baker."

Nellie went down the hallway and into one of the rooms.

Maeve saw a parlor to her right, a large room with a fireplace that wasn't burning now because the days were still warm. The furniture had once been good quality but was starting to show its age. Still, everything appeared to be clean and in good order. Maeve could see Louisa being satisfied with the accommodations.

A round little woman came out of the same door Nellie had disappeared into. She was smoothing her dress and patting her hair, like she wanted to make a good impression. Her cheeks were flushed, as if she was overheated, although the day was pleasant. "Hello, I'm Mrs. Baker. Have you come about the room?"

"Yes, I have. I've just taken a secretarial job in the neighborhood, and I'd like a place nearby, so I don't have to use the El," Maeve said.

Mrs. Baker looked her over. "Irish, are you?"

"No," Maeve said. She was an American. "Maeve Smith."

Mrs. Baker frowned. Maeve was an Irish name, but Maeve didn't even blink. "Well, if you pay your rent and follow the rules, it don't make no nevermind." She told her what the rent was. The rules were that the tenants weren't allowed to hang around the house during the workday— because that would mean they had lost their jobs and could no longer pay rent. They also could entertain gentlemen callers only on Sunday afternoon in the parlor. No men were allowed in the bedrooms ever. No strong drink on the premises and any girl who appeared intoxicated will be turned out. Rent was due every Friday. If you missed one week, you were out on your ear. Maeve nodded her understanding.

"That sounds reasonable. My family was adamant that I find a safe place to live."

Did Mrs. Baker grow a little pale at that? Maeve pretended not to notice.

"Oh, you'll be safe enough here," Mrs. Baker said with a little too much confidence. "I look after my girls."

"That's good to know. How many rooms do you have available?"

"Just the one right now."

Good, she'd be sure of seeing Louisa's old room. "Did someone get married?" Maeve asked as innocently as she could manage, which was pretty well.

This time the color rose in Mrs. Baker's face.

"No, uh, she had to, uh, leave. Her family needed her."

"That's too bad. May I see the room?"

"Oh yes. Nellie!" she called, startling Maeve.

Nellie came at once. She had probably been eavesdropping.

"Nellie, can you show Miss Smith Louisa's old room? My bunions are aching me something fierce and I don't think I can manage the stairs." Indeed, she did seem to be having a little trouble walking.

"I'd be happy to," Nellie said with so much enthusiasm that Maeve understood she wasn't just doing her landlady a favor. "It's downstairs. This way."

Maeve was a bit surprised, but she followed as Nellie led her down the hallway to a door under the main staircase.

This would lead to the first floor—the garden or terrace level—where the kitchen would be located.

"Don't worry, there's a window," Nellie said, having seen Maeve's hesitation. "It's a very nice room, even if it is down-stairs. It would normally be the cook's room, I guess."

"Does the cook not live in, then?" Maeve asked.

"We don't have one. Mrs. Baker just does for herself. The rest of us get our meals out except for a little breakfast."

Which was a trend in the city since there were now so many cafés and restaurants where people—including unac-companied females—could eat cheaply. Boardinghouses that supplied tenants with breakfast and supper were be-coming rooming houses only.

The kitchen was in the back of the house, a bright room that opened out into the back terrace. Nellie led Maeve to the front of the house, past a water closet. "You'd have that to yourself, but you'd have to go upstairs to get a bath," Nellie explained.

She opened a door and led Maeve into a nice-sized room furnished with a bed, a wardrobe, and a chest of drawers. A window looked out onto the patch of yard beside the front steps and the sidewalk beyond.

"Louisa liked being down here by herself," Nellie said. "She didn't want the rest of us bothering her when she was working."

"What was she working on?" Maeve asked, idly open-ing the wardrobe as if she wasn't very interested in the answer.

"She was a writer," Nellie said. "She was always writing things."

"Mrs. Baker said she left because her family needed her at home," Maeve said. "Was that the real reason?"

Nellie started to answer, then glanced at the door, which was still open. She went over and shut it before saying very solemnly, "Poor Louisa died." This was most likely the reason Nellie had been so willing to take Maeve to see the room. She had wanted to break this news herself.

"She *died*?" Maeve echoed, properly shocked. "How on earth did she die?"

"Someone killed her. Not here," she hastily added. "It happened at her office, the place where she worked. Late at night. She shouldn't have been out at that time of night, or at least that's what Mrs. Baker says."

"How awful. It must have been a shock for everyone here," Maeve said.

Nellie drew a breath and let it out in a tragic sigh. "It was awful. It still is awful, I mean. Louisa was my very best friend in all the world."

"I'm so sorry. You must have known her well, then."

"Oh yes. We told each other everything," Nellie assured her.

"Then she must have told you about the story she was writing for the magazine."

"Of course she did. She was always working on it when she was here. She never had time to go dancing or to see a show. I used to tell her, Louisa, I would say, you'll work yourself to death. And now . . ." She let her voice trail off and wiped a tear from her eye.

"Did she tell you about Clyde Hoffman, too?" Maeve tried.

Nellie looked down to where she had clutched her hands in front of her. "She talked about him all the time."

"Did she tell you they were engaged?"

Nellie looked up, startled. "How do *you* know that?"

"I know it was a secret, but Mr. Hoffman himself told us about their engagement."

Nellie's expression changed from surprise to shock, and she took a step back. "Who is this *us* you're talking about, and how do you know so much about Louisa?"

Maeve glanced at the door to make sure it was closed tightly. "I'm sorry to deceive you, but I'm a private investigator." Maeve found Nellie's wide-eyed reaction to that information a little insulting, but she didn't let it faze her. "Louisa's family hired our firm to investigate her death. I'm supposed to question the people here to see if they know of anyone who might want to harm her."

Nellie needed a moment to absorb this information. "You'd waste your time talking to the other girls, then. They hardly had a word for Louisa, and she hardly had a word for them either. Not her sort at all. It was just the two of us. We'd go out for a meal together and sit up late at night talking about our beaux. I'm the only one who knows anything about her at all. That's why Mrs. Baker trusted me to pack up her things after . . . Well, after, although somebody had already done it. One of the other girls, I guess, but I'm the one Mrs. Baker asked to do it because we was such good friends."

Maeve had pulled open a drawer in the dresser to find it empty, too. "Then you already sent all her belongings to her family?"

"Mrs. Baker wanted to let the room as soon as possible."

Maeve nodded. "Do you know if Louisa was having trouble with anyone? Was she frightened of someone?"

"Not a soul. Everyone loved her. She was happy as a lark and planning to get married to her Mr. Hoffman."

"What about the people she knew at the magazine? Did she ever talk about them?" Maeve asked.

Nellie looked up at the ceiling as if the answer were written there. "She complained about them some. They didn't appreciate her. That's always the way, isn't it? You work yourself near to death and they just want more."

This was the second time Nellie had mentioned death in relation to Louisa. Maeve managed not to point it out. "Did you see Louisa the day she died?"

Nellie frowned, trying to remember. "I saw her in the kitchen. Mrs. Baker lets us make toast in the morning. Louisa grabbed a piece before she left."

"Did you see her afterward?"

Nellie shook her head.

"I thought you had dinner together every night," Maeve said.

"Not every night. She worked late sometimes, and sometimes a fellow buys my dinner." Nellie smiled coyly. "Anyway, she never came in at all that day. The next morning Mrs. Baker was furious because Louisa was out all that night, and she was saying she couldn't have such a creature in her house, and she was going to send Louisa packing as soon as she showed her face. Then the police came, and Mrs. Baker was all sad and crying about losing such a wonderful girl like that."

"Thank you for telling me all this. I'll need to speak with Mrs. Baker, though. I'll have to confess to her why I'm here, too. Do you think she'll throw me out?"

"I'll vouch for you," Nellie promised. "I just want to see her face when she finds out you're a private detective."

Mrs. Baker's expression was everything Nellie could have hoped for.

"You better not be thinking anybody here did that girl harm," Mrs. Baker said when Maeve had properly introduced herself. "Louisa could get above herself sometimes, but nobody would kill her for that."

"What do you mean, 'above herself'?" Maeve asked sweetly.

Mrs. Baker sighed. "Thought she was better than the other girls here."

"She *was* better than they are, too," Nellie said. "She came from money. You could tell."

"Which is why I was happy to rent to her," Mrs. Baker said primly. "I knew she'd be able to pay."

"Mrs. Baker, did you see Louisa on Monday, the day she died?"

"See her? I probably did, although I don't remember exactly. All the girls come down to the kitchen for a piece of bread and jam in the morning. She might've been there, but I couldn't swear to it."

"What about later in the afternoon? Did she come here after work, say around three o'clock?"

"I didn't see her at all the rest of that day, but she wouldn't have come here at three. I told you the rules. I don't like the girls to be here during working hours. They should be at their jobs, shouldn't they?"

Except Louisa had quit her job that afternoon.

And if she hadn't come here, where had she gone?

Mr. Rodgers jumped to his feet and turned to the woman in black. "Hilda, this is Mr. and Mrs. Malloy. They are our guests," he said sternly.

Mrs. Rodgers looked at him as if she didn't know him for a moment, and then her expression cleared and she looked back at Sarah and Malloy, who had also risen. "Have we met?" she asked.

"No, we haven't," Sarah hastily assured her. "We're sorry to intrude at this difficult time, but we needed to speak with your husband."

She turned back to her husband, as if for an explanation. She was a small woman, delicately made, but her expression was hard.

He rubbed a hand across his face. "Remember, I told you I hired a private investigator to find out who . . ." He had to stop and swallow before finishing. ". . . who killed Louisa."

Her face crumpled at that. "Louisa," she said in despair.

When Mr. Rodgers made no move to go to her, Sarah did so. She took the woman's hand in both of hers. "This must seem like a nightmare to you. Perhaps we could go somewhere else while the men discuss their business."

Mrs. Rodgers looked down at where Sarah held her hand. "Yes," she said. "I should like to go back to my room."

"I'll take you," Sarah said, not even glancing at Mr. Rodgers lest he try to stop her. "Come along. You'll have to tell me where to go."

Sarah held her breath, hoping Mr. Rodgers wouldn't stop her, but perhaps he was grateful to have someone remove his wife from the room. Whatever his reasoning, he said nothing. Sarah took Mrs. Rodgers's arm and walked her out into the hallway.

"It's upstairs," Mrs. Rodgers said.

The two women made their way up the grand staircase to the second floor. This was probably where Mr. and Mrs. Rodgers had their bedrooms. Sarah let Mrs. Rodgers lead the way to the room that would face the back of the house. This was obviously a woman's retreat. The four-poster bed was draped with yellow silk and covered with a yellow satin spread. The wallpaper was a riot of daisies and the furniture French with gold leaf and many curlicues. A love seat sat in front of the ornate fireplace, flanked by two slipper chairs. A fainting couch had been placed beneath the window so the lady of the house could recline while enjoying a view of the garden.

"What a lovely room," Sarah said, helping Mrs. Rodgers sit down on the love seat. "Can I get you anything?"

Mrs. Rodgers glanced over her shoulder, in the direction of the bed, but she said, "No, thank you."

Her expression was so bleak, Sarah had to do something. "I'm very sorry about Louisa. She was a fine young lady."

"You knew her, then?" Mrs. Rodgers asked in surprise.

"Yes. I met her when . . . Well, did you know she was writing an article for the magazine?"

Instead of softening, as Sarah had expected, Mrs. Rodgers's expression hardened. "That girl. I knew she would come to no good. What an unnatural creature she was, always questioning and challenging. God ordained a woman's place to be a helpmeet to her husband and a mother to her children, but that wasn't good enough for Louisa. She was always rebelling. I warned her father not to send her to college. That place just filled her head with all sorts of nonsense. They made her think she could go out into the world and make her own way like a man, and now you see what that got her."

Sarah was shocked but not surprised. Many people reacted to a loss like this with anger, blaming the victim for causing the tragedy. "A lot of young women attend college," Sarah said gently.

"Which is exactly what is wrong with our society. Girls aren't constitutionally able to withstand the pressures of this world. That is why God put men in charge. They protect us from evil and keep us safe."

"Then you would have approved if Louisa wanted to marry," Sarah said, thinking of the secret engagement.

"Approved? I would have celebrated, but that girl insisted she was never going to marry. She wouldn't put herself in some man's control, or at least that's what she claimed."

Sarah could have spoken about the dangers of putting one's self in the control of the wrong man. She also could have mentioned Clyde Hoffman and the supposed secret engagement, but she decided Mrs. Rodgers wasn't in any condition to listen to either.

"Losing a child is so difficult. You have a son, too, don't you?" Sarah tried.

This time Mrs. Rodgers's expression did soften. "Yes, my Oscar. He's everything a mother could want. So different from his sister." She had been clutching a handkerchief in one hand and she pressed it to her lips. "I need my salts."

She got up and disappeared into an adjoining room. That would be a dressing room or a bath, a place she would logically keep smelling salts. Sarah didn't think she should follow her, so she waited, and after a few minutes, Mrs. Rodgers reappeared. She did seem to be a little calmer and the color had returned to her cheeks.

"I'm sorry to have burdened you with my problems," she said with more composure than she had shown before.

"That's perfectly fine. I'm a nurse and I felt obligated to help."

"A nurse?" Mrs. Rodgers echoed in disapproval. "But aren't you married?"

"I trained as a nurse and I'm also a midwife. I had to earn my living when my first husband died." Which wasn't the whole truth. She could have returned to her wealthy parents, but she, like Louisa, had been in rebellion back then herself.

"And now you're married to Mr. . . . . I'm sorry, I've forgotten the name."

"Malloy," Sarah said, knowing Mrs. Rodgers would probably turn up her nose at the Irish name.

This time Mrs. Rodgers simply let her expression speak of her disapproval, but she did purse her lips a bit to let it be known. "I see. And Mr. Malloy is a private investigator."

"Yes. You see, I gave Louisa my card in case she needed more information from me. She was interviewing me for the article she was writing. Your husband found my card in her purse and came to ask me what I knew about her that might help find her killer."

"And your husband just happened to be a private investigator," Mrs. Rodgers said, not even trying to hide her disapproval this time.

"Mr. Rodgers seemed intent on finding the killer himself since the police expressed little interest in doing so."

"And the police are right. We'll never know who killed Louisa. Through her own willfulness, she put herself in a dangerous situation and fell prey to some lunatic."

"Then shouldn't we try to find that lunatic to prevent him from killing some other innocent woman?" Sarah asked.

"If the police don't think they can do that, what makes your husband believe he can?"

"Because he's done it before."

That startled her into silence. Several emotions flickered across her face, too quickly for Sarah to identify them. Finally, Mrs. Rodgers said, "Good luck to him, then. But in the end, it doesn't matter. Nothing will bring Louisa back."

FRANK WAITED UNTIL THE WOMEN WERE GONE. HE WAS a little surprised that Rodgers hadn't objected to Sarah going off with his wife after the way he'd objected to the very thought of it this morning, but he was glad. If Mrs. Rodgers knew anything, Sarah would find out.

"My wife is devastated by Louisa's death," Rodgers said by way of explanation.

"She has every right to be."

Rodgers sat back down, so Frank did, too.

"Now, where were we?" Rodgers asked. "You said Louisa had resigned from her position at the magazine, which I find difficult to believe."

"Yes. She walked out of the office after Mr. Tibbot told her he wouldn't publish her article. We believe that she returned that night to collect the things from her desk. She had quite a few papers, some of which may have been notes for the article she was writing. She wouldn't want to leave them behind and she didn't want to return to the office during regular hours and face the other people in the office."

"How did you figure all that out?" Mr. Rodgers asked in amazement.

"I found a box containing everything that had been in her desk, all packed and ready to go except Louisa must have realized it was too heavy for her to carry. I could hardly carry it myself. Perhaps she intended to return later with help, but whatever her plans, that would explain why she was at the office at that hour of the night."

"But not who killed her," Mr. Rodgers said sadly.

"Not yet. I don't suppose you saw Louisa that afternoon, after she walked out of her office."

"Saw her?" he repeated, puzzled.

"Yes. We think she might have gone back to her rooming house. We have someone checking that. But we also thought she might have come here."

Mr. Rodgers sighed. "I doubt she would have come here. She would have had to tell us about her failure, and she was too proud to do that unless she was in extremis. I wasn't here, though, so I couldn't tell you. Normally, I would have been at my office in any case, but that day I was in Albany, meeting with legislators. There is some legislation being considered that our firm has an interest in. I didn't get home until almost midnight."

Louisa would probably have been dead by then. They both knew it, but neither man could say it.

"I suppose your wife would have mentioned it if Louisa had been here that day," Frank said.

Rodgers rubbed a hand over his face again. The poor man was obviously in agony. "If only to gloat. She never approved of the way Louisa chose to live her life. She believes a woman's place is in the home as a wife and mother. Hilda and Louisa were always at loggerheads. Hilda would have been crowing if she knew Louisa had left the magazine."

"Louisa was fortunate she had you to encourage her," Frank said.

"Was she?" Rodgers asked sadly. "If she had married and had a family, she would still be alive."

Mrs. Rodgers was right. Nothing would bring Louisa back, but perhaps finding her killer would save other lives. At least it would bring justice, which was so difficult to come by in this world. Sarah took a moment to think about what else they might learn from Mrs. Rodgers, who was blotting her eyes with her handkerchief.

"When was the last time you saw Louisa?" Sarah asked.

Mrs. Rodgers's head jerked up. "What does that matter?"

What an odd reaction. Sarah smiled innocently. "We know Louisa left the magazine office in the midafternoon on the day she died. We are trying to find out where she went and who she saw between then and when she was killed."

Mrs. Rodgers closed her eyes and sighed deeply, as if fighting off a wave of pain. When she opened her eyes again, she said, "I hadn't seen Louisa for weeks. She used to come on Sundays to go to church with us and have dinner afterward, but . . ."

Which probably made it unlikely Louisa had kept anything of importance in her room here, so there was no use trying to search it. "Did something happen between you?" Sarah prodded when Mrs. Rodgers hesitated, half expecting Mrs. Rodgers to snap at her for the presumption.

But she didn't. Mrs. Rodgers's back was ramrod straight and every muscle seemed to tense. "She said she was tired of listening to my advice." Mrs. Rodgers turned her head and looked straight into Sarah's eyes. "Do you have children, Mrs. Malloy?"

"Yes," Sarah said. Her children had not been born to her, but they were hers now.

"Then you know the pain I felt when my daughter chose to ignore everything I ever taught her. *Everything.* Louisa broke my heart. I wasn't sorry when she stopped coming to visit."

"Then she didn't come here on Monday afternoon?" Sarah had to be sure.

"Why would she have?"

Sarah had no answer. Mrs. Rodgers would hardly have offered Louisa comfort, and her gloating over Louisa's failure would have chafed.

"Now, if you don't mind, I'd like to lie down. The doctor has given me a sedative to take, and the oblivion of sleep is the only relief I can get right now."

THE COFFEE HAD ARRIVED, AND FRANK SIPPED HIS AS HE considered what other information Rodgers might be able to supply.

"Would it be possible to speak to your son, Mr. Rodgers? Louisa may have confided in him if she was having trouble with someone."

"Huh, she'd hardly turn to Oscar for help," Rodgers said in disgust. "The boy is worthless. Never could apply himself at school. Too lazy to complete his work. Hardly ever read a book if he could help it. Didn't even last one term at college. Not like Louisa, who excelled at everything."

"And now Louisa is dead," a young man said from the doorway. He was tall and slender with golden hair and a patrician face. "And you are stuck with me."

V

F<small>RANK AND</small> R<small>ODGERS BOTH LOOKED UP IN SURPRISE AT</small> the young man in the doorway. Frank rose to his feet, but Rodgers remained seated, his expression grim.

"Mr. Malloy, allow me to present my son, Oscar," Rodgers said, his dismay obvious.

"His worthless son," Oscar added with a bitter smile.

Frank said, "I'm very sorry about your sister."

Oscar's smile faded. "Poor Louisa. Such a bright light to be snuffed out so soon." Was he being sarcastic or sincere? Frank couldn't tell.

"Mr. Malloy is the private investigator I hired to look into Louisa's death," Rodgers said.

"Have you found anything?" Oscar asked, moving into the room and taking a seat in one of the empty chairs.

"I've learned some things about Louisa, but I had a few questions for your family. Had your sister mentioned having trouble with anyone? Someone at the magazine, for instance, or a spurned suitor perhaps?"

"If Louisa ever had a suitor of any kind, it would be a surprise to me," Oscar said. "She actively discouraged men from becoming interested in her. She was determined to live her own life without a man controlling her."

"If she did have a romantic interest, would she have told you?" Frank asked.

Oscar registered surprise at the question, and Rodgers said, "Of course she would have told us."

"Why did you ask that particular question, Mr. Malloy?" Oscar wasn't fooled. He knew Frank must have a purpose.

Frank gave them both a moment to think about it. Then he said, "I have reason to believe that Miss Rodgers did have a suitor."

Rodgers frowned and Oscar sat up straighter in his chair. "I don't believe it. Or wait, maybe I do," he said. "Mother's fondest wish was for her to marry, so Louisa would have taken great delight in keeping that news from her."

What an odd family.

"Who was this mysterious suitor?" Rodgers demanded.

"I'm not at liberty to say right now," Frank hedged.

"Could he have killed her?" Oscar asked.

"We're still gathering evidence, and until we have all the information, everyone is a suspect," Frank said.

"Even me?" Oscar seemed to find this amusing.

"Yes, even you. Where were you on Monday from three o'clock in the afternoon until about midnight?"

. . .

Since Mrs. Rodgers had made it clear she wanted Sarah to leave her alone, Sarah rose to leave. "If you think of anyone who might have wanted to harm Louisa, please let my husband know."

"I'm trying not to think about Louisa at all," Mrs. Rodgers said, rising to encourage Sarah to be on her way.

She escorted Sarah to the door and opened it.

"I'm very sorry about Louisa," Sarah said again, but Mrs. Rodgers's attention had shifted.

She was gazing out into the hallway, and Sarah realized they could hear men's voices coming from downstairs.

"That's Oscar," Mrs. Rodgers said, and pushed past Sarah, hurrying down the stairs.

Sarah hurried after her, and they arrived at the door to the parlor in time to hear Malloy ask Oscar where he had been the day Louisa was killed.

"He was at home with me," Mrs. Rodgers said.

The three men looked up in surprise and all of them rose, as good manners demanded.

"And what does it matter where he was?" Mrs. Rodgers went on. "You can't think he killed his own sister."

"We're all suspects, Mother," the young man who must be Oscar said. "Mr. Malloy has just confirmed it." His smile told them what he thought of the notion.

"That's nonsense," Mrs. Rodgers said. "Louisa put herself in danger and some lunatic took advantage of her carelessness."

"But I'm supposed to be the careless one," Oscar said. "Louisa is the embodiment of every virtue."

His seemingly casual words told Sarah he harbored a well of resentment, but why? As the only son and heir, he should, by rights, hold the favored status in the family.

"Oh, Oscar, stop," his mother cried, pressing her handkerchief to her lips as she began to weep.

The young man went to her immediately and tenderly escorted her to the chair in which he had been sitting. Sarah slipped in unnoticed and took her old seat beside Malloy on the sofa. She glanced at Mr. Rodgers, who was watching his wife and son with a somewhat jaundiced eye. Did he really feel no compassion for them?

"Mrs. Rodgers said Louisa didn't come here after she left her office on Monday," she told Malloy softly.

"I told you she didn't," Mr. Rodgers said, having heard her.

"Why would Louisa have come here?" Oscar asked. He was still absently patting his mother on the back as she wept. "I thought she said she was done with all of us."

"Not *all* of us," Mr. Rodgers said angrily. "She would have come to me if she needed comforting."

"Since when did Louisa ever seek comfort for anything?" Oscar asked.

"She . . . she had a disagreement with her employer," Mr. Rodgers said reluctantly.

"Then she probably went to her rooming house," Mrs. Rodgers said. "That's the only thing that makes sense. I don't know why you're bothering us when we know nothing about all this. It's very upsetting," she added tearfully.

"We certainly didn't intend to upset you," Sarah assured her.

But Malloy obviously wasn't deterred by Mrs. Rodgers's

tears. "Did Louisa ever mention a man named Clyde Hoffman to you?"

Mrs. Rodgers's head came up at that and even Oscar looked interested. "Who is this Clyde Hoffman?" he asked.

"He works at the magazine," Malloy said, his gaze taking in all three of the Rodgerses, watching for their reactions.

"What has he done?" Mr. Rodgers asked. "Do you think he's the one who . . . ? Or is he the suitor you were talking about?"

"Suitor? What suitor?" Mrs. Rodgers asked, her tears forgotten.

"So Louisa did have a lover!" Oscar said, delighted by the prospect.

"That's impossible," Mrs. Rodgers insisted. "She would have told us."

"No, she wouldn't have. You would never have approved," Mr. Rodgers said.

"How can you say that?" Mrs. Rodgers cried, rising to her feet.

"Mother, don't upset yourself," Oscar said gently. "We don't know what Louisa would have done or not done. Maybe she was going to surprise us."

Sarah doubted that very much, but Oscar did seem to have a calming effect on his mother.

"Let me help you upstairs," Oscar said. "You can take some of your medicine and lie down."

Mrs. Rodgers allowed her son to escort her from the room.

"My wife is in very delicate health," Mr. Rodgers said by way of excuse.

"We understand completely," Sarah assured him.

"This Hoffman, who is he?" Mr. Rodgers asked.

"Just someone who has come to our attention," Malloy said. "If Louisa never mentioned him, he probably isn't important. I'm sorry to have upset your wife. We'll be going now. Please give her our apologies." Malloy rose.

Sarah rose, too, and they didn't wait for the maid to show them out.

Once they were outside and safely seated in the privacy of the motorcar, Malloy let out a long sigh. "I probably shouldn't have mentioned Hoffman, but I wanted to see if Louisa had said anything about him, especially if she was afraid of him."

"Obviously, she didn't confide much in them at all. What a sad family," Sarah said. "It appears that the mother dotes on the son and the father dotes on the daughter."

"And each parent hates the other child," Malloy finished. "You should have heard the things Rodgers said about his son."

"I'm not sure I'd say *hate*, but they are certainly very critical of the other child."

"The children must know how the parents feel, too."

"Children always know," Sarah said. "Well, at least we learned a few things."

"Yes. We learned Louisa didn't go to her parents' house when she walked out of the office on Monday afternoon."

"And we learned that Louisa's family knew nothing about her engagement to Clyde Hoffman." Sarah considered that for a moment. "Do you think they really were engaged?"

"Why would Hoffman make up something like that?"

"You're right. He'd have nothing to gain, but maybe they were seeing each other but they weren't actually engaged yet. He might exaggerate to . . . to . . ."

"To what?" Malloy asked. "To make himself more important?"

"Perhaps to make himself more important in the eyes of her family," Sarah said, "although that seems a bit silly. That would be unlikely to gain him anything either."

"He did want to know when the funeral was being held and I . . ."

"You did what?" Sarah prodded when he hesitated.

"I encouraged him to make himself known to her parents. That was probably a mistake."

"After the way they reacted to your question about him, they probably won't believe him anyway."

"No, they wouldn't. I don't suppose you had a chance to look in Louisa's room."

"No, Mrs. Rodgers was so unstable, I didn't want to upset her by asking. She said Louisa hadn't been home for weeks, though, and since she was living elsewhere, I didn't think searching her room would profit us much."

"We can always go back if we decide it's necessary. Let's hope Maeve found something at the rooming house."

I'D LIKE TO SPEAK WITH THE OTHER LODGERS IF I MAY," Maeve told Mrs. Baker when she felt she had learned all she could from the landlady.

"They won't know anything," Nellie said. "I'm the only one who was friends with Louisa."

Mrs. Baker gave her a frown, then turned to Maeve. "You can try, but they usually eat their supper out and then go dancing. They won't be home until late."

And Gino would have a fit if she stayed out that late. It might do him good to worry a bit, but she wasn't too eager to be riding the El late at night herself. "When would be a good time to catch them in?"

Mrs. Baker shrugged. "Sunday mornings. They work a half day on Saturday and then go out to have fun. They like to sleep in on Sunday."

"What time do they get up?" Maeve asked with a grin. This would be a perfect excuse to miss Sunday dinner with the Donatelli family.

Maeve had thanked Mrs. Baker and Nellie and was going out the door when she remembered something she had forgotten to ask. "Did anyone come here on Monday evening looking for Louisa?"

Mrs. Baker shook her head and turned to Nellie.

"I didn't see anybody. Who would it have been?" she asked but then seemed to realize the answer. "Her Mr. Hoffman, you mean."

"Who?" Mrs. Baker asked. She seemed annoyed that Nellie might know something she didn't.

"Her fiancé," Nellie said importantly. "But if he came, I didn't see him."

"Maybe he talked to one of the other girls," Maeve said.

"It's possible, I guess, but I don't think they were home that evening," Mrs. Baker said.

Maeve thanked them again and took her leave. It irked her to have to wait until Sunday to speak with the other women in the house, but if Nellie was right, they wouldn't know much in any case.

G INO SET OUT EARLIER THAN HE NEEDED TO SO HE COULD go by Louisa's rooming house and make sure Maeve was safely away. When he saw no sign of her, he walked the few blocks over to the building where Louisa had been killed.

He arrived shortly before eight o'clock. Night was settling in and the streets here were quieting down. He strolled past the building to the next corner and found no businesses open on either side of the street. It was unlikely anyone would have seen Louisa returning the evening she died.

He walked back to the entrance on 26th Street and found the door unlocked. He stepped inside and was instantly challenged. A man in a uniform stepped out of the shadows. He looked Gino over and apparently decided he didn't pose much of a threat. Gino decided in turn not to be offended.

"The building is closed," the guard said.

"I know. I'm investigating the death of the young woman who was murdered here the other night, and I was hoping to speak to you."

The guard visibly winced. "I thought the police was finished with this." Gino just smiled apologetically, not bothering to mention he wasn't with the police. "I don't know nothing about that. I never even saw her."

"I know you didn't," Gino said to be agreeable. "I just wanted to ask you how things work here and who might have had access to the building that night. For example, is the outside door always unlocked?"

"We usually lock it when the next shift starts, around eight o'clock. Drunks are always looking for someplace to curl up out of the weather. And we've got a guard on duty all the time to keep people from going upstairs if they don't have business here."

"I understand Billy Funhouser was on the late shift on Monday night."

"Billy don't work here no more."

"I heard. I was told he wasn't at his post that night, though. Did he just not show up to work at all?"

"Oh, he showed up all right, like he did every night. He had to show up to get paid, and he needs to get paid. Only thing, he didn't always stay awake."

This was interesting. Gino glanced around the large open space. "Where did he sleep?"

"There's a janitor's closet over by the elevator. He would go in there to sleep."

Gino nodded. With the outside door locked, he probably wouldn't be bothered either. "If you know he did that, how did he get away with it?"

The guard shrugged. "See, he had to work two jobs. He has six kids. That's why he needed to sleep. But it's pretty quiet here. As long as nothing happened, nobody said anything."

Gino looked around again. "If Billy locked the outside door, how would Miss Rodgers—and presumably her killer—have gotten inside?"

The guard stiffened. "I don't know."

Gino didn't believe him. "Come on now. You must have a theory. I'll bet all the guards have been talking about it. You must've figured it out by now."

He glanced around, either looking for eavesdroppers or a way to escape. Then he cleared his throat. "Billy," he said, and then cleared his throat again. "Billy didn't always remember to lock the door."

"Forgetful, was he?" Gino guessed.

"Billy likes to take a little nip now and then," the guard said, not quite meeting Gino's eye.

"I see. When you mentioned drunks coming in to find a place out of the weather . . ."

"Billy found the best place."

Gino looked around again. "Let me get this straight. If Miss Rodgers returned to the building to get something from her office—which is what we think she did—she could have come in before eight o'clock because the front door was usually unlocked then."

"But she didn't because I was on duty and I would've seen her," the guard clarified quickly. Unfortunately, he sounded a little too certain, so maybe he might've missed her. In any case, he wouldn't want to admit it and possibly lose his job like Billy did.

"So, she must have arrived after eight o'clock."

"And Billy might have let her in," the guard added helpfully. "He said he didn't, but maybe he, uh, forgot."

Gino nodded. Drunk people often forgot things. "And if he locked the door after her, he would have had to let her killer in, too."

The guard scratched his head. "Yeah, that doesn't seem likely, unless . . ."

"Unless what?"

"Unless it was somebody who works in the building, too."

Like the fiancé, Mr. Hoffman, or one of the other employees of the magazine, although why would they kill Louisa? Still, it was a possibility. "Let's see if I've got this straight. Our Billy might have let both Miss Rodgers and her killer in, or he might have let Miss Rodgers in and forgotten to lock the door so her killer came in unobserved, or he might have left the door unlocked the whole time and they both just came in without his knowledge," Gino summarized.

"I hadn't thought about that, but you're right," the guard said.

"I guess the only people who know for sure what happened are Miss Rodgers, her killer, and Billy," Gino added. "Miss Rodgers can't tell us and I don't think her killer is going to offer his help, so that leaves our Billy."

The guard scratched his head again. "I guess you're right."

"I don't suppose you know where I can find him, do you?" Gino asked pleasantly.

"Oh," the guard said in surprise. "I thought the police already talked to him."

Had they? They did know he hadn't been at his post, which had gotten him fired, so they probably had. "I haven't talked to him, though," Gino said. "Do you have his address?"

The guard frowned. "No, but I can tell you where he lives." He gave Gino the street name and a description of the tenement building.

Gino thanked the guard and went on his way. On the sidewalk, he passed another man wearing a guard's uniform who entered the building, probably to take the next shift. If he knew exactly what time Louisa had returned to the office, he could be sure to check the neighborhood at that time to see who might have been around. But surely she hadn't gone out much past sunset. Unescorted ladies tended to stay close to home when it was dark.

Gino decided to take the Third Avenue elevated train down to Houston Street, which was the nearest stop to Billy's home. The El would be faster than a cab, which might not want to go into that part of the city in any case. He found the building the guard had described just outside the notorious neighborhood known as the Bowery. The tenements here were older and dirty and sad, and the residents as poor and run-down as their buildings.

Except for a few men smoking on the steps of the various tenement buildings, all the residents had gone inside since night had truly settled on the city now. Children would be in bed or at least Gino hoped they would, if Billy really did have six of them.

He asked the two men sitting on the steps which apartment belonged to the Funhousers.

"You a copper?" one of them asked.

"Yeah, we heard he was in some trouble and lost his night job," the other added.

Gino smiled. "I'm his lawyer and I'm here to get him out of trouble." They'd be more likely to cooperate if they thought he was here to help.

The men exchanged a glance, obviously impressed. "You won't find him here," the first one said. "He won't come home until all his little ones are sure to be asleep."

Gino chuckled along with the two men. "Any idea where I might find him?"

They named a saloon on the next block and sent Gino off with their best wishes for poor Billy. As Gino reached the saloon door, which was standing open to catch the air on this warm September evening, he realized he had no idea what Billy Funhouser looked like. Not only that but the clientele of this saloon was working men who all frowned when they saw Gino in his fancy suit. He'd have to watch his step.

The tables were filled with groups of men who had been talking and joking when he walked in, so he dismissed them. They were all too happy to be Billy Funhouser. He went straight to the bar and asked for a beer. Then he glanced at the other men standing at the bar. They all stared back at him except one. That man was leaning heavily on the bar, nursing a beer, and staring down into the glass as if he might find something there.

Gino took a chance and carried his glass down to where this fellow stood. He was a pitiful mess. Scrawny and un- kempt, his fair hair was greasy, his clothes wrinkled, and his cuffs frayed. Gino said, "Mr. Funhouser?"

The man looked up in surprise. He squinted a little, as if trying to bring Gino into focus. "Do I know you?"

"No, but I know you, Billy," he said, just to be sure he had the right man.

Billy looked Gino over. "You're another cop. I already told you, I never saw that woman. I never saw nothing."

"I believe you. I just need to ask you a few more questions if you don't mind. I'll be happy to buy you another drink," he added.

Billy perked up at that. "A whiskey?"

"Whatever you'd like." Gino signaled the bartender.

He waited while Billy was served and watched while he downed the drink in one gulp. Billy wiped a hand across his mouth and said, "That tasted like another."

Since Mr. Rodgers would be paying for this and a well-lubricated Billy was more likely to talk, Gino bought Billy another shot, but warned him that would be all until Billy answered his questions. When the second glass was empty, Gino said, "I understand that you were sleeping when Miss Rodgers returned to the building that night."

Billy frowned. "I never said that."

"What did you say? Just for curiosity."

"I told them I was patrolling the rest of the building. She must've come in when I was up in the power plant."

"But how would she get in if the outside doors were locked?"

Billy upended his beer glass to get the last drops and set it down with a clunk. He gave Gino a hopeful glance.

Gino signaled the barman to refill the beer glass.

When Billy had taken a gulp, he wiped the foam from his upper lip and said, "I might've left the door unlocked."

"Don't the tenants have keys to the outside doors?"

Billy shook his head. "The owners don't give those keys out. Too easy for them to fall into the wrong hands."

So, Louisa may have had a key to the magazine offices but not to the building itself. If she was able to walk in unnoticed, her killer could have, too.

"Who found Miss Rodgers's body?"

"I did," Billy said, affronted to be asked. "I'm the guard, after all."

The guard who had done a pretty poor job of guarding, but Gino wouldn't mention that just yet. "I thought the beat cop spotted it."

Billy grunted in disgust. "That's what he claims. He woke me up with his hollering and I was the one officially found her. He only saw her through the window."

A very fine distinction. "What time was this?"

"I don't know. Around dawn. It's pretty dark in that building. A lot of shadows. You couldn't see her until the sun started to come up."

Or until he woke up that morning, but Gino didn't bother to say that. No sense in alienating Billy. "How did you know she was dead?"

"I didn't!" Billy said, affronted again. "How could I? She was just laying there, not a mark on her. I thought she fainted or something."

"Or was drunk," Gino said.

Billy frowned. "She didn't look like a drunk. Anyway, I called out and gave her a little nudge with my foot, but she didn't move. Took me a minute, but then I realized she must be in a bad way. The beat cop is the one decided she was dead."

"I understand that you might have been in the janitor's closet beside the elevator at some point during the night," Gino said, holding up a hand to stop him when Billy would have protested. "We both know you sleep in there. I'm not here to condemn you, just to get the facts. If someone had used the elevator, would you have heard it?"

Billy took another swig of his beer and set the glass down carefully, using both hands. "I might not have heard," he admitted, staring into his beer again. "I came straight here after my day job that day. Had a fight with the wife that morning. She was complaining that she had no money for food and the kids was all crying, so I never went home at all before I went to Rose Hill that night."

"You've spent a lot of time in that area," Gino said, choosing not to comment on Billy's drinking habits or his worth as a husband and father. "Can you think of anyone who might've been around and could have seen Miss Rodgers or her killer that night?"

Billy drained his glass. "There's an old man who lives on the streets up there. He sleeps out when the weather is good. He tries to get into the building when it's not. But the weather was nice that night, so I don't know."

"Do you think he might've killed her?" Gino asked. It was certainly possible a stranger had done it, after all.

Billy gave him a disgusted look. "Maybe, but he's a feeble old thing. Arms like matchsticks. She could've pushed him off with one hand."

Still, Gino would keep the old man in mind. "Where does he sleep when he's outside?"

"Lots of places. Doorways or under stairways, mostly. Folks run him off, so he moves around a lot."

"Does he have a name?"

Billy smiled sadly. "They call him Trapper."

Gino would be making another trip to Rose Hill.

He pulled out one of his cards. "If you think of anything that might help, let me know." He handed Billy the card and slid his untouched beer glass over to him. "Have a nice evening, friend."

. . .

FRANK WENT INTO THE OFFICE EARLY THE NEXT MORNing and found Gino already at work. He had finished sorting the papers from Louisa's desk and was reading through the ones related to the article she had been working on about patent medicines.

"I found Billy Funhouser. Did the rest of you find out anything?" Gino asked as Frank came into his office.

"I think we found out that we don't know a lot of things. What did Funhouser have to say?"

"He was drunk and sleeping in a janitor's closet where he didn't hear if anyone came or went. He also probably forgot to lock the outside doors, so Louisa and her killer could have come and gone unseen. He apparently didn't wake up until around dawn when the beat cop saw Louisa's body and started shouting for him. One thing for sure, the guard on duty until eight says he never saw her come back to the building during his shift, so she might well have arrived after that when Billy was on duty but not paying attention."

"I don't suppose anybody else could've seen Louisa."

"Not a soul around that late. Billy said there's a man who sleeps on the streets who might've been in the area, though. I'll go back tonight and try to find him and ask him if he saw anything, but I don't hold out much hope."

"Any chance he might be the lunatic killer the police seem so sure about?"

"Billy didn't think so, but I'll judge for myself when I see him. What did you and Maeve find out?"

"Louisa's friend at the rooming house confirmed the engagement story, and she knew Louisa was working on an article. Nobody there saw Hoffman looking for Louisa on Monday evening like he claimed, but not all of the tenants were there. Maeve is going back on Sunday to talk to them."

"Why Sunday?" Gino asked with a frown.

"Because the girls are very busy and that's the only time she will catch them at home. Why?"

Gino's frown deepened but he said, "No reason."

Uh-oh. Trouble in paradise, but Frank wasn't going to ask. "Sarah and I met Mrs. Rodgers and their son, Oscar, though."

"And what did you think?"

Frank pulled one of the client chairs up closer to Gino's desk and sat down. "I think the Rodgers family is very unhappy. Louisa was obviously her father's favorite child and Oscar is his mother's, but it's worse than that. Each parent seems to actively detest the child they don't favor. Mr. Rodgers was actually cruel in the things he said about his son, and he wasn't at all disturbed that Oscar heard him."

"My brothers and I argue all the time about which one is the favorite, but we know, deep down, that our parents really love all of us," Gino said. "I can't imagine what it would be like to know for a fact that wasn't true."

"I'm sure it would be awful, but would it make you hate your sister enough to kill her?"

"Do you really think he could have?" Gino asked in surprise.

"At this point, anybody *could* have. His mother said he was home with her all that day and night, though."

Gino grinned. "And you believed her?"

Frank grinned back. "I didn't say I believed her. I'm just reporting what she said."

"Did Mrs. Frank find out anything from the wife?"

"Just that she didn't approve of Louisa's job and ambitions. She thinks all women should be happy being wives and mothers. Are you learning anything from these?" Frank gestured to the piles of papers on Gino's desk.

"I'm learning a lot about patent medicines, and most of it is convincing me to never swallow another drop of any of them."

"I know the claims they make are outlandish and most of them taste awful."

"According to Louisa's notes, most of them are almost all alcohol and the rest heroin or cocaine," Gino said, "but nothing that could really cure you if you're sick."

"I see. You don't get well but you feel better because of the alcohol and drugs."

"And maybe you don't even care if you're sick anymore. According to this, people can get addicted to these medicines, just like they get addicted to opium."

Frank frowned. "Which would be very good for business, wouldn't it? People would just keep buying the stuff."

"And information like this, given to lots and lots of people in a magazine, could be very bad for business," Gino added.

"Tibbot, the owner of the magazine, said he refused to even consider publishing Louisa's article. If the patent medicine companies pulled their ads, it would bankrupt him."

"But some other magazine might take the chance. This is important," Gino argued.

"You're right, it is, which makes it a reason someone might not want Louisa to write about it. Does she mention any companies in particular?"

"I haven't read all her notes, but she's got them pretty well organized. She has a list of several brands with the amount of alcohol and other drugs listed, but so far, I've only found detailed information about one particular brand, Watson's Blood Purifier." Gino riffled through one of the stacks and pulled out a folder that was thicker than all the rest. "It looks like she actually interviewed Mr. Watson himself. He has a manufacturing plant in Brooklyn."

"I've seen their signs all over the city," Frank said, taking the folder Gino offered. He flipped through the handwritten pages, which appeared to be notes Louisa had taken.

"What does it cure?" Gino asked.

"Pretty much everything, according to the signs. Have you read all this?"

"I skimmed it. A lot of it is about how they manufacture the stuff, but she somehow found out what the ingredients are, and it's pretty damning."

"I'm sure Louisa didn't tell Mr. Watson what her article was really about, but maybe he found out."

Gino nodded. "And if he did, he might have been very unhappy with her."

"But would he have been unhappy enough to kill her?"

"Unhappy enough to come all the way from Brooklyn or to send somebody else and track her down late one night?"

It didn't sound likely, but Frank knew people were often killed in the most unlikely ways and for the most unlikely reasons. "Why don't we go to Brooklyn and ask him?"

They both looked up at the sound of the front office door opening. A moment later Maeve came in. She would have taken Catherine to school by now and was reporting for duty in the office.

"Did you find out anything?" she asked Gino, gesturing to the papers.

"Yes, we're going to visit the plant in Brooklyn where they make Watson's Blood Purifier," Gino said. He knew this would irritate Maeve, who wouldn't be included.

But Maeve was unmoved. In fact, she looked quite smug. "We'll have to close the office, then, because Mr. Malloy has assigned me to an undercover job." She gave Frank a conspiratorial look.

"Doing what?" Gino asked, straightening in his chair.

"The *New Century* magazine has an immediate opening for a secretary. Mr. Malloy thinks I should apply."

VI

Sarah was enjoying her morning solitude by drinking a second cup of coffee while she read a newspaper. Maeve and Mother Malloy had taken Brian and Catherine to school, Malloy had gone to the office, and Maeve would join him there after dropping Catherine off.

The newspaper reports on the president's recovery from the assassination attempt were promising. He'd survived for a week now, and his doctors were certain he would recover. She wondered if her old friend Theodore Roosevelt was relieved or disappointed by the news. He would hardly wish another man dead, of course, but he would certainly have been excited by the prospect of being elevated from the obscurity of the vice presidency to the presidency itself. She had no doubt Theodore would run for the office himself eventually.

Sarah heard the doorbell, but her maid, Hattie, was already hurrying to answer it. Sarah was pleased to see her neighbor Mrs. Ellsworth come into the breakfast room unannounced.

"Good morning," Sarah greeted her before noticing her rather harried expression. "Is something wrong? Is it the babies?" Sarah asked anxiously. Mrs. Ellsworth's daughter-in-law had delivered twins about six months ago, so she hadn't seen much of her neighbor lately.

"No, no, the babies are fine. Everyone is fine except . . . Oh, Mrs. Malloy, we had a bird in the house."

"A bird?" This was not unheard of, of course. When the weather was warm and the fireplaces not in use, occasionally a bird would fall down the chimney.

"Yes, a swallow," she said ominously.

Sarah bit her lip to keep from smiling. Mrs. Ellsworth was notoriously superstitious, and Sarah suspected this would turn out to be an omen of some kind. "I'm sure that caused quite an uproar."

"Oh yes. It was flying all over the parlor, crashing into the mirror we have over the sideboard and bumping into the windows. Nelson had already left for work, so Theda and I had to deal with it ourselves. We opened the front door and all the windows and then we both chased it with brooms. The babies were crying, and the poor bird kept trying to escape but slamming into things instead."

"Did you get it out or have you come looking for reinforcements?" Sarah asked.

Mrs. Ellsworth sighed. "We finally managed to get it to fly out the front door, but it was too late by then, of course."

"Too late for what?"

Mrs. Ellsworth looked at Sarah in amazement. "The damage was already done, you see. A swallow in your house means someone is going to die."

From her expression, Mrs. Ellsworth must believe that *someone* would be a member of her family, all of whom were extremely precious to her. "But not necessarily someone in that house, I'm sure," Sarah said. "Everyone in your family is very healthy."

"Death can strike at any time," Mrs. Ellsworth said gloomily.

Sarah knew that only too well. She tried a sympathetic smile. "Perhaps the death is the one Malloy is working on right now," she tried, to distract her neighbor. "A young woman was murdered, and the police aren't interested in investigating. They think she was killed by a stranger who will never be caught."

"You see," Mrs. Ellsworth said. "Death can come at any time!"

Sarah mentally kicked herself for confirming Mrs. Ellsworth's worst fears. Instinct told her to explain to Mrs. Ellsworth that her superstitions were silly and unfounded, but she also knew she would be wasting her time and offending a dear friend into the bargain. Nothing was going to change her mind.

But Mrs. Ellsworth had noticed the newspaper Sarah had laid on the table when her guest had come in. She pointed at the headline. "I thought perhaps it was an omen of the president's death, but mercifully, he seems to be recovering."

"Yes, he does. Mr. Roosevelt must think so, too. He and his family are on a camping trip, I understand."

"I was quite worried at first," Mrs. Ellsworth said, "but when I heard Mr. Roosevelt had left town, I knew things would be all right."

"Of course they will. Are you sure the bird was even a swallow?" Sarah asked, getting up to fetch a clean cup and saucer from the sideboard. "We don't see them much in the city."

"Well, now that you mention it, I may have just assumed it was a swallow. But any bird in the house is bad luck."

Sarah filled the cup from the coffeepot and slid it over to Mrs. Ellsworth. "Yes, they can really leave a mess," Sarah said.

"Oh, Mrs. Malloy, that's not what I meant," Mrs. Ellsworth said, but she was smiling in spite of herself. "I knew you could cheer me up."

"I'm glad you came over, then. Tell me how the little ones are doing."

"Arthur is sitting up on his own," the proud grandmother said, "and Alice is trying her best, but she keeps toppling over. Boys do develop a little more quickly, though, don't they?"

"Sometimes," Sarah said diplomatically. "Soon they'll both be crawling and then walking. Theda will be grateful for your help."

"And I will be grateful to give it." She glanced down at the newspaper again. "I do so hope the president will recover."

"Yes," said Sarah. "We all do."

. . .

MAEVE WALKED OVER TO THIRD AVENUE AND TOOK THE elevated train to the 23rd Street station, which was just two blocks from the building where the *New Century* had its offices. She had dressed to look like exactly what she was, a young woman with experience working in an office who was looking to better herself. She wore a dark brown skirt and matching bolero jacket over a crisp white shirtwaist. Her hat was stylish but conservative. A plain brown tie completed her outfit. Working girls didn't have a lot of money to waste on fripperies.

A man in a guard's uniform asked her what her business was when she entered, which told Maeve he was doing his job. Had he been so diligent about challenging strangers before a young woman was murdered in this very lobby? That's something she hoped to learn if she could get herself hired by the magazine.

The guard directed her to the enormous elevator that carried her to the fourth floor. The room she entered was larger than she had expected, and more people were working there than she had imagined. All of them looked up to see who had come in.

Maeve smiled politely and scanned the room for someone who looked like they were in charge. A woman who had been moving pictures around on a long table sighed wearily and came to greet her.

"May I help you?"

"I hope so." Maeve gave her a grateful and charming

smile. "I heard that you might be hiring a new secretary and I'm looking for a position."

The woman appeared to be in her late thirties and wore no wedding ring, which told Maeve she was like Louisa, a New Woman. She winced a little at Maeve's explanation, probably because of why they needed a new secretary. Maeve hoped that was the reason, at least.

"Do you have any experience?" the woman asked skeptically.

"Oh yes. Two years of doing general secretarial work, typing and filing and answering telephones." Two years was a bit of an exaggeration, but really, how long do you need to do those things to get good at them? "I have a letter of reference from my employer." Signed by Mr. Gino Donatelli after Maeve had composed and typed it for him.

Maeve reached into the bag she carried and pulled out the envelope containing the letter.

The woman didn't accept it. Instead she stared at it as if it might bite her. "How did you hear about this opening?"

"A friend told me. She said the girl who used to work here left kind of sudden and you'd need to replace her quickly."

One of the dozen or so men and women working at the rows of easels over by the windows coughed and seemingly all of the others shifted uncomfortably in their seats. The wave of emotion was palpable although no one said a word.

"Is something wrong?" Maeve asked, carrying on her pretext of not knowing about the murder.

The woman gave all of her coworkers a glare and they quickly went back to sketching. "Come with me," she told Maeve.

When they had gone a few steps, the woman looked back over her shoulder and said, "I'm Vivian Yoder."

"Maeve Smith," she said. "I really appreciate this."

Miss Yoder just rolled her eyes.

When they reached the end of the room where space had been walled off to create offices, Miss Yoder said, "Wait here." She stepped into one of the offices and closed the door. She was inside for only a minute or two, and then she came out and motioned for Maeve to enter. "This is Mr. Tibbot. He owns the magazine."

Tibbot was rather imposing with his lumberjack beard and his fierce expression, but Maeve knew better than to acknowledge it. "Thank you for seeing me, Mr. Tibbot. I understand you have an opening for a secretary and I'm hoping you'll consider me for the position."

"You're awful young," he said, looking her over with a frown. At least his expression wasn't lecherous.

"I'm older than I look, and I have two years of experience. I'm a very speedy typist, too. Here is my letter of reference."

She laid it on his desk in case he decided not to accept it as Miss Yoder had.

He looked at the envelope for a moment but made no move to pick it up. "How did you know we needed a secretary?"

"A friend told me. I'm sorry, Mr. Tibbot, but is there something strange about your last secretary? Miss Yoder asked me the same thing."

"No, not at all," he lied, trying to pretend he wasn't lying but without much success. "We just . . . we haven't advertised it yet, that's all."

"I know. My friend told me I should be quick, before you hired someone else."

Tibbot was frowning again. With his black beard and bushy hair, he reminded Maeve of a thundercloud. "Why are you looking for a job? Get fired, did you?"

"Oh no, not at all. My previous employer explains it in his letter of reference. You see, he's getting married and moving his business to Albany, which is where his wife's family is from. I didn't want to leave the city, so I'm looking for something else." Being an undercover detective was very much like being a con artist, Maeve observed. She was the last in a long line of con men, and although she had never actually conned anyone out of money, she had learned to lie well and make up stories on the spot, skills every good detective needed.

Tibbot considered her story for a long moment, and Maeve stood calmly under his thunderous gaze, secure in the knowledge her story would hold up under scrutiny. Finally, he said, "Do you have any ambitions to be a writer?"

"A *writer*?" she echoed in amazement, although she should have expected the question, considering Louisa's history. "You mean writing articles for the magazine? Heavens, no!"

Tibbot nodded in satisfaction. "You're hired. *Vivian!*"

Maeve jumped at the shout, but Miss Yoder seemed unmoved when she reentered the office.

"Set this little lady up with a desk. She's our new secretary."

Miss Yoder glanced pointedly at the unopened letter of reference lying on his cluttered desk.

He snatched it up. "We'll give her a thirty-day trial," he hedged. "Tell her what she needs to know."

"Thank you, Mr. Tibbot. I won't let you down." Now Maeve was lying, but maybe Tibbot would be too grateful to remember when they solved Louisa's murder. Anything was possible.

FRANK CHOSE TO DRIVE THE GASOLINE-POWERED MOTOR-car out to Brooklyn. Gino drove much too fast for Frank's taste and the electric might not have enough charge to take them out and back. Finding the Watson's Blood Purifier factory was a bit challenging, but the people in Brooklyn were a friendly lot, unlike those in the city proper, and with some help, they eventually found it.

"Maybe we should've made an appointment," Gino said when they pulled up outside of the massive building that housed the business they were looking for. Watson's Blood Purifier took up an entire city block with its redbrick factory. The words WATSON'S LABORATORY were painted large on the sign in front, and an elaborate cornice over large double doors seemed to mark the main entrance.

"If we telephoned to make an appointment, Watson would've had time to change his mind and not be available when we showed up," Frank pointed out. "There's a lot to be said for the element of surprise."

A prim female of indeterminate age and a generally disapproving expression greeted them when they entered the lobby, rising from the chair behind her massive desk. She wore an operator's headset, and a large, complicated switchboard covered the wall behind her. "May I help you, gentlemen?"

Frank had taken care to wear his best suit, which the woman had apparently noticed and which may have been why she didn't call for a guard to throw them bodily into the street. "Yes, we'd like to see Mr. Watson."

Her expression remained disapproving. "Which one?"

This was a quandary. "The one in charge," Frank tried.

"That would be Mr. Watson Jr. Mr. Watson Sr. is semi-retired. I assume you have an appointment."

"Actually, we do not," Frank admitted without apology. "But I think he will want to speak with us. We would like to talk to him about his visit with Miss Louisa Rodgers and the article she was writing."

Plainly, the woman recognized the name, and if anything, her expression grew even more disapproving. She asked Frank his name and then said, "Please have a seat." She gestured to some chairs placed against the side wall of the entryway.

When they were seated, she turned to the switchboard behind her and apparently spoke with someone. A few minutes later, during which the receptionist gave them not so much as a glance, a young man in a suit came into the lobby area. He was tall and pleasant-looking, with light brown hair and a thin mustache. He asked, "Mr. Malloy?"

Frank and Gino rose and shook his hand.

"I'm Karl Spangler, Mr. Watson's secretary. Please, follow me."

He led them through a door and down a short hallway to an elevator that carried them to the third and top floor of the building. This was obviously the floor where the executives worked, far above the manufacturing process. The floors here were polished and the walls hung with artwork. Young men were moving from office to office, carrying papers, and young women were typing. Mr. Spangler led them to the end of the hall and into an outer office, which was presumably his. He continued to another door and knocked before opening it. "Mr. Malloy and his associate are here, Mr. Watson."

Watson said something Frank couldn't hear, but apparently he had granted them admittance. Mr. Spangler motioned for them to enter.

Archibald Watson was younger than Frank had expected, probably not yet forty, but then he had inherited the business from his father, as Frank had just learned. He was a fine-looking man, well dressed and clean-shaven. His brown hair was thinning on top, but he had combed and pomaded it carefully to cover the spot.

"Thank you for seeing us, Mr. Watson," Frank said.

Watson didn't smile or rise from his chair. Plainly, he wasn't receiving them graciously. "You left me no choice, did you?"

"I beg your pardon?"

"When my secretary told me you wanted to see me about Miss Rodgers's magazine article, I understood the implied threat all too well."

"I'm sure I don't know what you're talking about," Frank said, although he could figure it out pretty easily.

"Miss Rodgers did a very good job of misleading me into believing she wanted to do an article about how my father happened to invent our product and become a successful businessman. It was only after she had learned everything she possibly could about our company that she revealed her true intentions, which—as I'm sure you know—were to ruin me."

"Did she actually tell you that was her intention?" Frank asked in amazement. Louisa was rather foolish if she had.

And it could have led to her murder.

Watson gave Frank a pitying look. "Not in so many words, but she was rather smug when she explained at the end of our interview that she intended her piece to be a warning about the dangers of patent medicine and my product in particular."

Frank and Gino were still standing since Watson had not yet invited them to sit and probably didn't intend to. "Are you under the impression that my associate and I are here to somehow continue her professed mission?"

This time Watson did smile but it was more like a feral grin. "I'm not a fool. I expect you're here to negotiate some sort of arrangement."

"What kind of arrangement?"

Watson slapped his desktop impatiently. "An arrangement in which I pay you a sum of money to stop the story from being printed."

Gino gasped in surprise. He was still new to this business.

"I'm sorry to disappoint you, Mr. Watson," Frank said, "but that is not at all why we are here, and we have no intention of accepting any payment from you."

"Then what is it you want?" Watson asked skeptically.

"We are private investigators. We are investigating Louisa Rodgers's murder."

. . .

This is your desk," Miss Yoder told Maeve. "I assume you know how to type."

She indicated the large machine taking up most of the desktop.

"Oh yes." After many painful hours of practice.

"The last girl . . ." Miss Yoder's voice broke and she had to stop and clear her throat. "The last girl answered the phone and handled the mail. Can you do all that?"

"Of course. Normal office duties, but . . . What's going on?" Maeve added in a whisper. "There's something strange about the last girl, isn't there?"

"I guess you need to know," Miss Yoder said with a sigh. "She . . . she died."

"Oh!" Maeve said sympathetically. "Now I understand. Was it some kind of accident?"

Miss Yoder studied her for a moment, and Maeve concentrated on looking innocent and ignorant of the facts. "You'll hear about it eventually, so it's better you hear it now. Louisa was murdered."

"How awful!" Maeve said quite sincerely. "The poor thing. Who did it?"

"That's just it. We don't know. She . . . she was killed downstairs in the lobby."

"Right here in this building?" Maeve asked, suitably horrified.

"Yes, but it was late at night. She came back to the office for . . . for something, and the guard wasn't there and someone . . . But you don't have to worry. You'll never need to come to the office late at night, and during the day, it's perfectly safe."

"Why are you telling her all that?" Mr. Tibbot growled from the doorway of his office. "You'll scare her off."

"She should be warned," Miss Yoder replied, not the least intimidated by him.

"I appreciate knowing," Maeve assured them. "It's shocking, but I see Miss Yoder isn't afraid to work here. And these other ladies." Maeve gestured to the two women sitting at easels.

"That's right," Mr. Tibbot said before Miss Yoder could contradict him. "They're not afraid."

Or else they need the work so badly, they can't afford to be. But Maeve pretended to believe him. "Then I'm not afraid either. Murder is a terrible thing, but if a woman is sensible, she is in no danger." Which was the biggest lie she had told so far today.

"That's right," Mr. Tibbot said, looking almost happy or at least satisfied that he had convinced her. "You don't have anything to worry about."

Miss Yoder said nothing, but her expression told Maeve that she disagreed with Mr. Tibbot's rosy view. Still, she went back to instructing her new employee when Mr. Tibbot returned to his office. She told Maeve the working hours and the salary (she'd have to ask Mr. Malloy for a raise after this) and told her how to use the telephone system.

"Can you stay for the rest of the day and come back on Monday?" Miss Yoder asked when she'd finished instructing Maeve. "We'll pay you for the full day today if you do. I'm behind on everything because I've had to answer the telephones since Louisa . . . Well, since she's not here, and we have an issue to get out."

"Sure, I'll stay."

The telephone rang and Maeve picked it up and told the caller they had reached the *New Century* magazine office. Miss Yoder watched until Maeve had satisfactorily directed the call.

"Very good," she told Maeve. "I'll leave you to it."

Maeve sat down at the desk and started looking through the desk drawers. It had been stocked with paper and pencils and pens. There was a stack of mail on the corner of the desktop, and she opened all the envelopes, sorting it into piles by subject and setting the bills aside for whoever would handle them.

All the while, she was glancing at the other employees, wondering why Miss Yoder hadn't bothered to introduce her to them. Which one was Clyde Hoffman? She amused herself by trying to guess, but then a man came out of one of the other offices and asked if she was the new girl and when she said she was, handed her something to type without even asking her name.

The afternoon passed quickly after that. She figured out that the people in the offices were the writers, and the ones at the easels were the illustrators. Considering how heavily illustrated the magazines were, the illustrators were quite busy. As near as Maeve could figure out, Miss Yoder's job was to decide where all the pictures went in the magazine, a tedious task to be sure.

At five o'clock all the illustrators laid down their pencils and began to gather their things. The men put on their suitcoats—Maeve found it amusing that they worked in shirtsleeves—and the women put on their hats. The writers also emerged from their offices and filed out. She waited until almost everyone had left, not wanting to appear to be in a hurry to leave. When she had gathered her own things, she went to where Miss Yoder was still puzzling over her illustrations.

"Will we see you back on Monday?" Miss Yoder asked.

"Oh yes. I look forward to it. Everything is so interesting."

"Is it?"

"I think so. I typed an article for Mr. . . . . Well, he didn't tell me his name, but I learned so much about the Aztecs."

"Were you telling the truth about not wanting to be a writer?"

Maeve feigned surprise. "Yes, why?"

"Because Louisa—she's the one who, well, whose place you're taking—she really wanted to be a writer."

"Lots of magazines have female writers, though, don't they?"

"Yes, but Louisa . . . I shouldn't say anything. We can't know for sure. Just be careful and don't come to the building after hours."

"Don't worry. I'll be careful," Maeve said. Maybe Miss Yoder would be willing to say more on Monday.

Maeve shared the huge elevator with some people from the other offices located on the third through the sixth floors. The lobby traffic had thinned out as most people had already left the building, but one man had taken a station near the outside doors and appeared to be waiting for someone. Maeve was a little surprised when she realized she was the one he was waiting for.

"Excuse me, miss. We haven't been introduced, but I work at the *New Century*, too. I'm Clyde Hoffman."

*M*URDER?" WATSON ECHOED WITH JUST THE APPROPRI-ate amount of surprise. "What are you talking about?"

"Miss Rodgers was murdered last Monday evening. We have been hired to find her killer," Frank said.

Watson seemed even more shocked at this news. "Do you think I had something to do with her . . . her death?"

"We're retracing her movements during the past few weeks to see if something she did might have offended anyone."

"She certainly offended me," Watson admitted, "but I don't go around killing people for that."

"Perhaps you would answer a few questions for us, then, just so we can mark you off our list of suspects," Frank said as pleasantly as he could manage.

"*Suspects?* I've never heard of such a thing. I'm a respected member of the community. No one would dare accuse me of murder," Watson insisted.

"Then you'll want to help us find the real killer so no one does, won't you, Mr. Watson? We won't take up much of your time, but I am getting a little tired of standing."

Watson huffed his annoyance, but he said, "Sit down, then. But I can't give you more than a few minutes. I'm a busy man."

"Of course you are," Frank said, taking one of the visitor

chairs that had been placed in front of Watson's desk. Gino took the other one and pulled a pad and pencil from his jacket pocket to take notes.

Watson eyed him uneasily, but he said, "What is it you'd like to know?"

"When was it that Miss Rodgers visited you?"

"She first came a few weeks ago. She told me her magazine was doing a series on Americans from humble beginnings who achieved great success, and she wanted to feature our company."

"Did you start from humble beginnings, Mr. Watson?" Frank asked.

Watson frowned at that. "I was a boy when my father developed the formula for our blood purifier. He was satisfied with selling a few bottles to friends and neighbors, but I saw the potential. I took over management of the company about fifteen years ago and turned it into a major industry."

"Congratulations," Frank said with no apparent irony. "Was that the only time you met Miss Rodgers?"

Watson winced. "No. That time she interviewed me about our family and the history of the business. She wanted to tour the factory, too, so I arranged for her to return one day last week so she could."

"What day was that?"

"I don't know. Wednesday or Thursday. What does it matter?"

"As I said, we're trying to retrace her steps."

"Spangler will know the date," Watson said grudgingly.

"And did you see her that day?" Frank asked.

"Oh yes. She made a point of stopping by my office after

her tour. She said she wanted to thank me for my help. She said she had learned a lot about Watson's Blood Purifier that she knew her readers would be interested to learn," Watson said, not bothering to hide his anger.

Frank pretended to be puzzled. "I thought you said she was planning to ruin you."

Watson's face had already been pink with indignation but now it flushed scarlet. "She was going to publish the secret formula. She claimed our product was mostly alcohol and really offered no healthful benefits. She was going to tell people not to buy it."

Frank glanced at Gino, who was scribbling notes on his pad.

Gino took his cue and looked up. "But isn't your product really almost half alcohol?"

Watson gave him a withering look. "We must use the alcohol to suspend and preserve the healing herbs, which are what purify the blood and prevent disease."

"And you think that if people knew this, they would stop buying your product?" Gino asked, sounding as naive as he possibly could.

"No, I do not. We sell thousands of bottles of Watson's Blood Purifier every day. Our customers know its benefits. They aren't going to be persuaded by some upstart magazine when they already know our product works."

Gino turned back to Frank, who said, "Then why did you say Miss Rodgers was going to ruin you?"

"I said she was going to *try* to ruin me. The very idea infuriates me."

"I can see that," Frank said, managing not to grin.

"But you really don't believe she could?" Gino asked.

"Certainly not! In fact, I would have bought extra advertising in that magazine because any mention of my product helps increase sales."

Frank didn't know much about advertising, but he was sure Watson did. Could he be right? It seemed unlikely but who knew?

"So," Gino said, "you weren't really afraid Miss Rodgers's article would ruin your business."

"Absolutely not. I do hate to be bamboozled, but I was not *afraid* of anything she might do, and I certainly had no reason to kill her. When you are successful in business, you are always dealing with disgruntled people who want to take away what you have earned. I've learned to deal with it, but not by murdering anyone."

"Is it true that your product contains ingredients that people can get addicted to?" Gino asked.

"Who told you such a thing?" Watson demanded, but he didn't wait for a reply. "Watson's is safe enough for a baby."

Frank didn't think alcohol was safe for babies, but he didn't mention that because Gino was already challenging Watson.

"Miss Rodgers had interviewed a lot of people who use your product. Some of them said they need to drink two or even three bottles a day. They crave it the way opium smokers crave their drug."

This news did not seem to surprise or alarm Watson. Instead he smiled smugly. "That just proves the benefits of Watson's. It makes people feel so good, they take more, although the package clearly states that the correct dose is one spoonful three times a day."

"There are dozens of patent medicines on the market," Frank said. "Do you have any idea why Miss Rodgers chose your company to write about?"

Rodgers frowned his disgust. "None at all. As I said, she claimed she was writing about my father's and my rise to success, but that was obviously a lie. I've tried to think of a reason she singled us out, but it could just be as simple as the fact that our factory is near Manhattan while most other companies are located in distant states."

"Can you think of anyone at your company who knew about Miss Rodgers's article and might have taken matters into their own hands to protect you?" Frank asked, thinking of the receptionist and her negative reaction to Louisa's name. Plainly, others knew about Louisa's plans.

"Do you think I employ murderers, Mr. Malloy?" Watson asked, outraged.

Frank shrugged. "Maybe somebody tried to convince her not to publish the story and got angry when she refused. It happens."

Watson didn't seem to think his theory was correct. "I employ hundreds of people here, so I can't speak for everyone, but only a handful of people met Miss Rodgers. Even fewer knew about her threats, and I can personally vouch for all of them. None of them are killers, Mr. Malloy. You've wasted your time coming out here today."

VII

"I hope you won't think me too forward, introducing myself to you like this," Clyde Hoffman said when Maeve did not respond to his greeting. "Miss Yoder should have introduced you to everyone, but I'm afraid that while she is very efficient at her job, she lacks some of the finer social graces." He was a very ordinary-looking man except that his pale eyes—somewhere between gray and blue— were a little too intense. His smile seemed nonthreatening, though, so Maeve decided to play along.

"I'm not offended. In fact, I'm grateful. It was a bit awkward for me this afternoon, not knowing anyone's name."

"I'm sure it was. I heard Miss Yoder telling you the sad news about your predecessor. I hope that won't keep you from returning next week."

Well aware that she might be speaking with Louisa's

killer, Maeve weighed her answer carefully. "Miss Yoder assured me the building is perfectly safe during the day."

"Yes, it is. Sometimes a few staff members work late when we have a deadline approaching, but you wouldn't have to. But I'm keeping you from leaving. Do you live nearby? I'd be happy to escort you home."

Now that *was* a bit forward, since a proper young lady might not want a man she had just met to know where she lives, but Maeve pretended not to notice. "I'm afraid I live in Greenwich Village, but if it's not out of your way, we can walk together to the El station."

"It's not out of my way at all," Hoffman assured her.

The crowd in the lobby had thinned to a trickle of people just making their way downstairs. Hoffman hurried to hold the door open for Maeve.

"Did you know my predecessor well?" Maeve asked when they were outside.

"Oh yes. Louisa . . . I mean, Miss Rodgers and I were great friends," he assured her solemnly.

"Her death must have been a shock to you, then. To everyone at the magazine, too, I'm sure."

"To me especially, I'm afraid," he said, then glanced around as if checking for eavesdroppers. Apparently finding none, he added, "You see, Louisa and I were secretly engaged."

"I'm so sorry!" Maeve exclaimed. "This must be terrible for you."

"Yes, especially since I can't share my grief with anyone and must hide it from the world."

"May I ask why you were keeping it a secret?" Maeve asked.

"It was Louisa's wish."

"I see," Maeve said, although she didn't. "It must have been difficult to hide your feelings from the other staff members, though."

"Louisa prided herself in keeping her personal business private. We were quite discreet."

"And her family didn't know, either?"

"She especially did not want her family to know," he said, as if that were quite common.

Maeve wasn't engaged, and she was only casually keeping company with Gino, but they still managed to spend time together. How could a couple see each other if their relationship had to be kept secret from everyone? Mr. Hoffman wouldn't be calling at the Rodgerses' house or taking Louisa for a walk in the park. Heaven knew her landlady wouldn't have allowed them to meet at her rooming house either.

But maybe they could meet after hours at the office where they both worked. He had told Mr. Malloy that he went to Louisa's rooming house after he got off work the day she died, but Nellie and the landlady hadn't seen him there, so maybe he had lied. Maybe they were set to meet at the office that night. And if Louisa had needed someone to carry a heavy box, wouldn't she have asked her lover for help?

Do you believe him?" Gino asked when they had left Watson's Laboratory and were walking to where they had left the motorcar.

"I believe Louisa set out to write a story that would prove

Watson's elixir or whatever he calls it was a fake. She shouldn't have told him that, but she wasn't really a reporter so she probably didn't realize it could put her in danger. She would have been thrilled to have such a big story to tell, too thrilled to keep it secret even from the man she intended to ruin."

"Yeah, I believe that part, too, but does Watson really think an article like that would have been good publicity for him?"

"Now, that is a whole different issue. He obviously wants us to think he believes that because then he would have no reason to wish Louisa harm. On the other hand, he was awfully angry about something he claims wouldn't have hurt him."

"That's what I thought."

"Also," Frank said, "he claimed no one would care about how much alcohol is in his stuff, but I'm guessing there are a lot of straightlaced temperance ladies taking daily doses of Watson's whatever-it-is who would be shocked to their core to learn they had been tricked into taking the demon rum."

"I never thought of that. The temperance movement has been around for a long time and those people would be horrified."

"There's a lot of them, too. You're too young to remember, but there was a woman who used to go around to saloons with a hatchet and chop up the bars. Just imagine what they might do to Watson's Laboratory."

"Which could explain why Watson is so angry at Louisa."

"And why he might want to kill her."

"Yeah," Gino said, "but I can't figure out how it could've

happened. How would Watson know that Louisa was going to be in the office building that night? Or that the guard wouldn't be around? And why would he even go into the city to try to find her at night? She shouldn't have been in the office then and he wouldn't have known where she lived either."

"He wouldn't have done it himself. Men like that don't do their own dirty work," Frank said. "But if he'd sent someone, that man could have been following her, waiting for his chance."

"So, we'll have to keep Mr. Watson on our list of suspects."

"And so far, nobody we've talked to had a better reason to want her dead."

MALLOY HAD EXPLAINED HIS PLAN TO HAVE MAEVE apply for a job at the magazine before he left for work that morning, so Sarah knew she would have to escort Catherine home from school at the end of the day. She had decided to visit her mother in the meantime, since Catherine's school was near her mother's house. She drove her electric motorcar. Catherine loved riding in it.

Her mother welcomed her and ordered tea for them both in the family parlor. Elizabeth Decker was aging well. Sarah hoped she had inherited that ability herself. When they had drunk their tea and devoured all the best items on the tea tray and Sarah had reported the children's every recent accomplishment, her mother said very casually, "Is Frank working on any interesting cases?"

Sarah smiled at that. "Do you mean any cases you might get involved in?"

"Heavens no," her mother said in feigned amazement. "Why would you think such a thing?"

"No reason," Sarah said with her own feigned amazement.

"But you do know I'm always available if I can be of assistance," her mother said quite sincerely.

"I do know that, and I appreciate it. I also know Father might not approve."

"What he doesn't know won't hurt him. Now tell me. I know you have a case. I can see it in your eyes."

Sarah was certain her mother couldn't see anything in her eyes, but she said, "You may have read about it in the newspaper, the young woman who was murdered in an office building in the Rose Hill neighborhood last Monday evening."

"I did see that, but mainly because your father mentioned it. It seems he knows the young woman's father."

"He does?" This was interesting news. "Are they friends of yours?" The Rodgers family didn't seem like they would be in the Deckers' social circle, but you never knew.

"Not friends. Your father insures his ships through her father's company, I believe."

Which seemed quite possible. Hadn't Malloy said Mr. Rodgers was in insurance?

"Then it's just a business connection," Sarah said, a little disappointed.

"Yes, although it would be only kind to pay our respects to the family, or have we already missed the funeral?" Her mother looked quite hopeful that they hadn't.

"No, it's tomorrow, but will Father think it's appropriate for you both to attend?"

"I think I can convince him it would be. Tell me everything you know about this murder."

Sarah did so.

When she was finished, her mother said, "I can't believe anyone in her family would murder her."

"Really? Because that is usually the case when someone like Miss Rodgers is killed. She certainly wasn't involved with any criminals or in any activities that might have put her in danger."

"Except possibly for the article she was writing."

"Yes," Sarah said. "Gino is reading through all of her notes to see if she might have been focusing on anyone in particular."

Her mother frowned. "You said she was writing about patent medicines. Could that offend anyone enough to strangle her?"

"Maybe, if her article was published and it resulted in people choosing not to buy them anymore, but it hadn't been published. I don't think she had even written it yet."

"So, it was unlikely to have caused her death, then. And I'm going to eliminate her family from consideration, although I'm sure Frank can't. But I'm not a detective, so I can do what I want. I think that leaves her lover, does it not?"

"It does," Sarah said with some amusement.

"Do we know why Louisa was keeping the engagement a secret?"

"No, we do not."

"Then we must find out. When we do, I think we'll know who the killer is," her mother decided.

Sarah could only hope it would be that easy.

. . .

MAEVE WAS THE LAST TO ARRIVE HOME THAT EVENING. Sarah and Mother Malloy had gotten home first with the children. Malloy and Gino were next, returning from Brooklyn. Gino would be joining them for supper so they could all discuss the case afterward, when the children were in bed. Maeve found them in the parlor, waiting for her. Sarah noticed she looked awfully pleased with herself.

"Did they make you start work immediately?" Gino asked as she took the seat beside him on the sofa.

"Of course they did," Maeve said. "Poor Miss Yoder was having to answer the telephone herself, and she couldn't get her own work done. We're on a deadline, you know. We have to get the layout to the printer, or the magazine won't go out on time."

Gino looked very impressed. "Sounds like you learned a lot on your first day."

"I did, but that will have to wait," Maeve said when they heard a loud thump and a wail of protest from the upstairs nursery. "It sounds like my services are required."

"I'll go with you," Sarah said. "You had a busy day."

After they'd eaten and the children were safely tucked away, they all gathered in the parlor. Mother Malloy, who liked to pretend she wasn't involved in discussing the case, sat off in her usual corner, knitting away.

"Did you learn anything important today, other than how to run the magazine?" Gino asked Maeve. They were once again seated together on the sofa, while Sarah and Malloy had taken the easy chairs across from it.

"Yes. While I did learn a few things about magazines, more importantly, I had a nice long chat with Mr. Clyde Hoffman."

Sarah saw her own alarm reflected in Gino's and Malloy's faces. "I hope you didn't put yourself in danger," Sarah said. "He could be the killer, you know."

"Anyone could at this point, but I know how to take care of myself," Maeve reminded them. "He was waiting in the lobby when I left—along with at least a hundred other people, if you're worried—and he introduced himself. He also offered to walk me home."

"That's pretty forward of him," Gino said in disgust.

"It certainly is," Maeve said, apparently gratified by his disapproval. "I made sure he knew I lived much too far away to walk, but I did let him escort me to the El station so I could get him talking."

"Did you find out why his engagement was a secret?" Sarah asked. Her mother would certainly want to know.

Maeve sighed. "He just said it was Louisa's wish. Before he left me at the El, he did tell me Louisa lived in a rooming house nearby and I might want to rent her old room so I could be closer to the magazine offices."

"How strange," Sarah said, thinking this was even more forward. Mr. Hoffman sounded very odd indeed. Hardly like a grieving fiancé, at least.

"Maybe he was just being helpful," Malloy said, although his tone told them he was joking.

"I saw my mother today," Sarah said. "She is sure Mr. Hoffman is the killer."

"You told your mother about the case?" Malloy asked in dismay.

"She specifically asked what you were working on," Sarah defended herself. "It's been in the newspapers. I didn't think it was a secret. And good thing I did, because it turns out my father insures his ships through Mr. Rodgers's company."

"Are they friends?" Maeve asked excitedly.

"Not friends exactly, but Mother thinks they should attend Louisa's funeral to show their support."

"Your father will never do that," Malloy predicted. "He doesn't like it when your mother gets involved in our cases."

Maeve and Gino exchanged an amused glance.

"What was that?" Malloy asked, frowning.

"You weren't here when Mr. and Mrs. Decker helped us with a case," Gino said with a grin.

"He loved it," Maeve said. "That was actually our first case as a detective agency."

"No, it wasn't," Malloy said. "We didn't have a detective agency then."

"Not officially, but it did turn out to be our first case," Maeve said with a little too much satisfaction.

"All right, that's enough," Sarah said to end the discussion. "We don't have to wonder if my parents will attend the funeral or not, because they aren't involved in this case, and if they do attend and they do find out something, then we won't complain."

"Fair enough," Malloy said. "Did you learn anything else from Hoffman?"

"Not really, but I was thinking about the things he said,

about being secretly engaged, and it occurred to me that if he and Louisa were having a romance, they would want to be together at least sometimes. I know her landlady didn't approve of gentleman callers, and her parents didn't even know about him, so they weren't meeting at their house. I can't imagine that a woman like Louisa would meet a man at his lodgings, so where else could they be alone?"

"You're right, Maeve," Sarah said. "A couple doesn't get engaged unless they've courted, so they must have been meeting somewhere."

Gino was nodding. "And Louisa at least may have had a key to the office, which would be empty every night."

"And the night watchman wasn't often at his post," Malloy added. "Not a very romantic place for lovers, but needs must, I guess."

"And," Maeve said dramatically, drawing everyone's attention again, "if I needed help carrying a heavy box, I would certainly ask my secret fiancé to carry it."

"If you had one," Gino pointed out. Maeve ignored him.

Malloy shook his head at them, but he said, "Maeve is right. If Louisa and Hoffman were used to meeting at the office, it would be only natural for him to be there to help her."

"Let's hope I can find the man Billy Funhouser told me about, then, the one who sleeps in the doorways. If Hoffman was there that night, maybe this fellow saw him."

"Are you going out tonight to look for him?" Malloy asked.

"I am. If he can identify Hoffman, our case will be solved," Gino said.

"My mother will be so relieved," Sarah said. "She is sure the secret lover is the killer."

"You said that before. Why is she so sure?" Malloy asked.

"Because she doesn't want to believe someone in Louisa's family killed her, and neither of us could believe someone who didn't like the article she was writing would resort to murder to stop her, since the article hadn't even been written yet, much less published."

Malloy and Gino exchanged a knowing look this time.

"Did you find out something about that?" Sarah asked Malloy.

"We certainly did. Gino, would you like to explain?"

"When I read through Louisa's notes, she had lots of information about the formulas used in several different brands of patent medicine, but she had only really investigated one company in particular, Watson's."

"What do they make?" Maeve asked.

"Blood purifier," Mother Malloy informed them from her corner.

"Don't tell me you take it, Ma," Malloy said in dismay.

"Not me, but half the women in our old neighborhood did. Swore by it, too."

"What is it for?" Gino asked.

"Whatever ails you, I guess," Mother Malloy said. "Female complaints. Consumption. Liver failure. Catarrh."

"What is catarrh?" Gino asked.

"Who knows?" Mother Malloy said.

"Anyway," Malloy said a little impatiently, "Louisa seemed to be very interested in Watson's Blood Purifier."

"She actually went out to Brooklyn where they have their factory," Gino said.

"I wonder how she got off work to do that," Maeve said.

"You'll have to ask your new boss," Gino said. "It seems Louisa told Mr. Watson she was writing a series of articles about successful men, so naturally he agreed to talk to her. She toured the factory, too."

"And then she informed Mr. Watson she was going to tell everyone his product was a fake," Malloy said.

"He tried to convince us he didn't care, but he couldn't hide how angry he was," Gino added.

"Angry enough to murder a young woman, though?" Sarah asked.

"That's what we don't know," Malloy said. "And Gino is having a hard time believing Mr. Watson traveled into Manhattan and just happened to find Louisa alone at the magazine office at night."

"It does sound far-fetched," Sarah agreed.

"Unless he hired someone to do it," Maeve said.

"Which seems even more far-fetched," Gino said. "One magazine article isn't going to ruin a company like Watson's. Why go to such drastic lengths to stop her?"

"Because," Mother Malloy said, not even looking up from her knitting, "it would send a message to anybody else who might think about doing the same thing."

THE NEXT MORNING, FRANK WENT OUT BEFORE BREAKfast to get some newspapers. The children had eaten earlier and gone back to the nursery with Maeve since they were off school for the weekend. His mother always got up early and had eaten with them, so Frank had been looking forward to a leisurely morning with Sarah, reading the newspapers and discussing the news.

But that was before he had been offered an extra edition being hawked by a newsboy on the corner.

The regular newspapers didn't have the story yet, but he bought a few of them, too, just in case. Frank hurried back home with the awful news.

He found Sarah already seated in the breakfast room. "The president is dead."

"Good heavens," she exclaimed, taking the sheet of newsprint he offered. "But his doctors were so sure he was going to recover."

"Looks like they were wrong," Frank said, taking his seat.

"What's this about the president, Mr. Frank?" their cook, Velvet, asked, coming out of the kitchen with a tray of food for them.

"I'm afraid the president died sometime in the night. The newsboys were selling extras with the news," Frank said.

"That poor man," Velvet said, shaking her head as she set the tray on the table. "Who'll be the president now?"

Frank exchanged a look with Sarah.

"Our friend Mr. Roosevelt will be the president," Sarah said with all the amazement Frank himself felt.

"Won't that be nice," Velvet said. "You can go visit him in Washington City."

Frank doubted they'd be invited to the White House, but it would be entertaining to watch how Roosevelt conducted himself. When he'd been the governor, he'd managed to make the crooks in the New York capital so angry that they had convinced McKinley to choose him as a running mate. They'd thought getting him out of New York would end his reform work, but now Frank was pretty sure Roosevelt would set out to reform the whole country.

"I don't think we'll be visiting Mr. Roosevelt in Washington City, Velvet," Sarah was saying, "unless he needs a private investigator."

"I'm sure he'll need all the help he can get, Mrs. Frank," Velvet said. "Running a whole country is a big job."

Frank couldn't argue with that.

"Oh dear, poor Theodore," Sarah said when Velvet had gone back to the kitchen.

"I think we should be saying, *poor Washington City*," Frank said.

"You're probably right. I should telephone my mother to make sure she has heard the news. She and Theodore's mother were great friends. It's a shame Mrs. Roosevelt died so young, before she could see her son's success."

"And find out if your parents are going to the funeral today," Frank said, hoping Mr. Decker had convinced his wife they shouldn't attend. "If they do, tell them not to mention our relationship."

"Why not?" Sarah asked.

"I just don't want to distract Mr. Rodgers. He might think I sent your parents to spy on them or something, since they aren't the kind of friends who would naturally attend Louisa's funeral."

"That makes sense. I'll tell my mother she's working undercover. She'll love that."

. . .

Funerals like this are so sad," Sarah said as Frank pulled the electric motorcar up to the curb near the Rodgerses' house that afternoon.

"Aren't all funerals sad?"

"I suppose, but it's especially sad when a young person dies. Louisa had so much promise, and now she'll never do the things she dreamed of."

"Which is why my job brings me satisfaction. I can't stop people from killing one another, but if I can bring the killer to justice, then that's making the world a little better."

"And preventing them from killing anyone else, which makes the world a *lot* better," Sarah said, giving him an adoring smile that he felt to his toes. How had he ever managed to actually marry her?

"Stop that. I can't kiss you in public and certainly not here. What will people think?"

"They'll think we're in love," she said with a laugh. "Which reminds me, do you think Mr. Hoffman will show up?"

Frank sighed. "I'm ready for anything."

The black wreath was still on the door and a maid admitted them. The mood inside was suitably somber. The Rodgerses obviously hadn't expected a lot of people, or they would have had the funeral at a church, but the crowd was a respectable size.

Frank saw some familiar faces from the *New Century* office. The woman he had spoken with, who he now knew was Miss Yoder. Tibbot was there, and he recognized some of the illustrators. Were the Rodgerses pleased the magazine staff had come or would the family consider it insulting since they had, indirectly at least, been involved with Louisa's death?

One person he didn't see was Clyde Hoffman. Hopefully, he had ignored Frank's foolish advice and stayed away. His presence could only cause a disturbance if he insisted on making himself known to the Rodgers family.

Louisa's casket had been placed in the formal parlor and most of the furniture had been removed. Folding chairs were set up for the service. People were filing by the casket to view the body and then stopping to speak to Louisa's parents, who were standing vigil nearby. Frank noticed that Oscar stood beside his mother as if to offer support, although Mrs. Rodgers didn't look the least bit distressed. She greeted each person in the line quite properly and merely nodded at their expressions of sympathy.

On the other hand, Mr. Rodgers appeared appropriately grief-stricken. His eyes were red and his cheeks pale. He shook hands with each mourner and whispered his thanks for their attendance.

"Is Mr. Hoffman here?" Sarah asked softly as they waited for their turn to view the body.

"I haven't seen him. Some of the other magazine staff are, though."

"I assume most of the people are friends of the Rodgerses', but . . . Oh, look. Could that be a friend of Louisa's?"

Frank looked over and saw a young woman whose clothes marked her as far less affluent than the other mourners, but he didn't recognize her from the magazine. She was accompanied by an older woman whose sour expression indicated she would rather be anyplace else.

"You'll have to chat with her and find out," Frank said.

Frank sighed when the Deckers came in next. Mrs. Decker gave them a quick smile before resuming her solemn expression, suitable for funerals. Frank noticed her speaking to the young woman he was wondering about. She was just in front of them in line. Maybe Mrs. Decker would find out who she was.

Tibbot had passed the casket with hardly a glance, as if he couldn't bear to look at Louisa. Maybe he couldn't. He introduced himself to Mr. Rodgers as Louisa's employer.

"I hope you're proud of yourself," Mrs. Rodgers said before her husband could speak. "If you hadn't fired Louisa, she would still be alive."

"I didn't fire her," Tibbot said, not intimidated in the least. "She walked out. I fully expected she'd come back the next day when she had a chance to cool off."

"That's not what she said," Mrs. Rodgers said.

"Mother, please," Oscar said. "You're making a scene and this gentleman had nothing to do with Louisa's death."

A lesser man would have left the house then, but Tibbot merely nodded and moved on to find a seat.

Several other members of the magazine staff quickly expressed their condolences without even stopping to shake hands, lest they be chastened as well. Mrs. Rodgers glared at all of them.

Now Frank and Sarah had reached the casket. Frank realized that Sarah was the only one of the four of his team who had actually met Louisa. She looked down at the still, cold figure and brushed a tear from her eye. Frank, in turn, studied the young woman for a long moment. She looked much as he had imagined. Not conventionally pretty, but her features were pleasant and her expression, even in death, was determined. If given the chance, she might well have accomplished wonderful things.

Frank let Sarah speak to the Rodgerses first since she always seemed to know the right thing to say.

"Louisa was a remarkable person," Sarah said to Mr. Rodgers. "I feel privileged to have known her, however briefly."

"Yes, yes, she was remarkable," he replied, taking her hand in both of his. "Our lives will never be the same."

To Frank's amazement, Mrs. Rodgers made a huffing sound that indicated she didn't share his feelings. Sarah, of course, pretended not to notice. Her expression was still appropriately solemn when she turned to Louisa's mother.

"My deepest sympathy," Sarah said pointedly yet impersonally, to be proper but also to acknowledge that Mrs. Rodgers probably wasn't feeling the same level of grief as her husband.

Mrs. Rodgers stiffened at the subtle snub and made no move to shake Sarah's hand, which was fine since Sarah hadn't offered it.

"I don't know why you're here," Mrs. Rodgers said to Frank.

"Just doing what we were hired to do," Frank said pleasantly but softly so others couldn't hear.

Mrs. Rodgers gave him a murderous glare.

Unfazed, Sarah turned to Oscar, who was watching the whole little drama with some amusement.

"I know how difficult it is to lose a sibling," Sarah said. "My sister died too young."

"Perhaps you loved your sister, Mrs. Malloy, which would make it much more difficult, I imagine," Oscar said. "I'm afraid I feel more relief than grief."

"Then you truly do have my sympathy, Mr. Rodgers," Sarah replied.

Oscar was still gaping at her when she and Frank walked away to find a seat.

They chose chairs very near where the Rodgerses were standing so they could overhear the rest of the mourners, in case someone said something incriminating.

Frank had been watching the poorly dressed young woman as she made her way up to the casket. She was nervously fingering the brightly colored scarf tied in a bow at her throat and clutching a handkerchief, although she didn't appear to be weeping. When she reached the casket and looked down at Louisa's body, though, she burst into tears.

"Poor Louisa, my dearest friend in all the world," she sobbed.

Frank glanced at Sarah, who was staring wide-eyed at the spectacle. People around them were murmuring their disapproval at such a vulgar display, and the older woman who had accompanied the girl was frowning. She grabbed the girl's arm and jerked her away, urgently whispering something to her, probably an admonition to get ahold of herself.

The whole Rodgers family was appalled, if their expressions were any indication. The girl didn't seem to notice, though. She turned to Mr. Rodgers and said, "Louisa and I lived at the same rooming house. She was my dearest friend."

"Was she?" Mr. Rodgers said uncertainly.

"Yes. I'm Nellie Potter. She must have told you about me."

Sarah turned to Frank, silently acknowledging that this was the young woman who had spoken with Maeve at the rooming house.

"I . . . It's very nice to meet you, Miss Potter," Mr. Rodgers managed. Plainly, he had never heard of her but was too polite to mention it. "Thank you for coming."

The older woman with her introduced herself as Louisa's landlady, and Mr. Rodgers greeted her appropriately.

The young woman turned to Mrs. Rodgers, who had been watching her with undisguised disgust.

"I'm Nellie Potter," she said unnecessarily, grabbing Mrs. Rodgers's hand to shake it, even though Mrs. Rodgers hadn't offered it. "I was Louisa's very best friend. She told me everything. She was a wonderful person, so good and kind to me. And smart. She was so very smart."

But Mrs. Rodgers's expression had slowly changed during Nellie's little speech. She was staring at the girl with growing horror. "That scarf you're wearing. That's Louisa's scarf. I bought it for her."

VIII

If Nellie was embarrassed, she gave no indication. Instead, she touched the scarf as if to verify that it was still there. "Yes, it was. She gave it to me. I told you, we were friends."

"She wouldn't have given it away. It's silk," Mrs. Rodgers insisted rather ungraciously.

"Nellie," the landlady said in a warning tone, "we should move along."

"It's mine now," Nellie insisted. "Louisa gave it to me."

"I'm sorry," the landlady said to Mrs. Rodgers, and gave Nellie a little shove to get her going.

Nellie was pouting but she walked on to find a seat.

"Do you think Louisa would be friends with a girl like that?" Frank whispered.

"She might have felt sorry for her," Sarah whispered back.

Which might explain the scarf. But was Louisa that soft-hearted? Certainly not where Archibald Watson and his patent medicine were concerned.

The Deckers were offering their condolences now. Mr. Rodgers seemed impressed that Mr. Decker had come to pay his respects. He introduced the two of them to his wife, who also seemed impressed, as well she might. When they weren't helping Frank solve one of his cases, the Deckers were a socially prominent couple.

Mrs. Decker had taken Mrs. Rodgers's hand, and she said, "I know what you must be going through. We lost a daughter, too. If I can be of any help to you, please don't hesitate to contact me."

Frank reached over and clasped Sarah's hand, offering silent comfort at the mention of her lost sister. She squeezed his fingers in gratitude. He had to glance over to see Mrs. Rodgers's expression, though. Oddly, *she* didn't look very grateful even though she murmured her thanks. He was pretty sure Mrs. Rodgers wouldn't feel the need to share her grief with anyone, although his mother-in-law was certainly generous to offer.

A few more latecomers filed by and then found seats. The Rodgers family took their places in the front row, and a man in a clerical collar welcomed everyone and began the formal service.

He had just started reading a prayer from the book he held when someone pounded on the front door. The minister stopped midsentence and, like everyone else, looked toward the parlor door. A maid hurried to open the front door, and in a few seconds a young man appeared in the parlor doorway. He looked a bit harried and chagrinned at seeing all eyes on him, but he nodded to silently apologize and quickly took a seat in the back row.

"Could that be Mr. Hoffman?" Sarah whispered.

"It could," Frank replied. Why hadn't he arrived with the other people from the magazine? If they couldn't find out, Maeve surely would. Placing her at the magazine had been a good idea.

The minister continued the prayer, reading from a prescribed funeral service. Then he spoke of the joys of heaven and eternal life but made no mention of Louisa in particular. Frank couldn't see the faces of Louisa's family members from where he was sitting, but Mr. Rodgers's shoulders were shaking as he wept silently. Mrs. Rodgers and Oscar sat completely still, their shoulders stiff as if they were enduring a trial.

Frank tried to imagine a family so estranged that they could resent the inconvenience of a member dying. He had seen more than his share of such families, of course, but he could never understand it. At least he didn't have to worry about his family growing to hate one another. Sarah would never allow it.

The minister prayed again. Then he invited everyone to come to the gravesite and return here for a repast afterward.

"Aren't you even going to say her name?" a voice cried from the back.

The minister looked alarmed, and everyone turned to see who had spoken. Frank could have guessed. Clyde Hoffman was on his feet.

"A wonderful woman is dead, and no one said a word about her at her own funeral," Hoffman pointed out.

"Hoffman, sit down," Tibbot said. His voice was soft but obviously angry.

Hoffman did not sit down. "Doesn't anyone have a good word to say about her?"

The clergyman glanced at the Rodgers family, seeking some guidance, but he must not have gotten any because when he looked back at Hoffman, he was still quite flustered. "Perhaps you would like to say a word or two," he suggested tentatively.

Mrs. Rodgers's sigh of dismay was audible to all, but Hoffman was unfazed.

"I certainly would. Louisa was a magnificent woman. She was honorable and loyal and smart and pretty. I am proud to say that she had accepted my proposal and had planned to become my wife."

Many people gasped and Mrs. Rodgers stood up and turned to face Hoffman across the room. "That is a lie. Louisa would never have agreed to marry someone without telling her parents. Oscar, see this man out."

Oscar gave his mother an exasperated look, obviously unwilling to do such an unpleasant task, but he didn't have to. Several other men, including Frank, were already on their feet and moving toward Hoffman.

"Are you going to throw your daughter's fiancé out of her own funeral?" Hoffman nearly shouted, his anguish evident.

"You can't go on making a scene," Mr. Tibbot said, taking one of Hoffman's arms.

Hoffman tried to shake him off, but Frank had his other

arm now and the two men, with the help of several others, escorted Hoffman into the hallway and out the front door.

"I'll make sure he gets home and doesn't cause any more trouble," Tibbot said when they were on the sidewalk.

"I'm sure Mr. Rodgers will appreciate that," Frank said.

Hoffman was weeping softly by now and didn't look like he'd be much of a threat, but Frank watched until Tibbot and Hoffman had disappeared around the corner before following the other men who had come to help as they went back inside.

People were getting up to leave by that time. Some women had gathered around Mrs. Rodgers and were trying to comfort her, or maybe they were trying to calm her down, since she looked more angry than grieving. Frank recognized only one of them, his mother-in-law.

Sarah made her way through the crowd to where he was waiting. "Did he cause any more trouble?"

"No, he went quietly. Tibbot said he would take him home."

"Had he been drinking?"

"I didn't smell it on him, but what else could explain his behavior?"

"I hate to think." She glanced around, obviously looking for someone. "It's too bad we didn't bring our other motor. We could have offered someone a ride." The electric could hold only two comfortably, three in a pinch.

"Who did you have in mind?" he asked.

"That girl Nellie who was Louisa's friend. I would like to get to know her a bit."

"Maeve is going back to the rooming house tomorrow," Frank reminded her. "She can ask her anything you want."

"I felt sorry for her when Mrs. Rodgers practically accused her of stealing Louisa's scarf."

"Louisa must have felt sorry for her, too."

Just then, the Deckers walked by on their way out of the room. Sarah didn't look at them and they didn't look at her, but she said a little too loudly, "Yes, I wish we had our larger motorcar so we could have offered Louisa's friend a ride."

Her parents would have their carriage with plenty of room for guests.

"That was subtle," Frank teased.

Sarah didn't have a chance to reply because Mr. Rodgers appeared at Frank's side.

"Mr. Malloy, will you be going to the cemetery?"

"Yes, and returning here afterward. I find that people speak more freely when they are at a gathering, and we might hear something important."

"I think we all heard that young man," Rodgers said with a troubled frown. "He's the one you asked about, isn't he? Hoffman, was it?"

"Yes, he works at the magazine," Frank said. He didn't add that he had been the one who suggested Hoffman attend the funeral.

"Why would he make such an outrageous claim about Louisa, though? Certainly if she had really been engaged, we would have known."

"We'll certainly try to find out the truth of it," Sarah said before Frank could think of a reply. "This must be very difficult for you, Mr. Rodgers."

He sighed wearily. "I don't know how I'll go on. Louisa was the light of my life."

Most of the mourners had left the house by now. Those who were going to the cemetery would be finding their carriages or motorcars and lining up.

Mrs. Rodgers and Oscar had put on their hats and were ready to go. They were standing in the parlor doorway expectantly.

"Bernard," Mrs. Rodgers said sharply. "People are waiting."

"Promise me you'll find Louisa's killer, Mr. Malloy," Rodgers said so sadly that Frank had to reach out and put a comforting hand on the man's shoulder.

"I'll do everything I can, Mr. Rodgers. Louisa deserves justice."

"Thank you," Rodgers said.

"Bernard," Mrs. Rodgers said again, this time more loudly and impatiently.

Rodgers joined his family and they left, with Frank and Sarah close behind.

Although they had parked near the house, they were the last in the funeral procession line. Most of the vehicles were horse-drawn, including the undertaker's hearse and the carriages for the family. Only two of the vehicles were motorcars, and Frank was glad he'd brought the electric because the noise of the other vehicle, which was gasoline-powered, made the horses uneasy.

The trip out to the cemetery was slow, and they learned nothing at all since the graveside service was brief. At least the minister mentioned Louisa's name this time, although he obviously inserted it only to avoid further criticism. Frank did notice, however, that the Deckers had taken Nellie Potter under their wing. She and Mrs. Decker were chatting like old friends.

NONE OF THE MAGAZINE STAFF RETURNED TO THE HOUSE afterward and even Louisa's landlady failed to appear. Only the young woman who had proclaimed she was Louisa's best friend remained to be questioned.

And Louisa's family, of course.

Sarah served herself from the buffet and left Malloy to his own devices. She wandered over to a group of ladies who were chatting.

"I don't think we've met," one of the women said, looking Sarah up and down. She apparently approved of Sarah's gown. "How did you know Louisa?"

"I'm Sarah Malloy," she said. "My husband is a business associate of Mr. Rodgers's."

She knew the Irish name would raise eyebrows, which it did.

"What sort of business?" the woman asked, no longer quite as approving.

"Louisa was a remarkable young woman, wasn't she?" Sarah said, ignoring the question.

None of the women agreed with her. In fact, they suddenly looked very uncomfortable. One woman even glanced around as if she was afraid someone might have heard Sarah's remark.

"Did you know Louisa *well*?" the woman who had obviously appointed herself the spokesperson for the group asked.

"She interviewed me for one of the articles she was writing for the magazine," Sarah said. "I was quite impressed with her."

"Why on earth did she interview *you*?"

Sarah did take offense but only silently. "She was writing about women's health, I believe, and I am the patron of a maternity clinic on the Lower East Side." All of that was true, as far as it went.

"I had no idea Louisa was writing articles for the magazine," another woman said. "Hilda said she was just a secretary."

"I'm sure they quickly recognized Louisa's potential," Sarah said.

"I read the *New Century*, but I never saw her listed as the author of any articles," the first woman said.

"Perhaps she used a pseudonym," Sarah suggested. "I understand her parents didn't approve of her taking a job."

"Oh, her father didn't care," the second woman said. "He always let her do anything she wanted to."

"Yes, she was terribly spoiled," the first woman said. "A girl can have too much freedom, I always say. It only leads to trouble."

"As Louisa discovered," the second woman added.

"Yes," a third woman said smugly. "If she had married and settled down, she would still be alive."

Sarah had to grind her teeth to hold back what she really wanted to say, although she had to admit that Louisa's desire to have a career might well have led to her murder if her writing had offended the wrong person. She didn't have to admit it out loud, however. "Are you blaming Louisa for her own death?"

Someone in the group gasped, but the first woman refused to be shamed. "A woman needs to be careful in this world. If she puts herself in danger, she deserves what happens to her."

"It was very foolish for her to be out alone at that time of night," the second woman agreed.

"So, you think being foolish is an act punishable by death?" Sarah asked, knowing she was making lifelong enemies, but past caring.

"Certainly not, but . . ." The first woman hesitated when she could not think of anything to say that wouldn't be equally as offensive.

"Did you ladies know Louisa?" a cheerful voice asked.

They all looked up to see that Nellie Potter had joined them. She apparently had not heard their previous conversation, because she was smiling.

"Louisa was my very best friend," Nellie went on without waiting for an answer to her question. "She gave me this scarf just because I told her how pretty it was. She told me all her secrets, too. I even knew she was secretly engaged. I never met him, but it must have been that man who stood up at the funeral, don't you think? I don't expect she was engaged to more than one man, do you? She used to let me read the articles she wrote before they were printed in the magazine, too. She'd ask me what I thought, and she'd make changes if I suggested it."

Sarah knew she was gaping, but she couldn't help herself. Nellie Potter was a force of nature, and perhaps not a completely honest one. In spite of Sarah's hints to the contrary, as far as they knew, Louisa had never written any articles for the magazine, unless the staff hadn't been completely honest with Malloy. Someone was lying, but who?

Sarah was afraid she wouldn't have a chance to question Nellie more closely, but the other ladies, their expressions strained, began to murmur their excuses and drifted away, leaving Sarah and Nellie alone.

"I'm Nellie Potter," the girl said, undaunted by the snub. Perhaps she didn't even realize she had been snubbed. "Louisa was my very best friend."

"I'm sorry. I didn't know her well, but I liked her very much."

"She was so smart," Nellie said. "She was always writing stories. I couldn't write a story to save my life."

"Few people could. Did she talk to you about her work?"

"All the time. She had lots of ideas."

"I'd love to know what they were."

Nellie frowned and fingered the scarf at her throat. It was an expensive item, and had probably cost more than the rest of her outfit combined. "I'm not sure I should tell."

"Why not?"

"She said . . . she said they were a secret," Nellie said a little desperately.

"They probably were, but no one can steal her ideas now, can they? Louisa won't be writing any more articles."

"I . . . Still, I don't want to break her confidence. They were good ideas, though. I always told her so."

"You were very kind to encourage her."

Nellie frowned again. "I don't think she needed any encouragement. She had too much already."

FRANK WALKED SLOWLY THROUGH THE ROOMS, NIBBLING at his lunch while casually eavesdropping, but all the men were talking about the president's death and what it would mean to business, and the women were gossiping about people he didn't know. No one, it seemed, was thinking of Louisa.

Finally, he found Oscar Rodgers out on the back porch alone, smoking a cigar.

"Why are you still here? Haven't you upset my mother enough?" he asked when Frank joined him.

"I did not intend to upset your mother, but I have to do my job."

"Do you? I can't see how harassing a grieving family will help find who killed Louisa."

"That's just it," Frank said. "Not everyone in your family seems to be grieving."

Oscar jerked the cigar out of his mouth and turned to fully face Frank. "What do you mean by that?"

"I mean your father is obviously distraught, but you and your mother seem almost . . ."

"Almost what?" Oscar challenged angrily.

"I'm not sure how to describe it, but you certainly don't seem sad that Louisa is dead."

"Maybe we don't have any reason to be sad," Oscar said.

"What do you mean?"

"I mean I've spent my entire life in Louisa's shadow. She was better at everything than I was, except for sports. She wasn't interested in sports, but neither was my father, so he scoffed at my accomplishments. The only thing he cared about was education, and I didn't have any accomplishments there. I hated reading, and arithmetic made no sense to me. My father ordered Louisa to help me with my schoolwork, but no one wants a girl telling them how stupid they are, so she only made things worse. She never let me forget that she excelled at everything my father valued and I didn't."

"And this killed any affection the two of you might have had for each other," Frank guessed.

Oscar flushed scarlet. "We could hardly stand the sight of each other. I was glad when she moved out. She said it was to be closer to her office, but I knew she wanted to get away from Mother."

"And from you, too?"

"By the time we were grown up, we simply ignored each other." He turned away and jammed the cigar back in his mouth.

"Were you really at home with your mother the evening Louisa was killed?"

When Oscar turned back to Frank this time, his scowl was murderous. "To me it seems like simple laziness that you have decided to accuse Louisa's family members when she obviously was killed by an opportunistic stranger."

"It isn't that obvious to me," Frank said.

"Then you aren't worth the money my father is paying you."

"We'll see, won't we?"

Oscar shook his head in mock despair. "Mother was right."

"About what?"

"She told Father he was a fool to hire you, that you'd never find the killer and you'd just keep bleeding him for money while you tortured him with the hope of bringing Louisa's killer to justice."

"And she advised him to dismiss me," Frank guessed.

"Of course she did. It's the only sensible thing to do, and it would end this torment so we can get back to our lives."

"Without Louisa."

"Which would not be such a bad thing, at least for me."

"Do you think you will finally win your father's approval now that Louisa is gone?" Frank asked.

Oscar winced. "I don't want my father's approval. I never have." Which contradicted everything he had said up to now.

"And what if I do find Louisa's killer?" Frank asked.

"Do you really think you can do what the police said they couldn't?"

"I've done it before," Frank said. "In fact, I think I'm getting pretty close." It was a lie, but it had the desired effect.

Oscar scowled at him, threw his cigar out into the yard, and stomped back inside.

But why should that news have made Oscar angry if he had nothing to hide?

WHAT DO YOU MEAN WHEN YOU SAY LOUISA HAD TOO much encouragement already?" Sarah asked Nellie.

The girl shrugged and forced a smile. "I don't know. I don't know what I say half the time. Louisa was a good friend to me. Oh, there's her father. I should speak to him."

Nellie scurried away, leaving Sarah frustrated, but her mother soon wandered over.

"Hello, Mrs. Malloy," Elizabeth Decker said with a completely straight face.

"You're getting very good at this, Mrs. Decker," Sarah replied, equally expressionless.

"At attending funerals?" her mother said. "Sadly, yes, one does have to attend so many."

"I noticed you had an extra passenger in your carriage on the ride out to the cemetery."

"Nellie is a lovely girl. A bit of a chatterbox, but one must admire her spirit. She just lost her *very best friend in all the world*, after all." Her mother's expression made it clear she was quoting Nellie's oft-repeated claim.

"I don't suppose she mentioned any reason why someone would want to kill her *very best friend*, did she?"

"According to Nellie, none of the other girls at the rooming house liked Louisa. She thought she was too good to associate with them or at least that's what they believed, although Nellie thought Louisa was the sweetest person she knew."

"Of course she did. Louisa gave her that scarf, didn't she?"

Sarah's mother frowned. "So she said, but who's to say?"

"Not Louisa, certainly. Did Nellie say anything else?"

"She adored our carriage, and she thinks your father is very handsome," her mother reported with a twinkle.

"Poor Father."

As if she had conjured him, he appeared at her mother's side. "If we are quick, I believe we might leave without encountering Miss Potter again," he said softly.

"I'm sure she'll be heartbroken if you desert her," Sarah said.

He gave her a glare that didn't faze her in the slightest. "You are already in my black books for enlisting your mother's help in this. Attending a funeral is not how I like to spend my Saturday afternoons."

Her mother smiled sweetly. "But being admired by a pretty young girl more than made up for it, I'm sure."

Her father's eyebrows shot up, but he was nonplussed for only a moment. "You don't need to worry. If I were to take a mistress, she wouldn't be quite that chatty."

Her mother needed only a moment to retaliate. "Attending funerals is so instructive, though. I'll be glad for all I learned when I plan yours."

He didn't even bat an eye. "I have no intention of dying."

"Not ever?" she asked in amazement.

"Not ever, and especially not before you do."

"Then you are the one who should be taking note," her mother said quite reasonably. "I certainly want the minister to mention me at my funeral, and I expect at least five or six friends or relations to speak about what a wonderful person I was."

"But you wouldn't want to appear immodest, would you?" he chided.

"If I'm dead, I'll hardly be concerned with that. I'll just want your mistress to know she can never replace me."

Her father broke first, his lips twitching as he fought to

keep from smiling. "I'll be sure and tell her. Now, are you ready to leave? I believe Miss Potter was occupied in the other room, but we must act quickly."

"Why don't you both come for Sunday dinner tomorrow," Sarah said. "The children will be thrilled to see you, and you can tell us everything you learned."

"I may have already told you everything," her mother said, "but we'll never miss a chance to see the children."

When they had gone, Sarah looked around for Malloy. The crowd that had returned to the house after the cemetery was smaller than those who had attended the funeral, and now almost all of them had left or were in the process of leaving.

Nellie Potter had cornered an elderly man who was sitting in a corner of the parlor, and she was undoubtedly telling him what great friends she and Louisa had been. Mrs. Rodgers had spotted her, too, and was giving her a look that should have killed her on the spot.

When she realized Mrs. Rodgers intended to confront Nellie again, Sarah stepped into her path.

"I wanted to offer my condolences again, Mrs. Rodgers. It was a lovely service."

Mrs. Rodgers turned her anger on Sarah. "It was a ghastly service. First that young man barged in late and then he had the nerve to challenge the minister. I've never been so embarrassed in my life."

"Isn't he the one who should have been embarrassed?" Sarah asked. "Everyone knows his actions were his alone."

Plainly, Mrs. Rodgers didn't want to be mollified. "And that girl." She jerked her chin in Nellie's direction. "Louisa

never gave her that scarf, and she would never have culti-
vated a friendship with a girl like that."

"Perhaps Louisa felt sorry for her," Sarah suggested.

Mrs. Rodgers gave a mirthless laugh. "Louisa never felt
pity for anyone. If you knew how she mistreated her
brother . . . Well, let's just say that Louisa believed she was
more intelligent than everyone else, and she had no patience
for those she deemed less worthy. Which, I assume, would
include that girl."

That girl, blissfully unaware of Mrs. Rodgers's tirade, appeared beside them. "Mrs. Rodgers, I know how much
you're going to miss Louisa, and I just want to say that I
would be happy to come and sit with you anytime you're
feeling especially sad or missing her too much. We could
talk about Louisa together. That would help us both, I
think. Don't you?"

"No, I do not," Mrs. Rodgers said. "Seeing you is an
annoyance, and I'll thank you to leave my house and never
return."

"Oh dear, I never thought of that," Nellie said, apparently oblivious to the insult. "Seeing me must bring back all
sorts of painful memories of Louisa. I'm so sorry. I never
meant to disturb you."

Was Nellie really so naive that she could misunderstand
what Mrs. Rodgers was telling her? Her sympathetic smile
seemed to indicate she was.

"Nellie, could my husband and I give you a lift home in
our motorcar?" Sarah said in an attempt to rescue her from
further abuse.

"A motorcar? Really?" Nellie exclaimed. "I've never rid-den in a motorcar. The girls at the rooming house will be so jealous."

While Nellie chattered on, Mrs. Rodgers turned and walked away. Malloy found them, and Sarah told him they were taking Nellie home. It wasn't exactly on their way, but it was at least in the right direction. They were a little cramped with three adults in the electric, but Nellie was thin. She also kept them entertained the whole way by telling them how excited she was to ride in a real motorcar and recounting her ride in the Deckers' carriage and how nice those very rich people had been to her.

"I'm sorry Mrs. Rodgers embarrassed you about the scarf," Sarah said when Nellie finally paused for breath.

"She didn't embarrass me, although I thought it was sad that she didn't believe Louisa had given me the scarf. Louisa was very generous. She'd let me wear her clothes sometimes, too, and help me fix my hair. I always wanted a sister, and I think Louisa did, too."

"Was it true that she and her brother didn't get along very well?" Malloy asked, surprising Sarah. She wouldn't have thought of asking Nellie about Oscar.

"They used to fight when they were little, like all brothers and sisters, but when they got older, they were very close. Louisa was such a kind person, and she was the oldest, so she looked after him."

"It's odd that he didn't give a eulogy, then," Malloy remarked.

"He was probably afraid he would break down in tears," Nellie said with great certainty. "He must be feeling her loss."

"Yes, he is definitely feeling her loss," Malloy said in a tone that made Sarah aware he knew something she didn't.

With Nellie's instructions, they finally arrived at the rooming house.

"This looks like a very nice place," Sarah said, although she noted the house was not quite as well kept as its neighbors.

"Mrs. Baker keeps things very clean, although the other girls can be mean," Nellie reported. "I don't know what I'll do without Louisa."

"I'm sure you'll find a new friend," Sarah said.

"Not one like Louisa," Nellie said. "Can you wait here for a minute? Mrs. Baker won't believe I rode in a motorcar if she doesn't see it."

They agreed and Nellie hurried inside.

The older woman who had been at the funeral earlier came out reluctantly, a few minutes later. Nellie was pulling her by the hand. The woman allowed Nellie to pull her only as far as the front gate, but Nellie waved so Sarah would wave back, confirming that she knew Nellie. Mrs. Baker would probably remember seeing them at the funeral.

Sarah noticed another young woman had appeared in the doorway and was craning her neck to see them better. Nellie would have two witnesses to testify to this historic event.

When Mrs. Baker turned to go back inside, Malloy pulled away from the curb.

"Can ears wear out?" Malloy asked her half seriously, rubbing his own ear to illustrate. "I was worried there for a minute."

Sarah grinned at his nonsense. "That girl can really talk,

can't she? But I think she was just nervous because of the situation."

"She was wrong about Louisa and Oscar being close," he said.

"I know they didn't get along because of their parents, but sometimes children in that situation learn to rely on each other," Sarah said, trying to be fair.

"Except that I talked to Oscar today, and he said Louisa used to lord it over him that she was smarter at everything than he was."

"That's an ugly thing to do."

"Very ugly. Oscar made it clear he hated Louisa for it, too. He was apparently good at sports but not at school-work. Their parents made Louisa help him with it, but she mocked him instead."

"Yes, his mother said the same thing. This is not the kind, loving sister that Nellie described."

"So where did Nellie get the idea that Louisa and Oscar were close?"

"Maybe Louisa lied to her," Sarah said. "No one wants to brag about how mean they were to their siblings, do they?"

"They don't brag about how *good* they were to their siblings either."

"No, they don't usually, but Nellie knew about the secret engagement and the article Louisa was writing. Louisa must have confided in her."

"But maybe she didn't always tell Nellie the truth."

IX

Gino had helped Maeve with the children while the Malloys were at the funeral, but they had plans for the evening. Gino was taking her out to dinner and then to a play. They lingered only long enough for Gino to report he hadn't found the homeless man the previous night, although he felt sure he had looked into every doorway and alley in a ten-block radius of the magazine office. He would, he said, search again on Sunday night.

Mother Malloy helped Sarah put the children to bed later, and only then did Frank and Sarah have a chance to talk more about what they had learned that day.

"I'm having a difficult time figuring out who Louisa Rodgers really was," Sarah said when she and Frank were alone in their private parlor.

Frank nodded. He knew exactly what she meant. "I don't think Oscar was lying when he said he hated Louisa, which means she may have had a bit of a cruel streak, at least for her brother."

"And if she was as mean to him as he indicated, I can certainly understand why he hated her. But why would Nellie claim Louisa and Oscar were close unless Louisa had lied to her about her relationship with Oscar?"

"Well, we do know Louisa wasn't above lying when it suited her purpose. She lied to Watson to get his cooperation for her story. She said she was going to write a flattering article about him and his family."

"You could also call it a lie that she kept her engagement a secret from her family," Sarah said. "Although I can't understand why she did. Her mother apparently wanted nothing more than to see Louisa married."

"Maybe a lowly magazine illustrator wouldn't have suited her mother, though," Frank suggested.

"Maybe, but Mrs. Rodgers doesn't have a very high opinion of her daughter, so she might have welcomed any young man, regardless of his prospects."

"What we know for sure is that Louisa could be ruthless when it came to getting her story and that she may have been mean to her brother."

"We also know she had a temper if her reaction to her editor's rejection of her story is any indication. On the other hand, her father thought she was a perfect daughter, and Nellie said she was kind and generous."

Frank shook his head. Something wasn't right. "If Louisa

didn't have any patience with her brother because she thought he was stupid, would she be kind to Nellie, who also isn't very bright?"

"I'm not sure we can judge Nellie's intelligence on such short acquaintance," Sarah told him with that saucy smile he loved. "But she *can* be quite annoying."

"She probably annoyed Louisa, too, which makes me wonder why Louisa would've given Nellie that scarf or been friends with her at all."

"Mrs. Rodgers apparently wonders the same thing. She practically accused Nellie of stealing the scarf, but I suggested Louisa may have just felt sorry for her."

"Nobody has suggested Louisa was softhearted about anyone or anything, though," Frank reminded her.

"Nobody except Nellie," Sarah reminded him right back.

"I guess it's up to Maeve to find out what the other girls in the rooming house thought of her, then."

"I'm sure she will, and speaking of Maeve, she didn't even get defensive when I teased her about going out with Gino tonight."

"Uh-oh, things are getting serious."

"I think they've been serious for a while. Maeve just hasn't admitted it. What are we going to do if they get married?"

Frank rubbed his chin as he considered this odd question. "Attend the wedding?"

"No, I mean what are we going to do about Maeve. She won't be living here anymore, and we'll need to get someone else to look after the children. You may need a new secretary at the office, too."

"I hadn't thought of that," Frank said, wishing he didn't

have to think about it now. "She'll probably still want to help with investigations, though."

"I'm sure she will, but they'll probably have babies. She won't be as much help then."

This was going to be a problem. "We'll have to make sure they don't get married, then."

Sarah gave him a pitying look, and he knew there was no hope.

Maeve took the elevated train up to Rose Hill late the next morning. Sunday was a day of rest for most people, so the El wasn't as packed as usual. This gave her time to think about the previous night. She and Gino had enjoyed the play and had a lovely dinner. He had told her all about his nephew, baby Robert, and his accomplishments and expressed regret that she wouldn't get to see the baby if she didn't come to Sunday dinner. Maeve smiled to herself when she remembered Gino saying he was pretty sure she had scheduled this meeting at the rooming house so she wouldn't be able to see his family. How silly. She had scheduled this meeting because she could get information that would help with the case. If she had to miss Sunday dinner, too, then that was just a bonus.

As much as she would have loved to see Gino's nephew, little Robert, she definitely didn't want to see Gino's mother. Not even when Gino told her that his mother had mentioned she wouldn't mind having some red-haired grandchildren. That had made her blush to the roots of her red hair, even though she was pretty sure Gino had made it up.

When she got off at the 23rd Street station, she found the neighborhood was even quieter than the train, with many people probably still at church. She was determined not to think about the Donatellis any more today.

Mrs. Baker answered her knock at the rooming house. Instead of welcoming her, Mrs. Baker just sighed with resignation and stepped aside so Maeve could enter.

"Are your guests awake?" Maeve asked.

"Just barely. Two of them are down in the kitchen and the other is getting dressed. You can find your own way. My bunions are aching this morning."

With that, she toddled off into what was obviously her bedroom. Or rather she stumbled off. She didn't seem to be quite steady on her feet. Sore bunions must be a trial.

Undaunted, Maeve made her way downstairs to the kitchen. She found two young women there, sleepily nibbling toast, and also Nellie Potter, looking bright-eyed and eager.

"Miss Smith, I told the girls you'd be back, but they didn't believe me."

"We believed you," one of the girls said in disgust, but Nellie ignored her.

"I told them I already answered all your questions about Louisa," Nellie went on. "They hardly knew her, not like I did. She was my very best friend in all the world." She touched the colorful silk bow at her throat. "She gave me this scarf."

One of the girls snorted, earning a scowl from Nellie, and while Nellie wasn't talking for a moment, Maeve seized the opportunity to say, "I wonder if I could speak with you both privately about Louisa."

"You don't need to speak privately," Nellie tried. "We don't have secrets here."

"Just because you don't know what they are doesn't mean we don't have them," the first girl said with a smirk. "I'm Gertie. Nice to meet you."

The other young woman introduced herself as Susan. Both wore simple skirts and shirtwaists that were a bit worse for wear. Susan was plump and pleasant with light brown hair and a winning smile. Gertie was thin and serious and a bit suspicious.

"Come up to my room, Miss Smith," Gertie said. "We can talk in private there." She gave Nellie a meaningful glance, making her scowl again.

As happy as she was for the opportunity to speak with the other women without Nellie's interference, she also couldn't alienate the girl. Nellie might have more valuable information she hadn't thought to share yet. She gave Nellie an apologetic smile and said, "I'll have some more questions for you, too."

That seemed to placate her, although she was still clearly not pleased. They should probably check to make sure she wasn't listening outside the door.

"We can go to my room," Gertie said as they climbed the stairs to the second floor. "Unless you want to talk to us separately."

"I don't think that's necessary," Maeve said. "Isn't there another lodger, too?"

"I'll get her," Susan said.

Gertie escorted Maeve into her room. It was sparsely furnished with a chest of drawers and pegs on the wall for hanging clothes. A single bed sat against the wall, and a small table with one chair sat against the opposite one. Gertie offered Maeve the chair, and she sat on the bed. Susan brought a straight-backed chair from her own room for herself, and another girl came in behind her with her own chair. They introduced her as Angie. She was a delicate little woman whose gaze darted nervously around the room, refusing to settle on any one thing.

"Have you lived here very long?" Maeve asked.

"I've been here a little over a year," Gertie said.

"It's about eight months for me," Susan said.

"Almost two years for me," Angie said, her voice barely audible.

"Angie is afraid of Mrs. Baker, but she's also too afraid to move," Gertie explained. Angie nodded her confirmation.

Maeve continued, undaunted. "How well did you know Louisa Rodgers?"

The women exchanged a glance. "Louisa wasn't very sociable," Susan said.

"Thought she was better than we were," Gertie added.

"We tried to be friendly, but she never wanted to go out with us," Susan said.

"She was always writing something," Angie said softly.

"In her room," Gertie clarified. "She didn't come upstairs to sit with us in the evening either."

"She was writing," Angie reminded her.

"Yes, we know, dear," Susan told her.

"But she was friendly with Nellie," Maeve tried.

This made Gertie and Susan laugh and Angie shake her head.

"Louisa hated Nellie," Susan said.

"All of us hate her," Gertie added. "She's a busybody and a thief."

"You don't know that for sure," Angie said, still speaking in little more than a whisper.

"Louisa thought she was. She said some things had gone missing from her room, and now Nellie is wearing her scarf and claiming Louisa gave it to her," Gertie said.

"Louisa wouldn't have given her anything," Susan said with certainty.

This wasn't making sense. "But Louisa told Nellie all about the article she was writing."

"Susan asked her one morning what she was doing in her room all alone, and she said she was writing an article for her magazine, and it was going to make her famous," Gertie said.

"I said I thought she was just a secretary," Susan said, "and she said she wouldn't be for long."

"Nellie was there, and she heard it," Gertie said.

"Then all of you knew she was writing an important article," Maeve said.

They nodded.

"Did you also know about her engagement?"

"Was Louisa engaged?" Susan asked, glancing at the other girls, who looked just as baffled as she.

"Who was she engaged to?" Gertie asked.

"Clyde Hoffman. It was a secret engagement, but Louisa told Nellie."

"Clyde Hoffman," Susan repeated thoughtfully. "Is he the one who—"

"Yes, I think he is," Gertie said.

"The one who what?" Maeve asked, thinking she might finally learn something important.

"He came to the house one evening and asked for Louisa," Susan said.

"Mrs. Baker would've had a fit except Louisa had one first," Gertie reported gleefully. "She told him he was never to come here and bother her again. She really put a flea in his ear."

"We all wanted to know who he was," Susan said.

"I didn't," Angie said. "I didn't like him."

No one paid her any mind.

"Who did Louisa say he was?" Maeve asked. This really could be important.

"She said he was some fellow who worked at the magazine. Seems like he was sweet on her or something, but she didn't feel the same," Susan said.

"She was plenty mad about it, too," Gertie added. "I don't think she would've said so much about him if she hadn't been."

"When was this?" Maeve asked. Could it have been the night Louisa died? Or maybe a day or two before? Could Hoffman have been so angry over being rejected that he had strangled Louisa?

The women conferred, trying to remember exactly when this had happened.

"It was still hot then," Gertie decided. "You know, from the heat wave."

The past summer had brought record-breaking high temperatures to much of the country for two months. The heat had finally eased in August.

"Do you think it might have been as long ago as July?" Maeve asked, a little disappointed.

"Or maybe early August, but it was still really hot that night he came," Susan said. "I remember how he was sweating."

"We were all sweating," Gertie reminded her.

Maeve shuddered at the memory of those awful weeks. Then she forced herself back to the matter at hand. "Did you ever see him again? I mean, did he ever come back looking for Louisa?"

"I saw him once," Angie said.

"So did I," Gertie said. "More than once, too, but he didn't ever come to the door again."

"What was he doing?" Maeve asked.

Angie shrugged. "Just leaning against the lamppost across the street there."

"That's all he ever did, just stand there, watching," Gertie said.

"By any chance, did you see him the day Louisa died?" Maeve said. "He claims he came here that evening, looking for her."

"Oh no," Angie said. "When I saw him, it wasn't long after the night Louisa gave him what for."

"And we were all out late the night Louisa died," Susan said, "so we couldn't've seen him that evening."

"Did any of you see him earlier that day?"

They shook their heads.

"He would've got an earful again if he did come, though," Angie said.

"If Louisa had been here, I'm sure she would have been

angry," Maeve said, remembering how furious Louisa would have been after having her article idea rejected.

"But she was here," Angie said with more confidence than she had previously shown.

Maeve frowned. "Mrs. Baker said she never came home that day at all."

"Don't you remember, Angie?" Susan said patiently. "Mrs. Baker was ranting because Louisa never came home. She was going to send Louisa packing for staying out all night."

"I know she wasn't here overnight," Angie said, "but I saw her come home around the usual time. I was about half a block behind her. She went into the house, and she must've gone straight to her room."

"Why didn't Mrs. Baker see her, then?" Maeve asked.

Angie shifted in her chair and refused to meet Maeve's eye. "She was laying down."

Obviously, this had a secret meaning Maeve did not understand. Gertie and Susan started snickering.

"She took her medicine, I guess," Gertie said slyly.

"Her *medicine*?" Maeve asked, thinking she might understand, after all.

"She's going through the change," Gertie informed Maeve. "She takes Watson's Blood Purifier."

Maeve remembered the main ingredient of Watson's was alcohol. No wonder she was stumbling and lying down.

"Let me get this straight," Maeve said. "Angie, you saw Louisa come home the day she was killed. What time was this, do you think?"

"Around five thirty, I'd guess," Angie said.

"And Mrs. Baker was, uh, *resting*, so she didn't see Louisa arrive."

Angie nodded.

"Did either of you see Louisa that afternoon or evening?" Maeve asked Gertie and Susan.

They had not.

"Could she have left the house without anyone noticing?"

"Sure," Gertie said. "She could've gone out the kitchen door. Her room was in the basement, and the rest of us only go down there for breakfast since Mrs. Baker doesn't serve lunch or dinner."

"She might not have wanted the rest of you to see her leaving," Maeve mused. "She had quit her job that day, and she wouldn't want Mrs. Baker to find out."

"Oh no," Susan agreed. "Mrs. Baker would've put her out."

"She could've just gone home to her family, though," Gertie said. "It's not like she would've been sleeping on the street if she left here."

But would Louisa have really gone home to her family? She hadn't actually been fired, but she had been humiliated when Tibbot refused to publish her story. From what Maeve knew about Louisa's mother, she probably would have been happy to see her daughter finally put in her place. So, Louisa wouldn't have gone home where she would have had to admit her failure, and she wouldn't have told anyone here she had quit her job and risk being thrown out.

"Are you figuring something out?" Angie asked timidly, peering more closely at Maeve's face.

"Yes," Maeve replied. "I think I am."

. . .

Sᴀʀᴀʜ's ᴘᴀʀᴇɴᴛs ᴄᴀᴍᴇ ᴛᴏ Sᴜɴᴅᴀʏ ᴅɪɴɴᴇʀ ᴀs ᴛʜᴇʏ ʜᴀᴅ arranged. The children were on their best behavior during the meal, which went slowly because people had to stop eating to sign for Brian's benefit, and Brian had to neglect his eating in order to be able to follow the conversation. The Deckers were thoroughly impressed with Catherine's and Mrs. Malloy's ability to sign while they fumbled through with their limited vocabularies.

Still, seeing how hard her parents were trying to communicate with Brian brought tears to Sarah's eyes. They had welcomed him and Catherine as their grandchildren and she would be forever grateful to them for that.

When everyone had finished eating, the Deckers accepted the children's invitation to come to the nursery and view their toys. Maeve wasn't back yet, but Sarah's mother insisted they could manage the children without help. Maeve came in a short time later, fairly bursting to tell them what she had learned.

With the children safely upstairs with the Deckers, they sat down in the parlor with Mrs. Malloy in her usual corner. Maeve told them what the other women at the rooming house had told her about Louisa and her relationship with Nellie.

"But if they weren't really friends, how did Nellie know about Louisa's article and her secret engagement?" Sarah asked.

"They all knew she was writing something she thought was important," Maeve said. "That wasn't a secret at all, and they also knew Hoffman had tried to call on Louisa back in the summer and that Louisa had not been pleased. In fact, she told him to never come to the house again."

"If they were engaged, why would she do a thing like that?" Frank asked.

"If it was a secret," his mother said from her corner, "she wouldn't want all those girls to know, would she?"

"Mother Malloy is right," Sarah said, seeing the logic instantly. "Mr. Hoffman might have thought it was a romantic gesture to call on Louisa, but she would have been furious at him for almost betraying their secret, and she sent him away."

Malloy was nodding. "Thereby convincing the other women in the house that he meant nothing to her."

"But we still only have Hoffman's and Nellie's word for it that they really were engaged," Maeve reminded them. "So maybe Louisa was angry because she really didn't want him bothering her."

"Malloy is confident that you can find out the truth at the office," Sarah told her.

"Don't worry," Maeve said. "That is first on my list of things to find out. Oh, and I also learned that one of the girls saw Louisa come back to the rooming house around five thirty the night she was killed."

"I thought her landlady said she never came home at all that day," Malloy said.

Maeve cleared her throat to indicate she was going to report something momentous. Sarah found herself leaning forward in anticipation. "It seems Mrs. Baker is having *female problems*, and she medicates herself with Watson's Blood Purifier."

"How did you find that out?" Malloy asked in amazement.

"The girls told me, and I noticed she was a bit unsteady when she answered the door and retired immediately to her room to rest. Apparently, she was also *resting* the day Louisa died, so she wouldn't have noticed anyone's comings and goings."

"So, Louisa left the magazine offices around three o'clock," Malloy mused. "Then she got back to the rooming house around five thirty."

"Because she couldn't go back to the house too early or Mrs. Baker would suspect she had lost her job," Maeve said.

"Where was she in between?" Sarah asked.

Malloy shrugged. "Probably walking and trying to work off her anger at Tibbot for rejecting her article."

"Or sitting in a park and planning what she was going to do next," Maeve suggested.

"Or just about anything," Sarah said. "The important thing is, she went back to the rooming house for a period of time."

"During which she must have decided she needed to collect her notes and things from her desk," Malloy said.

"When no one was around so she wouldn't be embarrassed," Maeve added.

"She might have known the late-night guard didn't pay much attention to who came and went on his shift and waited until eight o'clock to go back," Sarah suggested.

"The girls said she could have gone out the kitchen door, which is in the basement, and no one would have seen her," Maeve said.

"We know for certain she went to the office later that evening and packed up the things in her desk," Malloy said.

"But the box was too heavy for her to carry, so she left it there," Maeve said.

"Or did she?" Sarah said. "She might also have telephoned someone for help. I assume the magazine is on the telephone."

"Oh yes. I answered about a thousand calls on Friday," Maeve said. "But do we really think the person she called is the one who killed her?"

"That does seem wrong somehow, doesn't it?" Sarah said. "She would have called someone she trusted, who would be willing to come to her aid no matter what, so presumably not someone who wanted her dead."

"That eliminates her brother, I'd guess," Maeve said.

"Probably her mother, too. I can see her giving Louisa a lecture but no help," Sarah said.

"That leaves her father and her fiancé—if he really is her fiancé," Maeve said.

"We don't know if Hoffman even has a telephone, but I do know her father was out of town that night. He didn't get home until around midnight," Malloy said.

"So that also eliminates her father, who is also the only person who seems really sorry that she's dead," Maeve said.

"There's one more person who's mourning her," Malloy added with a grin, "her *very best friend in all the world*."

"Would she really have called someone she despised?" Maeve asked.

"If she was desperate enough," Sarah said. "And from

what I've heard about Louisa, she might not have hesitated to take advantage of Nellie's devotion to her."

"You're probably right," Maeve said. "And if Louisa thought Nellie had actually stolen things from her, she might think Nellie owed her."

"And of course there's the police theory that she was killed by some evil stranger who happened across her in the lobby that night," Malloy said. "Gilbride thinks I'm a fool for even looking for the killer."

"We do have to consider that Louisa might have been attacked by a stranger," Sarah said. "She could have encountered him in the lobby if she realized she couldn't carry the box herself, and she wasn't really engaged to Mr. Hoffman so she didn't call him for help, and her father was out of town so she couldn't reach him, and she didn't even think of calling Nellie for help because they weren't really friends, so she decided she would have to come back later and simply left, empty-handed."

"It also could have happened if Mr. Watson's hired killer had followed Louisa that night just waiting for a chance to stop her from ever writing her story about that company," Malloy said.

Maeve sat back in her chair and groaned. "I thought I'd found out something that would really help us figure out who killed her."

"Perhaps you did, and we just haven't realized it yet," Sarah said to comfort her.

"One thing you didn't find out, though, and which we still don't know, is why anyone would have killed Louisa at all," Malloy said. "She might have been mean to her brother and the women she lived with, and she might have spurned Hoffman's affections and even disappointed her mother, but these are things that happen every day without resulting in murder."

"People don't write articles that bankrupt businesses every day, though," Maeve pointed out.

"Do you suppose Louisa got the idea for her article from seeing Mrs. Baker taking her *medicine*?" Sarah asked.

"That would be interesting to know," Maeve said, "although I don't suppose it matters now. It's funny, though. Mrs. Baker is a teetotaler. She made it clear when I was pretending to rent a room that she didn't allow any drinking on the premises and if a girl came home drunk, she'd get kicked out."

"And yet she gets intoxicated herself on Watson's," Sarah mused. "Louisa might have recognized the irony and realized what a good story it would be."

"Someone should tell Mrs. Baker how much alcohol is in her medicine," Maeve said.

"Louisa wanted to tell *everyone* how much alcohol is in her medicine and look what happened to her," Malloy said solemnly.

X

On Monday morning, Maeve left early for her job at the magazine, Malloy went to the office, and Sarah drove Mother Malloy and Brian to their school on the way to dropping Catherine off at her school.

Sarah was really enjoying the freedom her electric offered her now. She could go wherever she wanted to without having to find a cab or hazard the El or a trolley.

Today she chose to visit her mother after Catherine was safely at school.

"That was cruel of you not to tell us what Maeve was doing yesterday," her mother said when Sarah had been welcomed and served coffee. "I knew it had something to do with the case."

"You know we don't discuss cases in front of the children," Sarah said to tease her.

"The children weren't always with us," her mother reminded her.

"No, they weren't, but when Father pointedly changed the subject after you asked if we'd identified Louisa's killer yet, I think we all understood he didn't want to hear any more about it."

"But I did," her mother exclaimed. "So, tell me what you've learned."

Sarah brought her up to date.

"Then you haven't actually eliminated anyone," her mother concluded. "I'm glad to know the secret lover is still a possibility."

"We aren't really sure he and Louisa were lovers, though. Maeve is going to try to find out now that she's working at the magazine."

"She's such a clever girl," her mother said. "Frank is going to miss her when she marries."

"What makes you think she's going to marry?" Sarah asked, just to see what her mother might have noticed that Sarah had not.

"It's plain as the nose on your face. Young Gino is besotted with her."

"Is she besotted with him, do you think?"

"Of course, although a young lady can't betray her feelings too openly. I kept your father dangling for months. Men appreciate you more if they have to work for your affection."

Sarah thought about how long she and Malloy had been dangling, thinking they could never be together. That must make their bond unbreakable.

"I'll miss Maeve at home, too," Sarah said, bringing the conversation back to that subject. "Although the children don't need much looking after, except for getting them to and from school."

"You could hire a chauffeur. I notice many families have."

"Rich families," Sarah countered.

"You are a rich family."

A fact that Malloy was still not comfortable with.

"We'll worry about it when Maeve and Gino tell us they're engaged. Tell me, Mother, have you experienced female problems?" she asked to change the subject.

Her mother gave her a sour look. "Do you mean am I going through the change?"

"Yes, that's what I meant."

"As a matter of fact, I am, although I haven't suffered the way some of my friends have. I get an occasional hot flash, and my monthlies . . . Well, nothing is quite the same."

"Maeve told us Louisa's landlady is taking Watson's Blood Purifier for it. Do you know anyone who takes a patent medicine to help with the discomforts?"

"I know several who take Lydia Pinkham's Vegetable Compound. They swear by it."

"What if I told you the main ingredient in most patent medicines is alcohol?"

Her mother blinked in surprise. "My goodness, I had no idea."

"Do you think your friends would be surprised? Or shocked? Or horrified?"

"Certainly surprised. Is that what Louisa Rodgers was writing about?"

"Among other things. We think her landlady's use of one of these patent medicines may have inspired her."

"But those medicines must work, or people wouldn't use them," her mother insisted. "And they're patented, so the government must check them somehow."

"I'm not sure about that, now that you mention it. I'll have to find out."

"I would hate to think that thousands of people are spending money on medicines that don't actually work. That's nothing but outright thievery."

"Yes, it would be."

"But I notice every advertisement has testimonials to how effective they are. They must work for some people, at least."

"Or else the company makes up the testimonials," Sarah said.

"Oh, Sarah, you're so jaded," her mother said in mock dismay.

"Experience has taught me to be."

"But why do they put alcohol in these medicines? If alcohol could cure disease, there would be no sick people on earth."

"That's true, but alcohol does ease pain and, well, perhaps the simple explanation is that while you may still be sick, you no longer care because you're intoxicated."

"What an awful thought, but you may be right."

"All you have to do is count how many saloons you see on nearly every block in New York City. A lot of people use alcohol for many reasons. We shouldn't be surprised if they use it to cope with illness, too."

"Even if they don't know they are," her mother said thoughtfully.

"Mother, you said your friends would at least be surprised to learn their patent medicine is mostly alcohol, but do you think learning that would convince them not to take it anymore?"

"I couldn't possibly know for certain. You know how people are. They believe what they want to believe, and if they still believed it brought them relief, I don't think anything could convince them to stop."

FRANK WENT TO HIS OFFICE TO FILL GINO IN ON WHAT Maeve had learned and find out if Gino had located the homeless man they'd been looking for.

"I'm starting to think this vagrant doesn't exist," Gino said when he finally arrived. He'd been out most of the night searching the Rose Hill neighborhood again for the mysterious homeless man who may or may not have seen Louisa's killer or even killed her himself.

"If he's the murderer, he might have hightailed it," Frank said. "No sense in hanging around to get caught."

"I don't think he's gone," Gino said. "I found some people who had seen him in the past few days, but they just didn't know where he was last night. One old woman told me he probably found a good spot and was staying put until somebody told him to move on."

"Gilbride, the detective who investigated—or didn't investigate—Louisa's murder, said she wasn't robbed or assaulted, which tends to rule out an attack by a stranger."

"That's true. I did find out something a little unsettling, though."

"About the murder?"

"Yes. Billy Funhouser told me the old man often tried to sneak into the lobby to sleep, but he would run the poor fellow off. Then last night, I stopped by the building to ask the new guard if he had seen anything, and he told me that Billy Funhouser often let the old man sleep in the lobby, or at least he just ignored him when he did, so long as he was gone before the building opened in the morning. Either way, that's not what Billy told us. Now we know the old man might have come in that night and run into Louisa."

"And if he did, she might have been frightened, maybe even screamed."

"The old man could have panicked and tried to make her stop and . . ." Gino shrugged.

"So, we definitely need to find him, even if it turns out he had nothing to do with it."

"Yes, because he also might have seen the person who did do it. If we had the slightest clue who was there that night, we could probably solve the case."

"I'll help you look for him tonight. We can cover twice as much territory that way."

Gino sighed. "Or with any luck, Maeve will find the killer today and we can both get a good night's sleep."

Maeve was used to typing up reports of their investigations, so typing the stories the reporters turned in was not a challenge. The telephone at the magazine rang much more often than it did at her real office, but the calls here were much more interesting. People complained a lot about the content of the magazine, although most of them just wrote letters. Hearing and reading the complaints was quite informative, though. Maeve learned that people had strong opinions but that those opinions weren't necessarily logical or even reasonable.

She had taken the initiative that morning and introduced herself to the other employees as they arrived for work. She gave Clyde Hoffman a smile and told him she was glad to see him again. He assured her he was even happier to see her in return. What a strange man he was, striking up an acquaintance with Maeve on Friday and then standing up at Louisa's funeral on Saturday to proclaim his grief over losing her.

Miss Yoder had also been excessively glad that Maeve had shown up on Monday morning and offered to treat her to lunch to express her appreciation. The office was too busy to allow for much gossip during working hours, so Maeve gratefully accepted her invitation, which would allow them to chat freely.

Miss Yoder took her to a small tea shop where ladies could dine unescorted and free from male interest.

"Mr. Hoffman introduced himself to me last Friday as I was leaving the building," Maeve said.

Miss Yoder looked up from her tea, startled. "He did, did he?"

"Yes, and he even offered to walk me home. I told him I take the El, but I let him walk me to the station. He is very upset over Louisa's death."

"Is he?" Miss Yoder asked without a drop of sympathy.

"Yes, he . . . Well, I don't know if I should tell you this, but he told me he and Louisa were secretly engaged."

Miss Yoder didn't look a bit surprised. In fact, she frowned. "I should have warned you about Clyde. I was too distracted on Friday, trying to do my own job and show you what to do as well, but that's no excuse."

"What should you have warned me about?" Maeve said, trying to look puzzled instead of triumphant at the possibility of learning some valuable information.

"Clyde Hoffman is a good illustrator, but . . ." Miss Yoder sighed. "He developed an . . . an attachment for Louisa."

"They fell in love, you mean," Maeve said in all innocence.

"Not at all. Clyde might have called it love, but Louisa had no feelings for Clyde except perhaps annoyance over his unwanted attentions."

"But Mr. Hoffman said the engagement was a secret. Maybe she was just pretending not to like him so no one would suspect," Maeve said, remembering their theory about why Louisa had been so angry when Hoffman showed up at her rooming house.

"Louisa wasn't pretending," Miss Yoder said. "She told me he had discovered where she lived, and he had actually come to the house. She'd sent him away, but she had noticed him loitering in the neighborhood several times. She thought he was watching her, and she was very irritated."

"Did she tell Mr. Tibbot?"

Miss Yoder snorted her derision at such a solution. "Tibbot wouldn't care. He'd probably tell Louisa she should be flattered by the attention. I said she should find another job or go back home to her family if she was worried, but she wasn't afraid of Clyde, just annoyed, and she was determined to be a reporter. She had an idea for a story that would make the world stand up and take notice, or so she claimed." Miss Yoder shook her head and rubbed at a stray tear. "Poor girl. Tibbot told her she was a fool, so she walked out, and now she's dead."

The waitress delivered their sandwiches, giving Maeve a chance to gather her thoughts.

When the waitress had gone, Maeve said, "Do you think Mr. Hoffman might have killed her?"

"Good heavens, no," she said quickly, obviously agreeing with poor Louisa's opinion of her admirer. "Clyde couldn't hurt a fly, so don't go imagining things. Louisa must have just encountered some tramp who wanted to have his way with her, and when she resisted, he strangled her. That's obvious, so don't go blaming anybody else."

But Maeve knew perfectly well that anybody might be driven to murder, especially a spurned lover.

On the way home from her mother's house, Sarah stopped at Malloy's office. She found him alone, having sent Gino home to take a nap before he spent another late night looking for the mysterious homeless man.

"I thought you could treat me to lunch if you don't have something important to do," she said, taking one of the client chairs sitting in front of his desk.

"I need to go see Rodgers and let him know what little

we've found out so far, but I can go after we eat, since I don't exactly have urgent news to deliver."

Sarah frowned. "I wish I could go with you."

"Why?"

"Because I can't understand why Mrs. Rodgers disliked her daughter so much, and I'd like to find out more about her."

"You might also want to find out why she lied when she said Oscar was home with her all evening."

"Do you think he wasn't at home that night?" Sarah asked in surprise.

"Does Oscar Rodgers strike you as the type of young man who spends his evenings sitting at home with his mother?"

"No, now that you mention it, but do you know who could tell us for certain?"

Malloy grinned. "The servants."

"Servants always know everything," Sarah said. "Do you think Mr. Rodgers would allow us to question them?"

His grin disappeared. "Maybe not. He'd probably be angry at any hint we believed someone in his family was responsible for Louisa's death."

"On the other hand, he might not be surprised at all to find out that one of them was," Sarah argued. "He certainly doesn't think much of his son."

Malloy thought this over for a long moment. "He might not like Oscar much, but that's a long way from believing Oscar could have killed his own sister."

"True. Still, I'd like the opportunity to at least talk to Mrs. Rodgers once more. I could ask her again where Oscar was that night and see if I think she's telling the truth or maybe get her to admit he wasn't home."

"The only problem is, how do I explain bringing my wife along to a business meeting?"

Sarah considered the problem, glancing around his office for inspiration. She noticed a pile of papers on his desk. He had been looking through Louisa's notes on patent medicines. "Didn't Louisa's box contain other things besides her notes for the articles?"

"Yes, Maeve and Gino separated them out."

"I could go along to take those things—Louisa's things—to her mother, then."

"Couldn't I just give them to her father, though?"

"Yes, but I understand how distraught Mrs. Rodgers must be over the death of her only daughter and how difficult it will be to receive this last remembrance of her, so I came along to offer what comfort I could, woman to woman."

"That's very kind of you, Mrs. Malloy," he said without a trace of sincerity. "It's also a little thin."

"But I don't think anyone would deny that a mother should be upset by her daughter's death and grateful to someone offering comfort."

"It's worth a try, I guess. We can put the papers and things in my briefcase."

"I think we should wrap them up in brown paper into sort of a package," Sarah said. "Make it look more like a gift."

He shrugged. "Whatever you think."

Sarah easily found some brown paper that Maeve used to wrap parcels with. Malloy gave her the pile of papers that

Gino had determined had nothing to do with patent medicines and wrapped them, tying a string around them to hold it all together.

"That reminds me, Mother asked me if there isn't someone who checks patent medicines to make sure they work before they're issued patents," Sarah said.

"You'd like to think so, wouldn't you? But according to Louisa's notes, it turns out the name doesn't mean they are patented at all or given any testing by anyone. Originally, in England, the people who made these medicines would patent the recipe so no one else could copy it, but even then nobody actually tested the medicines to see if they worked. In America, hardly any of the manufacturers even bother to patent their recipe."

"Probably because they don't want anyone to know what is in them," Sarah said, remembering what her mother had said about her being jaded.

"Probably, but the name *patent medicine* just stuck, and it sounds very official, so the manufacturers continued to use it."

When the package of papers was ready, Malloy drove Sarah in her electric to a nice restaurant where they enjoyed lunch without mentioning Louisa's death once. Then he drove them to the Rodgers house in Morningside Heights where the black wreath still hung on the door.

They stood on the front porch for several long minutes until someone finally answered the bell. The maid stared at them through red-rimmed eyes and said, "We are not receiving." How odd for her to still be weeping a week after Louisa's death.

"I know the house is in mourning," Malloy said gently, "but I have some news to report to Mr. Rodgers about the investigation into Miss Rodgers's death. I'm sure he'll want to see me."

"He can't," she said, choking on her tears. "He . . . he's dead."

Malloy and Sarah shared a horrified glance before he said, "What happened?"

"I don't . . ." the girl said, beginning to sob.

"That's enough, Florence," her mistress's voice called sharply from somewhere above. "Show these people into the parlor."

Florence choked down her tears and led them to the parlor before fleeing to weep some more. After a few moments, Mrs. Rodgers came in.

"Is it true?" Malloy asked, still as stunned as Sarah. "Is your husband dead?"

Her cheeks were flushed, and she was perhaps a bit unsteady, but she made it to a chair and sank down in it. "Yes, he is. We found him this morning."

"I'm so sorry, Mrs. Rodgers," Sarah said, giving Malloy a look that told him to let her handle it. "This must be almost more than you can bear."

Mrs. Rodgers stared at her coldly and said, "I'm glad you're here, though, Mr. Malloy. I wanted to tell you that you can end your investigation now."

"Mr. Rodgers already paid me to—"

"You may keep whatever fees my husband paid you. He was determined to prove that Louisa's death was more meaningful than it was. We all know she was killed by some stranger whose identity will never be known. I won't have my family—what's left of my family—disturbed anymore by your inquiries when they will never lead to any conclusion."

Sarah clutched the package of Louisa's papers more closely to her chest. "How did your husband die, Mrs. Rodgers?"

She turned her icy glare to Sarah, who she obviously felt had no business here at all. "We shall announce that he died of a heart attack caused by the grief of losing his only daughter, but you should know the truth since you helped drive him to it. My husband took his own life. He could no longer stand to live in this world without Louisa."

Sarah could only stare at her in shock, and although Mrs. Rodgers had made a point of not inviting them to sit down, she sank into the nearest chair.

"I'm very sorry to hear that," Malloy was saying.

"Are you sure he did it on purpose?" Sarah asked, earning another glare from Mrs. Rodgers. "I'm sorry. I know this must be difficult for you to think about, but could it have been an accident?"

"Yes, how did he die?" Frank asked.

Mrs. Rodgers sighed with annoyance. "The doctor had given me some powders to help me sleep after Louisa died. I did not use any of them. I have my own remedies, but my husband must have taken them from my room. He mixed all of them into the hot cocoa he drinks at bedtime, and he never woke up."

"Did he leave a note?" Sarah asked.

From Mrs. Rodgers's expression, Sarah knew she had gone too far. The woman rose to her feet, probably to order them out, but the sound of the front door opening distracted her.

"Oscar, is that you?" his mother called.

In a moment, the young man appeared in the parlor doorway. "What are you doing here?" he demanded, seeing the Malloys.

"They came to see your father," Mrs. Rodgers said. "I have just told them the news."

"I hope you're satisfied," Oscar told them, obviously angry. "If you hadn't kept on investigating Louisa's death, he could have come to accept it for what it was instead of . . ."

Plainly, his father's death had affected him strongly, although it was difficult to tell which emotions he was feeling besides anger.

"Mother, are you all right?" Oscar asked, hurrying to her. "You shouldn't be out of bed."

He glared at Sarah as if she were personally responsible for his mother's condition. Indeed, she did look awful.

"Come along, Mother. I'll get you your medicine so you can rest."

He helped her to her feet and slipped an arm around her waist to steady her when she faltered. He glared at Malloy.

"You can show yourselves out," he said ungraciously, and escorted his mother out of the room.

Sarah glanced up at Malloy, who was giving both mother and son the look he gave hardened criminals to intimidate them. Sadly, neither of them saw it, as they left the room and started up the stairs to the second floor.

"Oh my," she said.

"Let's go," he replied.

She stood up and let him take her arm to lead her from the house, since she was still feeling a bit disoriented after hearing the shocking news about Mr. Rodgers. Only when they were outside on the sidewalk did she realize she was still clutching the packet of Louisa's papers.

"Wait," she said when Malloy would have headed for their motorcar. "I didn't get a chance to leave these."

"Neither of them are going to see you again, at least not today," he said. "We can always mail them."

"I have a better idea. Let's drive away, in case someone is watching, but then go down the alley behind their house. I'll knock on the back door and deliver them to the—"

"—servants," Malloy finished for her with a knowing smile. "Mrs. Malloy, have I told you how brilliant you are?"

"Yes, and you really should put me on the payroll," she replied sweetly.

"We'll discuss it later. Right now, you have a job to do."

Malloy stopped the motorcar two houses away from the Rodgers house, and Sarah made her way down the alley, past the refuse cans. She ignored the stray cats and vermin who were busy trying to find something to eat. She let herself into the Rodgerses' backyard and went up the back porch and knocked at the kitchen door.

A few moments later, the tearful maid who had answered the front door opened the back door. She was no longer actively crying, but her eyes and nose were still red. She looked very distressed at finding a front-door guest at the back door.

"Is something wrong, ma'am?" she asked, glancing around as if she expected to see another disaster.

"Not really, but I had brought this for Mrs. Rodgers, and I didn't have an opportunity to give it to her." Sarah indicated the package she held. "I was wondering if I could leave it with someone."

"I don't know, ma'am. I . . . Would you mind coming in for a minute while I ask?"

Florence obviously felt uncomfortable inviting a guest to enter the kitchen, but coming in was exactly what Sarah had hoped to do.

A stout woman who must be the cook was rolling out pastry dough on the table, but she had paused to look at Sarah.

"She has a package for Mrs. Rodgers," Florence informed the cook.

The cook laid down her rolling pin and wiped her hands on her apron. "What is it?" she asked suspiciously.

"The things that were in Louisa's desk at the magazine where she worked. I thought the family might like to have them."

"Why did you bring them to the kitchen, then?" the cook asked with a frown.

"She and her husband came to the front door," Florence explained. "Mrs. Rodgers saw them for a few minutes, but when Mr. Oscar came home, he took her upstairs and sent them away."

The cook shook her head in disgust at Mr. Oscar's antics. "I don't know. We should ask Mr. Rodgers, but . . ." The cook's voice broke, and she rubbed her eye with the back of her hand, the part that wasn't covered with flour.

"That was a terrible shock, I know," Sarah hastily said. "Mr. Rodgers was a fine man." He must have been if his servants were mourning him.

"I'll never believe he done it," the cook said. "It must've been an accident."

"He didn't leave a note, did he?" Sarah tried. "Surely he would have if he had done it on purpose."

"You didn't see a note, did you, Florence?" the cook asked. "She found him this morning," she added to Sarah.

Florence shook her head as her tears started again.

"How did they know he took Mrs. Rodgers's powders, though?" Sarah asked.

"The papers," Florence whimpered. "The empty papers was in a heap on the table beside his bed."

The sleeping powders prescribed by the doctor would have been divided into individual doses and wrapped in small paper packets.

"Mrs. Rodgers said he put the powders into his cocoa," Sarah said.

"I always bring it to him, every night," Florence said, swiping at her tears. "The cup was empty this morning, sitting right next to the papers."

"Perhaps someone put some of the powders into his cocoa to help him sleep, without him knowing. His wife or his son, maybe, and he didn't realize it and put more in himself. Could that have happened?" Sarah asked hopefully.

Florence glanced at the cook, who was also waiting expectantly for her answer.

"It could have, I guess," Florence said reluctantly.

"Mr. Oscar couldn't've done it, though," the cook said. "He wasn't even home. He never is. Goes out every night, he does."

"Even the night Miss Louisa died?" Sarah asked, since this was one thing they really needed to know. "His mother said he was at home that night."

The cook gave a derisive sniff. "Not that night, not any night."

"He doesn't go out every single night," Florence said, a little irritated. "Sometimes he's still too sick."

"Because he's the worse for drink," the cook said in disgust.

"Did he go out last night and the night Miss Louisa died?" Sarah asked.

"He went out last night but came home early," Florence said. "Complained he lost all his money and didn't have any more credit or something. I didn't understand it all."

So, Oscar was a gambler. How interesting. "What about the night Miss Louisa died? Was he home that night?"

Florence shrugged, but the cook said, "Probably not. But why would he hurt his sister or poison his father anyway?"

"And it couldn't've been an accident," Florence said. "The papers . . . There was too many of them and all of them was empty."

"And no one would have accidentally taken that many," Sarah said sadly. "Is that what you mean?"

"But I can't see Mr. Rodgers doing it on purpose either," Florence said, her voice pleading. "Not Mr. Rodgers."

"He was grieving hard for Miss Louisa, though," the cook reminded her.

"But he had hired my husband to find Miss Louisa's killer," Sarah said, "and he told me he wouldn't rest until he found him."

"It don't make sense," the cook said. "No matter how you look at it."

No, it didn't, and the more they learned, the less sense it made.

Sounds like the servants believe it had to be suicide," Malloy said as he navigated the electric through the afternoon traffic.

"They certainly don't want to, but the evidence seems to confirm it. Mrs. Rodgers claimed she hadn't taken any of the sleeping powders herself. She said she has her own remedies, whatever that means."

"Patent medicine, do you suppose?" Malloy asked archly. "That would be interesting."

"I didn't even think of that, but you're right, she does act oddly. I thought it must be the shock of losing a family member, but it could have been something else entirely."

"Or it could have been shock. What else did the servants say?"

"He apparently didn't leave a note, which could have confirmed it, but the sleeping powders were in packets, and from what the maid who found him said, the empty packets were all on the bedside table along with his empty cup of cocoa."

"Would a killer have left the empty papers behind?" Malloy asked.

"Not likely, since Mr. Rodgers would certainly have noticed them and questioned why they were there."

"Yes, a killer would have put the powders in his drink and then taken the papers away, so he didn't notice anything unusual," Malloy mused.

"I know he was very upset about Louisa's death, but he just didn't strike me as someone who would end his own life."

"You can't always tell, of course, but I also think it was strange he didn't wait to see Louisa's killer brought to justice."

"But there also doesn't seem to be any reason for someone to kill him either. It's very confusing." Sarah shook her head.

"Yes, it is, but maybe if we could solve Louisa's murder, we can find the answer to his death as well. Did you find out anything about Oscar's comings and goings?"

"The cook claimed he goes out every single night, but Florence said that isn't necessarily true. Sometimes he is still too hungover to go out."

"Poor Oscar," Malloy said with a grin. "What about last night and the night Louisa died?"

"Neither the maid nor the cook could remember specifically about the night Louisa died, but he came home early last night. He complained he had lost all his money gambling and couldn't get credit or something."

"He'll inherit all his father's money. I wonder how long it will take for him to lose it as well."

"What are we going to do now?" Sarah asked with a sigh.

"You mean since Mrs. Rodgers fired me?" Malloy asked with another grin. "I'm paid for a month's worth of work, so

I think I need to give Mr. Rodgers what he paid for. Besides, I want to know who killed Louisa myself. If it was any of the people outside the family that we suspect or even the vagrant they insist it was, the Rodgerses should be glad we found him."

"What if it's someone *inside* the family?" Sarah asked.

"Then *we'll* be glad we found him," Malloy said with a grin.

"So, we just continue as if we were never fired?"

"Yes."

XI

Well after dark that night, Frank met Gino at the building where the magazine offices were located. Frank had to break the news to him about Bernard Rodgers's death.

"I can't believe it. Why would he kill himself?" Gino asked, as upset about it as Frank had expected.

"His wife believes he was overcome with grief over losing Louisa, but I thought that was why he hired us in the first place."

"And why would he kill himself when he was expecting us to find her killer?"

"I know, it doesn't make sense," Frank said with a sigh, "but the evidence does seem to point to suicide. Oh, and Mrs. Rodgers fired us."

Gino frowned. "Then why are we here?"

"Because Mr. Rodgers paid us to find his daughter's

killer, and I'm going to keep doing that as long as I think there's hope we might figure it out. At least he'll be able to rest in peace if we do."

"That doesn't seem like much comfort, but Louisa does deserve justice. I don't suppose Maeve found out anything today at the magazine."

"Yes, as a matter of fact, she did. Turns out that not only was Louisa not engaged to Clyde Hoffman, she was afraid of him. Remember, Maeve found out he'd tried to call on her at the rooming house, which made Louisa very angry."

"And we thought she sent him away to keep her engagement a secret," Gino said.

"Right, but it turns out she really was furious that he showed up because she didn't have any interest in him. He did, however, keep pestering her, and from what Maeve heard, he'd even been seen lurking in the neighborhood where she lived."

"That's spooky."

"More than spooky. We know how angry a man can get when the woman he wants doesn't want him. If he saw her leave the rooming house that night, he could have followed her back to the office."

"Then he's an even likelier suspect than he was before."

"I'd say so. One of us should ask him about his alibi for the night Louisa was killed."

"I'd be happy to oblige. Besides, I'd enjoy seeing Maeve at her new job."

Frank grinned. "I'm sure you would. Now, let's find this vagrant."

A quick check with the guard on duty told them the homeless man had not been around so far that night.

"Trapper knows all the hidey-holes in the neighborhood," the guard told them.

"Trapper?" Frank echoed.

"That's his name or at least the name he goes by," Gino explained. "I forgot to mention it."

"Why do they call him that?" Frank asked.

"Because that's what he tells people his name is, I guess," Gino said, and the guard agreed.

Armed with that nugget of information, they went back outside. The night was pleasant, which must be a blessing for those living on the streets. The two men discussed where each of them would search and when and where they would meet up again. Then they separated.

As Frank walked the quiet neighborhood, he recalled his days as a patrolman. Many of the police officers assigned to work at night would find a quiet place to catch a few winks on nights when the weather was good and nothing seemed amiss. If he wasn't careful, he might accidentally rouse one of them, which would probably get him run out of the neighborhood.

Some parts of town were overrun with homeless men, women, and children sleeping under bridges or squatting in abandoned buildings. This area of thriving businesses and well-kept homes was not as hospitable, however, which explained why so few homeless people could be found here.

After about a half hour of searching, Frank understood Gino's previous lack of success. Even though this part of the city had electric streetlamps, many areas were still in deep shadow, especially the doorways and alleys where a homeless man might seek shelter. He realized he needed one of those flashlights that the police were using. They produced only a single flash of light at a time, hence the name, but that would be enough to tell him at a glance if something was a person or a pile of trash. Instead, he had to go up and give whatever it was a nudge with his foot to find out, which wasn't very polite if it happened to be a person.

Every now and then, Frank would stop and just listen. In spite of the muffled din from the livelier areas of the city, he could often hear rustling in the alleys, but it usually turned out to be rats or stray dogs in search of a meal.

Then he ventured down an alley behind a row of stores, closed now and locked up tight. The light from the street barely penetrated this far, but he could make out a pile of something. When he nudged it, someone grunted, startling him. He jumped back a step, and said, "Trapper, is that you?"

"What?" a male voice asked groggily. "What do you want?"

"I just want to ask you a few questions," Frank said. "There's a dollar in it for you if you answer."

The man struggled to his feet. Frank could make out only a vague shape in the dark, but he could sense the fellow's wariness. "You the police?" he asked.

"No, a private investigator. I just need to ask you—"

"I never saw nothing. I never saw that girl, and I never killed her neither," he insisted in a panicked whisper.

"I know," Frank tried, although it was a lie. "I just want to find out—"

But Trapper punched him in the stomach, and before Frank could even think, the man was gone, his shambling footsteps echoing in the alley.

Doubled over and gasping for air, Frank realized the old man wasn't as feeble as he had been led to believe. He staggered back to the street, but it was empty, with no sign of where Trapper might have gone. With no one around to hear, Frank cursed eloquently.

Frank had no further luck at finding any people in general, much less Trapper in particular. By the time he met up with Gino again, he was able to breathe normally although he knew he would be sore for a few days. The worst part was having to admit to Gino what had happened.

"You're getting soft," Gino teased when he heard the story. "Too much time in the office."

"I don't suppose you had any luck," Frank said to change the subject.

"I found that old woman again. She said she told Trapper we were looking for him."

"Warned him, more like, judging from his greeting to me," Frank grumbled.

"She said he already knew the police were looking for him. Turns out Billy Funhouser told him they thought he killed Louisa."

"No wonder he ran, then," Frank said in disgust.

"But I never told Funhouser that," Gino insisted. "Did the police say they suspected him?"

"Not him in particular, although Gilbride is sure some stranger did it."

"Do you think our friend Billy knows more than he's telling?"

Frank shrugged. "Only one way to find out."

. . .

THE NEXT MORNING, MAEVE WENT BACK TO THE MAGA-zine and Sarah took Mother Malloy and the children to school in the electric again. Then she drove over to Louisa's rooming house. Malloy had suggested that perhaps she could get some information out of Mrs. Baker without her lodgers around.

She was really going to have to send Malloy a bill for her services.

Sarah had gotten only a glimpse of the house when she and Malloy had given Nellie a ride home after the funeral. It had once been a fine place, like its neighbors, but now it was looking a bit neglected. Obviously, Mrs. Baker didn't have a lot of extra money to spend on keeping the place up. Being left a widow was a sad fate for a woman who had probably never held a job or needed to.

Sarah had to ring the bell twice before Mrs. Baker answered it. She looked quite annoyed at having been disturbed, but whatever she had intended to say died on her lips when she saw who her visitor was.

"You were at Louisa's funeral," she recalled.

"Yes, I'm Mrs. Malloy. I was glad to see you and Nellie were there. I know her family appreciated it."

Mrs. Baker gave a derisive sniff. "They didn't show it if they did. That mother of hers . . . Well, I always thought Louisa was a little snooty, but she was nothing compared to her mother."

"She was probably just grieving for her daughter. People

can't be held accountable for their behavior under those circumstances."

Mrs. Baker looked like she was trying to think of a reply to that when something else caught her attention. "That motorcar," she said, indicating Sarah's vehicle parked at the curb. "Are you the one brought Nellie home that day?"

"Yes, as a matter of fact. She told me some disturbing things about Louisa, and I . . . Well, before I shared them with her family, I wanted to check with someone who would know what really went on here."

"What business is it of yours?" Mrs. Baker asked, suspicious now.

"Louisa's father hired our firm of private investigators to look into Louisa's death, so that makes it our business, too."

"Private investigators," Mrs. Baker echoed suspiciously. She looked Sarah up and down, probably wondering how Sarah could afford such an expensive outfit. "That girl who was here . . . What was her name?"

"Maeve Smith," Sarah guessed.

"Yes, that's her. She said she was a private investigator, too, but I never believed it."

"It's true. She works for our firm."

"She already talked to everybody who lives here, and besides, they're all at work now."

"She didn't speak with you, and you're here now. I was wondering if you would mind answering a few questions."

"I don't know anything about how that girl died," she said with a worried frown.

"I'm sure you don't, since she wasn't killed here, but I'd like to know more about Louisa as a person."

"I'm sure my girls told your girl everything about her already," Mrs. Baker hedged.

Sarah noticed Mrs. Baker's hand trembled a bit when she raised it to her forehead.

"But they are, as you say, just girls. I'm sure a woman such as yourself would have a much more mature understanding of Louisa's character. She was no longer a girl herself, after all. You must have observed things about her that your lodgers would have missed."

Sarah had long ago observed that most people responded to flattery, and Mrs. Baker was no exception.

"Well, if you don't think you'd be wasting your time, I can give you a few minutes, I suppose." Mrs. Baker stood back, allowing Sarah to enter the house. She followed Mrs. Baker into the parlor.

The room was a typical Victorian parlor with doilies on the tables and antimacassars on the furniture to protect it from gentlemen's hairdressing oils, even though gentlemen weren't very welcome here. The horsehair furniture showed wear, but the room was clean and rather homey.

Sarah took a seat on the sofa. Mrs. Baker took what must be her regular chair since it had a side table covered with what must be her personal items. "Now, what is it you want to know about Louisa?"

"First of all, I wanted to get your opinion on Louisa's love life," Sarah began with an apologetic smile. "I know you don't permit gentlemen in the house, but—"

"Louisa didn't want any gentlemen in the house. When one of them did come, she . . . Well, I suppose the girls told your girl—"

"Maeve."

"Yes, they must've told Maeve how Louisa pitched a fit when some fellow came calling for her. He was such a timid thing, I almost felt sorry for him when she told him to stop bothering her and that she didn't care for him and never would."

"She actually said that?" Sarah didn't have to pretend to be surprised.

"You can ask the girls. We all heard it. Sent him off with his tail between his legs."

Sarah pretended to consider this information. "Why then do you suppose she told Nellie they were secretly engaged?"

Mrs. Baker frowned and straightened in her chair. "I guess Nellie told you that."

"She told Maeve, yes."

Mrs. Baker shook her head. "You can't believe a word Nellie says. She's always making up stories. Mostly she talks about herself. Has all kinds of tales about how her family was rich but they lost all their money because somebody stole it from them and now she's the last one left and has to earn her own way. I never can figure out if she wants the girls to feel sorry for her or envy her."

"Is it possible that Louisa could have snuck out to meet a lover?" Sarah tried.

"Impossible. I keep a close eye on my girls," Mrs. Baker insisted.

"But isn't Louisa's room in the basement?"

"It was, yes," Mrs. Baker admitted reluctantly.

"And isn't there a back door down there?"

Mrs. Baker didn't like this at all. "In the kitchen, yes, but I keep it locked all the time."

"With a key?"

"No. It has a bolt."

Which meant someone could sneak out and back in again without needing a key or having to ask someone to let them back in. Mrs. Baker, with the bad bunions Maeve had told them about, would hardly run downstairs just to check the bolt.

"Nellie indicated at the funeral that she and Louisa were close friends," Sarah tried.

Mrs. Baker snorted. "Hardly. Nellie pestered her all the time, trying to do things for her or pretending to be interested in her writing, but Nellie can hardly read. Oh, she flips through magazines, but only to look at the pictures. Said so herself."

Hardly the kind of person Louisa was likely to befriend, and certainly not to confide in. That also meant Nellie probably hadn't read any of Louisa's writings either.

"Louisa's mother didn't seem to believe that Louisa had given Nellie that lovely scarf she was wearing at the funeral," Sarah said.

"Of course she never gave it to her," Mrs. Baker said. "I'd guess Nellie snuck down to Louisa's room the minute she heard Louisa was dead and snatched it. Wouldn't be the first time."

The other girls had mentioned they thought Nellie might be a thief. "What do you mean?"

"I mean Louisa had missed some things. Nothing big. A piece of jewelry. A handkerchief. Maybe something else. I don't remember. She wanted me to get the police in. Can you imagine how they'd laugh? Getting the police for a lost handkerchief?"

"Did she think Nellie had taken her things?"

"Everybody did, but I searched her room and didn't find anything. Even that didn't satisfy Little Miss Louisa, though. She told Nellie if anything else went missing, she'd get the police on her, even after I already told Louisa that would be foolish. I guess when Nellie heard Louisa was dead, she saw her chance. Heaven only knows what else she took."

"Did Nellie seem upset when Louisa threatened her with the police?" Something like that might have made Nellie angry enough to kill Louisa.

"She was mad. Said a few choice things to Louisa, who just laughed at her. Nothing much fazed Louisa."

"That must have made Nellie even angrier," Sarah guessed.

"Oh yes, it did. Never saw anybody so mad."

"When was this?"

Mrs. Baker frowned as she tried to remember. "Time runs together when you get older, but it must've been about a week before Louisa died, give or take."

So, Nellie did have a motive. But after all that, would Louisa have telephoned to ask Nellie—or anyone in this house, for that matter—to help her with her box? Because how else would Nellie have known Louisa was at the magazine office alone?

"Are you on the telephone?" Sarah asked, startling Mrs. Baker with the change of subject.

"Goodness, no. They charge six dollars a month for one of those contraptions. My girls can send a letter like everybody else."

So, Louisa couldn't have telephoned anyone here for help the night she died, even if she had wanted to.

But if Nellie had wanted revenge, she might have figured out another way.

GINO DIDN'T BOTHER TO STOP BY THE OFFICE THAT morning. He slept in after his late night and then headed down to Billy Funhouser's neighborhood. He needed to find out the real story about the old man named Trapper and whether or not he could have been in the lobby and killed Louisa.

This time he encountered none of the men who had directed him to the saloon where Billy had been drinking the first time Gino had come down looking for him. Those men would all be at work. Their wives were on the stoop today, gossiping as they did mending while they watched a gaggle of children who were too young for school and were playing in the street.

"Good morning, ladies," he began, giving them the smile that always charmed his mother. "How are you this lovely day?"

"Don't bother trying to flirt with us," the oldest woman said. Her hair was snow-white and she apparently had no teeth. "We know you're a copper. Who are you looking for?"

"I'm not a cop," Gino said, still smiling. "I'm a private investigator."

"Same thing," another of the women said bitterly.

"Not at all," Gino said. "I can't arrest anyone."

"Then why're you here?" the old woman asked, still unimpressed.

"I'm looking for Billy Funhouser."

The women made little humming noises in their throats as they all turned to the woman sitting on the bottom step and holding a gurgling infant.

The woman muttered something that might have been a curse. "He's upstairs, still in bed," she said. She was angry, but Gino didn't think it was at him. If Billy was still in bed, that probably meant he had lost his day job, too. No wonder his wife was mad.

"I hope he isn't sick," Gino said as if he meant it.

The woman laughed mirthlessly. "He's lucky I haven't murdered him, but he's not sick. What do you want with him if you're not going to arrest him?"

Plainly, the idea of having her husband arrested was not a particularly disturbing one. "I just need to ask him a few questions about things the police missed."

"Is this about that girl that got herself killed in the building Billy was supposed to be guarding?" the old woman asked.

"Yes, it is."

"He didn't do it," Mrs. Funhouser said, although she sounded more resigned than passionate in her defense of her husband.

"I know," Gino lied. They hadn't actually considered Billy to be a suspect, but maybe they should have. In any case, he wasn't going to mention that to Billy's wife. "I just need to clarify some things about that evening."

She shook her head in disgust. "Go wake him up, then. It'll serve him right." She gave him the apartment number.

The tenement stairway was dark, since it had no windows and it was too dangerous to run the gaslights that lined it because even a small flame could turn the building into an inferno. The smell of cooking cabbage and unwashed bodies sat like a cloud in the unventilated space. He did manage to locate the correct apartment, though, and he pounded on the door, calling Billy's name.

After a minute, Gino paused to listen, and he heard some groaning coming from inside. He pounded again.

"All right, I'm coming," a weary voice called.

Finally, the door opened, and a bleary-eyed Billy scowled out. He hadn't shaved in a few days, and his hair was a rat's nest. He wore a stained undershirt and had pulled on a pair of wrinkled pants. The suspenders hung down around his hips. "What on earth do you want? I paid the rent already."

"Remember me? I'm Gino Donatelli, the private investigator."

Billy muttered a curse. "You're not going to pin that girl's murder on me."

He tried to slam the door, but Gino had already put up his hand to stop him. "I just need to ask you a few questions about the homeless man you told me about."

Gino pushed on the door until Billy gave in, although he still blocked it so Gino couldn't come inside.

"I already told you what I know."

"You said the old man—Trapper, isn't it?—often tried to sneak in to sleep in the lobby, but you ran him off."

"That's right," Billy said, rubbing a hand over his messy hair. "Just like I told you."

"But the other guards told me you let him sleep in the lobby most nights."

"They're lying. I'd lose my job if I did that."

"You already lost your job," Gino pointed out. "It can't hurt now if you tell the truth."

Billy sighed and scratched his chest. "I don't guess it will. Yeah, I'd let him in whenever he came around. He said . . ."

"What did he say?" Gino asked when Billy hesitated.

"He said a gang of boys, street rats, would rob him if they found him sleeping out."

"Rob him of what?"

"He'd beg and you'd be surprised how much he could get in a day. Anyway, the boys would kick him a few times and take whatever money he had, so he liked to sleep in the lobby where he'd be safe."

"Did you happen to see him the night the woman was killed?"

"I told you, I didn't see anybody that night."

Billy was obviously not a good witness. "Where does he usually sleep when he's outdoors?"

"How do I know?"

"Maybe you've seen him," Gino pressed.

"I don't go prowling the neighborhood at night. I have to guard the building."

When you aren't sleeping in a closet, Gino thought, but he said, "Does he usually stay nearby, though?"

"He keeps to the neighborhood, I think. Some people feel sorry for him and leave food out. But he wasn't there that night, I tell you, or at least I never saw him."

"Then why did you tell Trapper the police think he's the killer?"

"I never!" Billy said, visibly shocked.

"Then why is Trapper hiding and telling people you did?"

Billy thought this over and looked a little sheepish. "I did tell him they'd probably try to pin it on him. That's what the cops do. They find some poor fellow who can't defend himself and lock him up. I knew Trapper didn't do it, so I warned him to make himself scarce."

"But still, you didn't lock the doors that night. Anybody could've gotten in."

"It's not my fault. I left it open for Trapper. How was I to know that woman would be there?"

"If you had been awake, you would've seen her," Gino pointed out, earning another scowl.

"I couldn't know somebody was going to get killed that night."

Gino returned his scowl and said, "The reason the building owner hires guards is to make sure that never happens."

Billy moaned and clamped both hands on the sides of his head as if to keep it from exploding. "Leave me alone, can't you? I didn't have anything to do with that woman and I don't know who did."

Gino just shook his head and let go of any suspicion at all that Billy might have been involved in Louisa's death. He was just too guileless to lie well. As for Trapper, he was still on the list.

. . .

Maeve had to go to lunch alone on Tuesday because Miss Yoder was too busy with the magazine layout to even take lunch. Maeve couldn't help noticing—mainly because she'd been keeping a close watch on him all morning—that Clyde Hoffman got up as soon as she started getting ready to go out. Pretending not to care, she put on her hat and gloves and told Miss Yoder she was leaving, then walked out the door.

Knowing Hoffman was probably following her, she didn't want to be alone in the stairwell with him, but people from other offices were also leaving for lunch at one of the numerous cafés and restaurants in the area, so she took the stairs along with them.

Once she was out on the street, she paused a moment to look around, as if trying to decide where to go. That gave Hoffman a chance to catch up to her.

"Miss Smith, well met. Perhaps you would join me for lunch."

She looked up, feigning surprise. "Thank you, Mr. Hoffman. I don't mind if I do."

Not the enthusiastic response he had probably been hoping for, but he managed a smile and indicated they should go to the left. "This is my favorite spot," he informed her when they reached a small Chinese restaurant on the corner.

The place was much more lively than the tearoom where she had dined yesterday with Miss Yoder, but that was fine. It also didn't invite intimate conversations. They found seats and ordered the one menu item, chop suey. If this was

Hoffman's favorite place, he certainly had a limited imagination.

"It must be difficult for you, coming into the office every day and seeing someone else at Louisa's desk," Maeve said in an attempt to introduce the topic she most wanted to discuss.

"Oh, it is," he agreed. "But one cannot mourn forever. Life goes on, doesn't it?"

"Hopefully," Maeve said with a smile, thinking that it had been only a week since Louisa died, which was not exactly forever. "How long had you been engaged?"

He frowned at that and looked away. "I, uh, I probably shouldn't have told you that."

"Why not? You don't have to keep it a secret anymore, do you?"

"It's not that. It's, well, we weren't really engaged. Not formally, I mean."

Maeve didn't have to pretend to be surprised by this. "But you did have an understanding."

"Louisa was a very independent woman, and as much as I might want . . . Well, she wasn't ready to settle down just yet."

"I can understand that," Maeve said. "There's a young man who is sweet on me, but I think I'm too young to get married. I want to enjoy my freedom for a while longer. I guess Louisa was too young, too."

"Oh no, it wasn't that. She wasn't young at all. She must have been nearly thirty."

Their conversation paused for a moment when the waiter plunked down bowls of chop suey in front of them. Hoffman dug right in.

"If she was almost thirty, wasn't Louisa afraid of becoming an old maid?" Maeve asked in horror, because that was supposed to be the worst fate a female could imagine.

"She wasn't conventional," Hoffman said a little apologetically. "She admired Ida Tarbell."

"Who's that?" Maeve asked, although she knew who Miss Tarbell was and admired the woman herself.

"A lady reporter for one of our rival magazines. Louisa imagined she could do the same sort of thing, but Mr. Tibbot made it perfectly clear to her that she could never accomplish such a feat. I had hoped . . ."

He stared off into space for a long moment.

"What did you hope, Mr. Hoffman?" she prodded.

"I had hoped that learning the truth would convince her she should give up her pipe dreams and accept my proposal." Now he sounded bitter and perhaps a bit angry.

Angry enough to commit murder? Maeve wondered as she ate her chop suey. It was surprisingly good.

"Surely she didn't turn you down again after she walked out of the office that day," Maeve said in false amazement.

"She never had the opportunity. I went to her rooming house when I finished work, and I waited outside all evening, but she never came out."

"Didn't you think to knock on the door and ask for her?" Maeve asked, which was a completely reasonable thing to do if he hadn't been thrown out the first time.

"She had forbidden me to call on her at the house," he said. "She didn't want to be the object of gossip, you see. Louisa was very particular about her reputation."

Which was a good explanation for her reaction to his visit.

"You can't blame her for that, which makes me wonder why she was out all alone the night she . . . she died. Miss Yoder said she had come back to the office late in the evening."

"Yes, she wanted to collect her things, but she would have been too proud to come back with all of us there to see her and feel sorry for her."

"If you didn't see her that night, how do you know that's why she came back?" Maeve asked as the hairs on the back of her neck prickled. Surely, knowing this proved he'd seen her that night.

"We saw the box with her belongings, all packed up and sitting on her desk, when the police finally allowed us into the office the next morning. She must have left it there and gone downstairs to flag a cab when she met her . . ." His voice broke and he pressed his fist to his lips as if to hold back the awful word *killer*.

"I'm sorry. It must be very painful for you to discuss this, even if you and Miss Rodgers weren't really engaged yet."

"Yes, it is, but it was kind of you to listen." He pulled out a handkerchief and wiped his eyes.

Maeve could almost feel sorry for him if she didn't know Louisa had been afraid of him.

"If Louisa knew how you felt about her, I wonder why she didn't telephone you to help her with her box instead of trying to find a cab herself that late at night," Maeve tried.

Hoffman actually looked surprised, but his expression quickly transformed. Now he looked stricken. "I hadn't thought of that. Perhaps she did try to telephone me, but I was never to know, because I was outside her rooming house, looking for her."

"Then you didn't go to the magazine to help her?"

"Of course not. I didn't even know she was there. How will I ever live with knowing I might have saved her?"

Maeve sighed in defeat. This wasn't exactly the conclusion she had envisioned for this conversation, but at least Clyde Hoffman now looked a little less likely as a suspect.

That is, if he was telling the truth about standing outside Louisa's rooming house all evening.

"I should apologize to you, Miss Smith," Hoffman said when he'd mopped his tears and started in on his chop suey again. "I didn't mean to bother you with my troubles and regrets."

"That's all right, Mr. Hoffman. I'm just sorry I couldn't offer much comfort."

"Your mere presence is a comfort, Miss Smith. So much in fact that I was wondering if you would allow me to escort you to the theater this Friday night. Just as friends, of course. It's far too soon after dear Louisa's death to consider anything more serious, and I wouldn't want you to think me unfeeling."

Maeve didn't bother to hide her surprise. She let her mouth hang open for a full two seconds, letting him know he had been unbelievably gauche. "I . . . I'm very flattered, Mr. Hoffman, but I . . ."

She couldn't possibly accept his invitation. He still might be Louisa's killer, after all. But on the other hand, did she dare refuse him? Louisa had and now she was dead.

XII

Frank had been looking through Louisa's notes about Watson's Blood Purifier again, wondering if it was really possible Watson was responsible for her death, when he heard the outer door of the office open. He was missing his receptionist. He needed to solve this case soon so he could get Maeve back. He got up and walked out to the front office to find Oscar Rodgers.

"Mr. Rodgers, what a surprise," Frank couldn't help saying since they had parted on such bad terms the last time.

"I'm sure it is," Oscar replied with an uncertain smile.

"I think you know your mother informed me that our services would no longer be needed." Which was so much nicer than saying she had fired them.

"Yes, I do know, but I am here to hire you myself, if that's possible."

Nothing Oscar Rodgers could have said would have surprised him more. He wasn't sure he trusted Oscar, but having his support would certainly make the investigation easier. "Then we should step into my office to discuss it."

Frank directed Oscar into his office and indicated he should take one of the client chairs. Oscar was dressed like a successful young businessman today in a well-made suit and a pristine shirt. His hair was pomaded into a dignified style, and he wore a black armband to indicate he was in mourning.

"I was very sorry to hear about your father's death. He was a good man."

Oscar winced a bit at that, and Frank remembered Mr. Rodgers hadn't been very good to his son. But apparently Oscar had decided not to dwell on that. "I knew he was distraught over Louisa's death, but I never imagined for a moment that he would break under the weight of it."

"I guess we never know how other people are suffering," Frank said, wishing Sarah were here. She always knew what to say in situations like this.

"No, but I do know how I am suffering, and I must confess, I have no wish to be a martyr in all of this."

"How would you be a martyr?" Frank asked, genuinely confused.

Oscar drew a breath and sat back in his chair as if settling in for a serious discussion. "Let me begin by reminding you that when my sister was murdered, my father hired you to find her killer. Then, less than a week later, he took his own life."

Frank nodded. He knew all of that, of course, and it still didn't make much sense to him.

"Now my mother's refusal to admit that Father took his own life has caused even more gossip than if she had announced it to the world."

"How could that be?"

"Because something like suicide cannot be kept a secret. Servants talk. Doctors talk. People guess. Then they begin to wonder why a man like my father would do such a thing. He must have been bearing a terrible weight. He must have known who killed my sister and why. Was it someone in our family? Her doting father was unlikely to have done it, but her jealous brother had always hated her. Everyone knew it, just as everyone knew our father despised me. So maybe I killed Louisa out of jealousy and maybe my father didn't take his own life at all. Maybe I killed him, too, because he had begun to suspect me."

"Mr. Rodgers, I think you may have let your imagination run away with you. Nobody could possibly—"

"But they *could* possibly, and more than possibly. A friend called on me a mere hour ago to tell me that was all the talk at my club last night. We only found my father's body yesterday morning. By tomorrow I won't be able to go anywhere in the city without being stared at and suspected of murdering half my family. I want you to find my sister's real killer, Mr. Malloy, because if you don't, I will never be able to hold my head up in this city again."

Frank gave Oscar a few moments to compose himself. His cheeks had flushed, and his breath was coming fast.

Plainly, he was sincere, and guilty people did not beg you to investigate them. But Frank still had a few concerns.

"I'm perfectly willing to continue looking for your sister's killer, Mr. Rodgers, but let me ask you some questions first."

Oscar drew a calming breath and sank back in his chair again. "All right."

"If you didn't kill your sister, why did your mother insist you were at home with her that night?"

"Oh, that," he said with a huff of relief. "You guessed, I assume, that I wasn't home at all. I think she was probably trying to protect me. She knew I'd been out all evening, and she didn't know where I'd been or if anyone could vouch for me, so she said I was with her so you wouldn't think I had killed Louisa."

"Is there someone who *could* vouch for you?" Frank asked.

"A number of people. I was at my club that night, and I lost a great deal of money gambling with some friends. I can give you their names if you think it's necessary."

"It will be necessary if I find the killer. We'll need to take our evidence to the police eventually. They often need to prove other people couldn't have done it, and as you say, there are reasons to suspect you."

"But I didn't do it, and I want to find out who did in order to clear my name, no matter what my mother says, no matter how long it takes, or how much it costs. I have my father's money now, and I intend to put it to good use."

"I must confess, Mr. Rodgers, we never actually stopped investigating."

"You didn't?" Oscar asked, obviously confused. "But my mother told you to stop."

"I know what she said, but I still wanted to honor your father's memory and avenge Louisa's death by finding her killer."

"That's very noble of you, Mr. Malloy," Oscar said uncertainly.

"Not noble at all. I just don't like to leave a job unfinished."

WHAT DID YOU SAY TO HIM?" SARAH ASKED MAEVE WHEN the younger woman had finished telling her about Clyde Hoffman's invitation. Maeve had just gotten home from work at the magazine. They were sitting in the parlor, waiting for Malloy and probably Gino to arrive, and taking advantage of a few minutes of privacy while the children were upstairs playing.

"I had a moment of terror when I debated whether to accept his invitation and possibly put myself alone in his presence or refuse and invite his wrath. It was a hard decision, so I finally admitted that I hesitated to see a man I worked with outside the office, but I would consider his offer because he was such a nice man."

"That was a good compromise, and hopefully you won't be at the magazine much longer. Did Mr. Hoffman convince you he wasn't guilty of Louisa's murder?"

"If he is, he is a good actor, although I'm also fairly sure he's a very strange man, so we can't rule anything out. He was actually weeping over losing Louisa one minute and inviting me to the theater in the next."

"That is more than strange. It's rather heartless," Sarah said. "Louisa was right to discourage his advances."

They could hear the front door opening, and Sarah called out to let Malloy know where they were. When he came into the parlor, he dropped a kiss on Sarah's cheek and sank wearily into a chair.

"Maeve had an interesting day today, and so did I," Sarah reported.

"You did?" Maeve asked, not having thought to even ask. "Where did you go?"

"To the rooming house. I spoke with Mrs. Baker, since you never had that opportunity."

"I'm willing to bet I had the most interesting day of all of us," Malloy reported.

"Did you?" Sarah asked. "Do tell."

"Oscar Rodgers rehired us to find Louisa's killer."

Before Sarah and Maeve could recover from their surprise, the sound of Catherine's shouting and Brian's screams—because he was deaf, he had no sense of how loud his voice could get—sent Maeve and Sarah on their way to settle the fight.

"We'll talk after supper," Malloy called after them.

Gino arrived later as Maeve and Sarah were putting the children to bed. When they had finished, all the adults gathered in the parlor to share their day's experiences, with Mother Malloy knitting her latest project.

Frank began by explaining why Oscar Rodgers had rehired them.

"You can't blame the man for not wanting that cloud of suspicion hanging over him," Gino said.

"It certainly didn't take long for the rumors to start," Maeve observed. "Mr. Rodgers only died yesterday."

"The rumors probably started a week ago, when Louisa died," Sarah said. "Then Mr. Rodgers's death would have given them new life. You have to admit, it makes a certain amount of sense that Oscar would have killed his father if he really had killed his sister."

"But now we know he didn't," Frank said. "Because if he did, he's the stupidest criminal I've ever run across."

"I don't think Clyde Hoffman did it either," Maeve said, earning everyone's attention. She told them about her lunch with Hoffman and her conclusions.

"He could be lying about watching the rooming house all evening," Gino said. "What kind of a man does something like that?"

"A lovesick one," Sarah said.

"Or a very strange one," Mother Malloy offered from her corner.

No one disagreed.

"At least we can be pretty sure that Louisa wouldn't have telephoned Hoffman for help that night even if he was at home," Frank said. "If everything we've learned about their relationship is true, she wouldn't have dreamed of asking him for anything."

"And I found out the rooming house isn't on the telephone, so Louisa didn't call there either," Sarah said. "That eliminates everyone she might have contacted, since we know her father wasn't home."

"Which means her killer either followed her there or encountered her by accident," Frank said.

"Or came with her," Mother Malloy said.

They all turned to look at her, but as usual, she didn't even glance up from her knitting.

Frank shifted uncomfortably in his chair, while Maeve voiced what he didn't want to admit.

"We never even thought of that," she said.

"Who would she have brought with her, though?" Sarah asked.

"Would she have taken advantage of Nellie's devotion and asked her?" Maeve asked.

Sarah shook her head. "Mrs. Baker told me today that Louisa had threatened to get the police to investigate the things that had gone missing from her room. She was sure Nellie was responsible and wanted to have her arrested."

"Then the scarf wasn't the only thing she stole?" Gino asked.

"According to Mrs. Baker, Nellie could only have taken the scarf after Louisa died, but some other small things were missing from Louisa's room before that."

"Why didn't they search Nellie's room if they thought she'd taken them?" Maeve asked.

"Mrs. Baker said she did and didn't find anything. Nellie may have been innocent, but Louisa didn't think she was, which makes it unlikely she would have asked Nellie for help," Sarah said.

"But we know how arrogant Louisa could be," Maeve said. "Is it possible she asked Nellie anyway? Maybe she promised not to tell the police if Nellie helped her, but Nellie might've seen it as an opportunity to get Louisa alone and take some revenge."

"I don't know if anybody would ask someone for a favor after threatening to call the police on them no matter how arrogant they were," Gino said.

"Besides, if Nellie and Louisa had left the house together, Hoffman would have seen them, assuming he really was watching," Frank reminded them.

"Not necessarily," Sarah said. "Another thing Mrs. Baker admitted to me is that the basement door—the one in the kitchen to which Louisa would have had easy access without anyone upstairs seeing or knowing—is locked with a bolt on the inside."

Maeve instantly sat up straighter, remembering what the girls at the rooming house had said about Louisa having access to that door. "She could have let herself out and the door would remain unlocked until she got back, and no one would have to know she was ever gone."

"Exactly," said Sarah with approval. "So, Louisa could have left the house without alerting anyone inside and she could have slipped away without Mr. Hoffman seeing her, since he would have been watching the front door."

"Which means Louisa and Nellie could *both* have slipped out without being seen," Frank said.

"I thought we decided Louisa would never have asked Nellie to help her," Gino said with a frown.

"But they didn't have to be together," Maeve said. "We know Louisa left the house at some point late in the evening to go back to the office, and we've decided she didn't tele-phone anyone to come and help her and that she probably didn't ask Nellie for help, so that means—"

"That she encountered her killer by accident," Gino said

confidently. "It was the homeless man, Trapper. Billy Fun-houser admitted to me today that he let Trapper sleep in the lobby a lot more often than he admitted the first time."

"*Or*," Maeve said, giving him a sharp look for having interrupted her, "someone followed her to the office and killed her."

"Someone like Nellie, you mean," Sarah said. "She could have seen Louisa leave and gone out after her. We know the other girls stay out late, and Mrs. Baker would have been resting from taking her *medicine*, so no one would have noticed either of them was gone."

"*Or* Clyde Hoffman might have seen her leave and followed her himself," Maeve suggested.

"*Or*," Frank said, "she could have been followed by someone hired by Archie Watson to protect his patent medicine empire."

THE NEXT MORNING, GINO COULDN'T HELP NOTICING THE number of motorcars seemed to increase daily in the city. You could hardly go out without seeing at least a few wending their way between horse-drawn vehicles in the crowded streets. Mr. Malloy had given him the gasoline-powered motor to use for his trip out to Brooklyn, although the train might have been faster. Mr. Malloy wanted him to arrive in style, though, if anyone happened to notice.

No one else had been as certain as he had last night that Trapper must be the killer, even though it made perfect sense. They still thought it was possible Nellie or Hoffman or someone else followed Louisa that night. But Trapper was used to sleeping in the lobby. Billy was too drunk to care and hadn't locked the doors. Louisa would have emptied the contents of her desk into the box, realized she couldn't carry it by herself, and either given up and decided to go home without it or gone in search of Billy or someone who could help her. Then she encountered Trapper in the lobby and did something to alarm him and he had accidentally killed her.

But Mr. Malloy was still wondering if Archie Watson could have hired someone to stop Louisa's article once and for all. It was possible, of course, but it still seemed a bit far-fetched to Gino. People with the kind of money Watson had usually used it in other ways than hiring killers.

In any case, Mr. Malloy had told him to return to Watson's factory and see what he could learn, so that was how he was planning to spend his day.

When he arrived at the enormous building where they produced Watson's Blood Purifier, Gino found the same officious woman on duty at the reception desk.

She obviously remembered him. "Do you have an appointment?" She also obviously knew he didn't.

Gino laid his card on her desk. "I would like to see Karl Spangler, please. You can tell him it's about the article for *New Century* magazine."

"Mr. Spangler?" Now she was confused because he had asked to speak to Mr. Watson's secretary and not the man himself.

"That's right. There are some details to clarify."

Did she look alarmed? She certainly didn't look quite so officious anymore. "Just a moment." She turned to the switchboard behind her and made a call. She spoke too softly for Gino to catch what she was saying, but in a few moments, she turned back and said, "Mr. Spangler will be right down."

She was right. Spangler had obviously wasted no time wondering what Gino wanted.

"Mr. Donatelli," he said with false cheer. "How nice to see you again."

Which was so much more polite than immediately demanding to know what on earth he was doing here. "Thank you for seeing me, Mr. Spangler. I needed some more information, and I didn't want to bother Mr. Watson. I know how busy he must be."

Spangler's phony smile never wavered. "Come with me. We can meet in one of the conference rooms."

As Gino had suspected, the conference room was miles from Mr. Watson's office, or at least a very long way. The factory was gigantic. It was also probably far from anyone else who might take an interest in Gino's visit.

Spangler did not offer Gino any refreshment, making Gino suspect he wanted the visit to be short, too.

"How can I help you, Mr. Donatelli?" he asked when they were seated at a tiny table in an equally tiny room. The room, which had no windows, must be reserved for very small conferences.

"As I told your receptionist, I had a few more questions about Miss Louisa Rodgers's visits to the factory and about the company itself."

"Certainly. I'll answer them if I can, but really, I'm sure

Mr. Watson told you everything there is to tell." Spangler was determined to keep this civil.

"We know a little more about Miss Rodgers now than we did the last time I was here. You see, we have determined that she had returned to her office late the evening she died. She was collecting some notes on the article she was writing." So far this was all true, as far as it went. "She was murdered in the building's street-level lobby as she was leaving."

"It's very distressing to think a young woman cannot go about the city alone without being in danger."

"Yes, it is. We have eliminated the possibility that she was killed by someone who knew her." Gino's first lie, although it wasn't very far from the truth. "This made us ask if someone who was not close to her might have wanted her dead."

Gino waited patiently while Mr. Spangler considered this information and realized how it might apply to Watson's.

"Mr. Donatelli, you can't think . . . I mean, that's outrageous! Mr. Watson would never . . . He simply isn't a violent person, not at all. He couldn't possibly—"

"We understand that men like Mr. Watson don't do foolish things like strangling a young woman to death just because she threatens to ruin the company to which he has dedicated his life."

Spangler had gone chalk white at the implication. "I . . . I'm glad you do understand that."

"However, we also know that men like Mr. Watson, who have unlimited resources—"

"Not unlimited!"

Gino ignored the interruption. "*Unlimited* resources, will sometimes use those resources to hire people to do unpleasant tasks for them, especially when the matter is as important as saving his business from disaster."

"Do you actually think Mr. Watson keeps hired assassins on his payroll?" Spangler asked. His outrage was as real as his pleasant greeting had been fake. "I assure you, Mr. Donatelli, no one in this company would ever dream of doing harm to Miss Rodgers or anyone else. She wasn't the first person to criticize Watson's and she won't be the last. Others have tried, and you are correct to assume that Mr. Watson found every instance disagreeable, but why on earth would he or anyone else resort to murder? If such a thing was ever traced back to him, it really would ruin him and his company more thoroughly and efficiently than anything Miss Rodgers could possibly write. Besides," he added, his stricken expression transforming into triumph, "Mr. Watson had already ensured that Miss Rodgers's article would never see the light of day."

"How did he do that?" Gino asked, although he had just realized he might already know.

"By telephoning the man who owns that magazine where she worked."

"Tibbot," Gino guessed. Louisa had made a terrible mistake when she told Watson what she planned to do with the information he had given her.

"Yes, that's his name. Mr. Watson merely had to point out that if the magazine published an article critical of any kind of patent medicine, he would not only cancel all his advertising in that magazine, but he would also make sure every other manufacturer did the same."

It was a different kind of death that Watson had threatened: If you kill my business, I will kill yours. Not the least illegal and probably more effective.

And it didn't involve actually murdering Louisa Rodgers.

Gino had one more point to make. "Mr. Watson still seemed very upset about Miss Rodgers's article when Mr. Malloy and I were here last."

"Of course he was upset. Miss Rodgers had misrepresented herself and outright lied, while Mr. Watson had shown her every courtesy and allowed her to learn all the secrets of how the company operates. He felt betrayed and—Well, he never admitted it, but I think he felt he had been made a fool of by a deceitful woman. He had a right to be angry."

"Angry enough to kill her in revenge?" Gino asked.

Spangler glared at him. "Angry enough to ruin her career so she would never be able to hurt another businessman. I believe I can safely promise you that he was quite satisfied with that outcome. Really, Mr. Donatelli, you are wasting your time looking for Miss Rodgers's killer here at Watson's. Even if Miss Rodgers had succeeded in publishing a critical article, it would only have brought attention to our product. Some people would have sworn never to use it again, but our regular customers would have laughed at any claims she made. Others would have made a point of trying our product to see if it worked as advertised. It would not have hurt us at all in the long run."

Gino had a feeling Spangler was correct. Publicity was a mysterious force that often worked just the opposite of how it was intended. Gino sighed in defeat. "Thank you for your time, Mr. Spangler, and give Mr. Watson my regards."

"If you don't mind, I won't mention this visit to him at all. He has already been bothered enough by Miss Rodgers."

Frank had left Sarah to her duties of seeing the children and his mother safely delivered at school while he took the El up to the magazine offices. Someone a little more threatening than Maeve needed to question Clyde Hoffman.

The *New Century* office was alive with activity. The illustrators were intently working on their drawings. Miss Yoder bustled about her table, moving pages from one place to another and then back again. Maeve was busily typing something, but when he stepped farther into the room, she looked up.

"May I help you, sir?" she asked, jumping up and hurrying over to meet him.

He handed her his card. "I'm a private investigator. I'm investigating the murder of Miss Louisa Rodgers, and I'd like to speak privately with Mr. Clyde Hoffman."

The room had gone still the instant everyone had heard Frank's announcement. They would remember him from last week, and now they would be wondering why he wanted to speak with Clyde in particular.

Maeve, bless her, played her part well. She glanced uncertainly at his card. "I'll have to ask Mr. Tibbot if that's all right," she said, and turned to do just that, but Clyde Hoffman had risen to his feet.

"Don't bother Mr. Tibbot, Miss Smith. I will see him." Hoffman looked oddly proud, as if he were a student who had been singled out for some honor, and he might have thought he had been. He had after all ordered Frank to report his progress on finding Louisa's killer. He probably thought this was why Frank was here.

"Is there a place we can speak privately?" Frank asked.

"We can step out into the hallway," Hoffman said haughtily. He might have been the owner of the entire building, granting Frank an audience.

Frank didn't care. He was enjoying himself. He followed Hoffman out into the hallway, pretending not to be amused.

"What have you learned about Louisa's death?" Hoffman asked the moment they were far enough from the office door to not be overheard. "Have you found her killer? It was that dirty old man, wasn't it? The vagrant who sleeps in the lobby."

"We haven't identified the killer yet, Mr. Hoffman, but I do have a few questions for you."

"For me?" Hoffman didn't like that.

"Yes, you told me you had gone to Louisa's rooming house after you finished work the day Louisa died."

"Yes, I wanted to check on her and make sure she was all right. She was very upset when she left here."

"Yet no one at the rooming house remembers you coming there or asking about her."

Hoffman's pompous air deflated a bit. "I didn't exactly knock on the door and ask for her."

"No, you didn't, because you had tried that once before and Louisa had told you never to come there again," Frank reminded him.

"Only because she wanted to keep our engagement a secret," Hoffman quickly explained. "I completely understood her reasoning and agreed with it. After that, we only met in secret."

"So much in secret that even Louisa didn't know about it," Frank said.

Hoffman frowned in confusion. "What?"

"Louisa didn't know you were meeting, just as she didn't know you were engaged. She didn't know you had a relationship at all. In fact, she considered your attentions annoying and maybe even a bit frightening."

"No, that's not true. We were in love . . ." He gestured helplessly.

"Mr. Hoffman, you have admitted that you weren't engaged to Louisa, and we know she told several people she didn't like you. You didn't knock on the door at Louisa's rooming house that night because everyone there knew you weren't welcome. Do you know what I think?"

"No," Hoffman said weakly.

"I think you did go to her house that night and you stood outside like you did many other nights, just watching, and you saw her leave and you followed her back to the office. Then you waited in the lobby for her to come out again and you took your revenge by strangling—"

"*No!*" he cried. "No, I never touched her, I swear! I didn't follow her that night. I didn't even see her, and I couldn't have killed her because I was standing across the street from her house that evening, all evening. I was hoping she would come out, but she never did."

"That seems like a very strange thing to do, Mr. Hoffman, standing outside a woman's house for hours. I don't suppose anybody saw you and can vouch for the fact that you were standing there from around five or six o'clock until . . . When *did* you finally give up and go home?"

"It was after ten o'clock, I know. And someone did see me. Someone in the house."

This was news and probably another lie. "Who?"

"I don't know, but it was a woman."

A good guess since all the residents were female. "But you don't know who it was?"

"It must have been the landlady. I'm sure she knew who I was. She kept checking all evening to see if I was still there."

"How did you know it wasn't Louisa?" Frank asked, trying to decide whether to believe him or not.

"I know Louisa's silhouette, Mr. Malloy. I could plainly see this woman's through the large front window. Lights were burning in that room, which I assume is the parlor, and she was not Louisa. I'm sure the landlady will confirm that she saw me several times throughout the evening. Of course, I don't know exactly what time Louisa was . . ." He paused a moment and closed his eyes as if fighting off a wave of pain. Then he shook himself and continued. "I do not know what time it was when Louisa met her end, but my own landlady can confirm I returned to my room at about ten fifteen or so. My home is about a ten-minute walk from here, and it was just after ten when the woman who had been watching me came out on the porch and told me Louisa wasn't there and I should go home."

"She actually spoke to you?" Frank marveled.

Plainly, Hoffman was chagrined by this. "Yes. I knew she had seen me standing out there from just after five o'clock until then. I suppose she felt sorry for me."

"Or just wanted rid of you," Frank muttered. "You're sure she was inside Louisa's rooming house?"

"Yes, of course. She should remember, too. It's embarrassing for me, but probably a bit memorable for her."

"No doubt." Was this just another story, like the secret engagement?

Hoffman rubbed his forehead and then jerked his chin up as if he had suddenly thought of something. "Wait a minute, who told you I wasn't engaged to Louisa?"

Uh-oh, Maeve and Gino will never let him forget this blunder. "Who have you told?" Frank countered.

"Only one person, one person in all the world," Hoffman said, not bothering to hide his outrage.

Before Frank could open his mouth to reply, Hoffman was off. He threw open the office door and marched in. Frank hurried after him, but Hoffman was almost to Maeve's desk when Frank caught up.

"You told this detective I wasn't really engaged to Louisa," he nearly shouted. "Who are you and what are you doing here, spying on us?"

Everyone in the main office had stopped their work to observe this unusual event. Tibbot and the people in the back offices suddenly appeared in their doorways, not to be left out.

"What's going on here?" Tibbot demanded.

"This girl is a spy," Hoffman said, gesturing to Maeve. "She came here to find out our secrets and report them back to *him*." He turned his fury on Malloy, who raised his hands as if to surrender.

"Miss Smith works for my agency," Frank said.

"And the only secret I've discovered so far is that you lied when you told people you and Louisa were engaged," Maeve said.

Someone gave a bark of surprised laughter that was quickly squelched.

"It's true, then?" Tibbot said. "You were spying on us?"

"I was trying to get more information about the office to see if anyone here might have killed Louisa."

Tibbot looked like he was going to explode with righteous indignation, so Frank decided to cut him off.

"Since it appears Mr. Hoffman is the only one here who might have wished Miss Rodgers harm and he can account for his whereabouts the night she died, I think our work here is done. Miss Smith?"

Maeve was already on her feet. She snatched her hat and gloves from the desk drawer and came out from behind her desk.

"Yes, you'd better leave," Tibbot said, obviously regretting having lost the opportunity to order her to do so. "And don't expect me to pay you any salary. It seems you were already being paid to pretend to work here."

Maeve smiled her most charming smile. "I didn't really expect to be paid. I did have a delightful time here, though, learning all about how magazines are published. I wish you much success, although I really think you should have at least considered publishing Louisa's article."

She turned to walk out and when she passed Hoffman,

who had stepped out of the way for her, she added, "I'm afraid I won't be able to accept your invitation to the theater after all, Mr. Hoffman, although I am flattered that you asked."

This time no one bothered to hide their snickers. Hoffman's face grew scarlet as Maeve breezed by him to precede him out the door.

As soon as they reached the lobby of the building, Maeve pulled Frank into a far corner so the guard wouldn't overhear them. "What did Hoffman say?"

"He claims he did go to Louisa's rooming house as soon as he left the magazine office and he stood outside it all evening, waiting in vain for her to appear."

"That's easy to say since most of the girls were out that evening, so no one would have noticed if he was there or not."

"He also swears the landlady saw him."

"Even if she did, it doesn't mean he didn't leave at some point and go back to the office. He could be lying about not seeing Louisa either. We know she went back to the house around five o'clock and left again later, probably close to eight o'clock. He could have followed her."

"Except he claims the landlady kept checking on him all night and finally went outside around ten o'clock to tell him Louisa wasn't there and he should go home."

Maeve frowned. "Why didn't Mrs. Baker mention this before?"

"I think we need to ask her."

XIII

Sᴀʀᴀʜ'ꜱ ᴍᴏᴛʜᴇʀ ᴡᴀꜱ ᴡᴀɪᴛɪɴɢ ꜰᴏʀ ʜᴇʀ ᴡʜᴇɴ ꜱʜᴇ ʀᴇ-turned home from taking everyone to school.

"You're up awfully early this morning, Mother," Sarah said, finding her in the parlor drinking the tea Hattie had provided for her. According to the rules of society, morning visits didn't start until the afternoon, so her mother usually slept late.

"I had to get here first thing and find out what happened to Bernard Rodgers. Your father and I were at a dinner party last night and our host told us he was dead. His heart, they thought, but I didn't think that could possibly be true."

"The family wants to keep the circumstances of his death private," Sarah said as tactfully as she could.

Her mother wasn't going to be fooled by a little tact, however. "Are you saying he was murdered? Oh, wait, they wouldn't be able to keep that private. Good heavens, did he take his own life?"

"I'm not saying anything," Sarah insisted.

"That's ridiculous. He was right in the middle of investigating the death of his beloved child. He would have spent the rest of his life searching for the truth."

"I believe his wife thinks he died from a broken heart after losing Louisa," Sarah tried.

"People don't really die of a broken heart, especially not men," her mother said. "And if he didn't die of a broken heart and he couldn't have even considered suicide, he must have been murdered."

"That's a rather reckless conclusion, Mother," Sarah said, more than a little shocked by her vehemence.

"It's the only one that makes sense, though. Really, Sarah, I can't believe you didn't reach the *same* conclusion, reckless or not."

"Actually, we did, but when we found out the circumstances, we had to accept the suicide theory."

"What circumstances?" her mother demanded.

Sarah sighed. "You can't tell anyone. Mrs. Rodgers will know where the information came from."

"If it's such a secret, how do you and Frank even know it?"

"We went over to their house Monday afternoon to give Mr. Rodgers an update on the case, and they had no choice but to tell us what happened. It seems he took the sleeping powders the doctor had given Mrs. Rodgers after Louisa died and put them all into the cocoa he drinks every night at bedtime."

"Someone else could have put the powders in the cocoa," her mother pointed out. "Didn't you think of that?"

"Of course we did, but the papers they came in were all in a heap on his bedside table, just where he would have left them if he had done it himself. And besides, who would want to kill him?"

"The person who killed Louisa, of course," her mother said.

"But how would that person have known about the powders or have gotten into the house unseen or even known Mr. Rodgers's bedtime habits?"

"That ne'er-do-well brother could have done it. Everyone knew he and Louisa were always at loggerheads."

"We thought of that, too, but Oscar Rodgers went to Malloy's office yesterday and rehired him to find Louisa's killer."

"Rehired?" her mother echoed. "Why did he have to rehire him?"

"Because Mrs. Rodgers had fired him after her husband died."

Her mother frowned. "I suppose I can understand that. Losing two close family members in the course of a week would be horrible. She probably didn't want anyone digging into the family's secrets anymore if she really thought her husband killed himself."

"That's what we thought, too, although Malloy had vowed not to stop investigating, even before young Oscar rehired him."

"I would have expected no less of him, but having Oscar's approval will help, I'm sure. You father will never believe Mr. Rodgers took his own life."

"I don't want to believe it either, but all the evidence we

have seems to indicate that he did. Who else in the household would want him dead?"

"Yes, I suppose it is a question of access, and if Oscar didn't do it, that just leaves his wife and perhaps the servants."

"The servants apparently adored him," Sarah said. "There also doesn't seem to be a good reason for Mrs. Rodgers to kill him, and while we did consider that Mrs. Rodgers and Louisa didn't get along, we couldn't figure out why or how she would have been at the office that night."

"A lot of mothers don't get along with their daughters without murdering them," her mother pointed out. "Besides, Mrs. Rodgers seemed quite protective of Louisa at the funeral. She certainly gave Louisa's employer a piece of her mind for dismissing her, didn't she?"

"She certainly did," Sarah remembered. "I couldn't help wishing Louisa could have heard it, although . . ."

"Although what?"

"Louisa wasn't dismissed from her job. She just walked out."

Her mother sighed. "Well, whatever happened, I guess we'll just have to accept that Mr. Rodgers took his own life, then."

"Yes, and in the meantime, we're still looking for Louisa's killer."

"I'm sure it's the secret lover," her mother said, not for the first time.

"Actually, Malloy is questioning him today, but he isn't the only suspect."

"Who else could have done it?" her mother asked eagerly.

Sarah knew she shouldn't be discussing this with her mother, but she also knew her mother wouldn't rest until she learned more. "I think I told you Louisa was writing an article about patent medicines and how they can cause more harm than good."

"Yes, you did, and I've been checking all the medicines we have in our house. None of them seem to be very effective, at least not the patent medicines. Do you think she might have been killed by someone who takes these potions?"

"No, by someone who *makes* them. She was focusing on one company in particular, you see."

"That's right. Blood purifier, if I recall."

"Yes, Watson's. Her landlady uses it, apparently."

"As do many other people. Do you think Louisa chose Watson's Blood Purifier because her landlady uses it?"

"It's the only connection we have found so far, although it's possible her mother takes it or something like it. She has some kind of nervous condition. But as you say, thousands of people use it. In any case, Malloy thinks the owner of the company might have hired someone to ensure that Louisa never published her article."

Her mother perked up at that. "Can you really hire people to do things like that? Commit murder, I mean?"

"Not in *your* social circles, Mother," Sarah said with a disapproving glare.

"I was just curious. You never know when a thing like that might be handy to know."

"Mother!"

"It does seem far-fetched, though," her mother said, un-ashamed. "Killing someone over a magazine article, I mean."

"We tend to agree with you, but we can't ignore the possibility. People in business can be ruthless. That's why Gino has gone out to Brooklyn where Watson's factory is to ask some more questions. Meanwhile, we're still looking at other people."

"Like the secret lover."

"Yes." Sarah decided not to encourage that line of conversation.

"Will you and Frank attend Mr. Rodgers's funeral?" her mother asked.

"I'm not sure there will be one. I haven't even seen an obituary for him yet. She may want to keep it private to discourage gossip."

"She'll only *encourage* gossip by keeping it private. Perhaps I should pay a condolence call on her. I'm sure she'll expect it after we attended Louisa's funeral."

"I'm not at all sure she'll expect it, Mother. You only just met her the other day at her daughter's funeral. Really, I promise to keep you informed if you will stay out of it."

"The way you kept me informed of Bernard Rodgers's death? Really, Sarah, how can I trust you after that?" her mother said in mock dismay.

"I've been busy. With Maeve working at the magazine office, I've had the children to look after," Sarah tried.

"But they're in school all day, and besides, you need to get used to caring for the children yourself, since Maeve is almost certainly getting married soon. Now, what would you like me to find out from Hilda Rodgers?"

. . .

Do you think she was drunk?" Maeve asked later, when she and Frank had reached the privacy of their office. They hadn't had much opportunity to discuss their brief visit with Mrs. Baker up until now, since they'd either been riding the El or walking on crowded sidewalks on the way back.

"I'm positive she was drunk, which is why she didn't dare invite us in, and you're the one who found out that she takes that blood purifier, so she's obviously been treating herself a lot recently."

"Still, she seemed very certain she hadn't seen Clyde Hoffman standing across the street on the night Louisa was killed."

"And what was it she said about shouting at strange men?" Frank asked, smiling at the memory.

"'I am not in the habit of shouting at strange men from my front porch,'" Maeve quoted, mimicking Mrs. Baker's outraged expression. "And besides, she would have been in her bed, sound asleep, by ten o'clock, according to her."

"Clyde didn't actually know who the woman was, though. He just thought it was the landlady. Maybe it was someone else."

"But none of the girls saw Hoffman that night," Maeve reminded him.

"Yes, but we do know at least one of them is a liar, and why would Hoffman make a claim like that if it wasn't true?"

They were still mulling this over when Gino came in, looking triumphant.

"Did you find out who did it?" Maeve asked before he could say a word.

"I found out who *didn't* do it," Gino said smugly, "which is always helpful in figuring out who did. Watson did not hire someone to kill Louisa."

"Did he tell you that?" Frank asked in amazement, wondering what had come over his partner to believe such a thing.

"Of course not, and I didn't even speak to him. I questioned his secretary. Remember him? Karl Spangler?"

"I remember."

"I figured he would be a little easier to deal with," Gino said.

"Because Watson would have probably thrown you out," Frank guessed.

"That was my reasoning, yes," Gino said, making Maeve laugh out loud. He ignored her. "Spangler informed me that Watson had no fear that Louisa would ever publish her article, because he had personally contacted Louisa's boss—"

"Mr. Tibbot?" Maeve guessed.

"The very same," Gino confirmed. "Watson told Tibbot that if the article was published, he would withdraw all his advertising and make sure all the other patent medicine manufacturers did as well."

"Which was probably why Tibbot was so aware of the possibility when Louisa brought the article idea to him," Frank said. "That was the very reason he gave her—and me—for rejecting it."

"So Watson had no reason to fear Louisa or her threats because he had already effectively silenced her," Gino concluded. "Spangler also pointed out that if a murder was ever traced back to Watson, that really would ruin the business, which means Watson had another reason not to have Louisa killed."

"Good work, Gino. We can't completely cross Watson off the list, but we can concentrate on our other remaining suspects now, at least."

"Who is left on the list?" Gino asked. "Besides the old man, Trapper?"

Maeve and Frank exchanged a look as they both considered the question.

"Hoffman claims he was standing outside Louisa's rooming house all evening and that a woman inside saw him there," Frank said. "He thought it was the landlady, but she denies it."

"Although she was probably drunk on Watson's Blood Purifier or something," Maeve added.

Gino frowned in confusion. "Was she drunk that night or was she drunk when you asked her about it?"

"Definitely when we asked her about it, and possibly both," Frank said. "But we'll need to question the girls at the house again to make sure it wasn't one of them and they forgot to mention it."

"Nobody would forget that," Maeve insisted.

"Well, *failed to mention it*," Frank conceded.

"So you still think it could be Hoffman," Gino said. "What about Nellie or one of the other girls, though?"

"None of the other girls had a reason to be angry with Louisa, but Nellie is still on the list," Maeve said.

"And don't forget Trapper," Gino said.

"How can we when you won't let us?" Maeve replied with a grin.

"Gino, come to dinner tonight and we'll go out looking for him again this evening," Frank said.

"And we won't go home until we find him," Gino said.

Frank and Maeve brought Sarah up to date that evening. Then Frank and Gino headed out, taking the electric. They parked it near the magazine office and went to the doors to seek admission. Frank was glad to see they were locked. The night guard recognized them from their first visit, though, and let them in.

"I don't suppose you've seen Trapper today," Frank said.

The guard shook his head, but he said, "I found out some more about him, though. The other people in the building, they knew all about him. Billy Funhouser let him sleep here every night for the past few months."

"*Every* night?" Gino echoed in amazement. "That's not what he told me."

"Some hooligans in the neighborhood had started bothering him, stealing from him and beating him up, so Billy would leave the doors unlocked for him." He glanced around to see if anyone was listening and lowered his voice. "They say the old man would lock the doors behind him so nobody else could get in, and that makes sense if he was scared, but nobody knows for sure if he did lock up or not the night that girl was killed."

They thanked him for the information and moved on, having already discussed how they would divide up the

neighborhood to search. This time they had brought bull's-
eye lanterns, which could be kept dark by twisting an inter-
nal cowl to cover the lens, effectively cutting off the light, or
twisting it back to uncover the lens and send out focused
light. They didn't want to draw attention to themselves, but
the lanterns would allow them to easily check the dark cor-
ners and alleys.

They also had armed themselves with billy clubs because
the hooligans who were robbing Trapper or others like them
might be a danger as well.

Thus equipped, they split up. Frank went immediately to
the alley where he had found Trapper the first time, but of
course he wasn't there. If Trapper knew he was being sought,
he would have logically hidden somewhere else.

Frank continued his search, shining his lantern into every
dark corner or entryway where a man might seek shelter.
After more than an hour of this, Frank stopped in his tracks
when he heard a sound he hadn't heard in quite a while. It
was the clatter of a policeman banging his nightstick on the
sidewalk as a signal for other cops nearby to come to his aid.
This was the other reason they had brought the sticks.

Frank took off running as fast as he could without spilling his lantern, in the direction of the noise. Was Gino in-
jured? Had the thieves bothering Trapper attacked him?

He came around a blind corner and almost tripped over
an obstacle on the sidewalk. It took him a moment to recognize it as two men. One lay flat on the ground and the
other was sitting on his backside.

Frank flipped open the lantern door and saw Gino grinning up at him. The man on the ground lay facedown and

still, although he was grumbling, so Frank knew he was alive and conscious. Only when he had assured himself of that did he notice another person standing nearby. He needed a minute to figure out it was a woman bundled up in as many old clothes as she could probably wear at one time and all of them were dirty. She was scowling at the two men on the ground.

"Mr. Malloy, may I introduce you to my friends Myrtle and Trapper?" Gino said pleasantly.

"You're sure that's Trapper?" Frank asked.

"That's him, all right," the woman apparently named Myrtle said.

Trapper grunted. "You're crushing me."

"Sorry, but I couldn't take a chance of you running away again," Gino said, shifting his weight a bit to make Trapper more comfortable. "You see," he continued to Frank, "I found Myrtle here and told her we were still trying to locate Trapper because we thought he might know something about Louisa's death."

Gino paused to make sure Frank understood he hadn't accused Trapper of the crime, at least not to Myrtle.

"Then Miss Myrtle here told me where to find him," Gino added.

"That was very kind of you," Frank told her.

She huffed in disgust and looked at Trapper. "Tell them what you told me, you old goat. Then they'll leave you alone."

"What did you tell her, Trapper?" Frank asked. "Did you tell her you killed that girl?"

Trapper bucked so suddenly, he almost dislodged Gino,

but Gino was made of sterner stuff than that and simply adjusted his position on Trapper again.

"Tell them, for heaven's sake," Myrtle snapped. "He saw something that night. He told me, but he doesn't think anybody'll believe him."

"Give us a chance," Gino said pleasantly. "We can usually tell if somebody is lying or not."

"At least let me sit up," Trapper whined.

Gino eased off Trapper's back while taking hold of one of his arms. Frank took the other, and they sat him up, keeping him from getting to his feet so he wouldn't be able to easily escape. Trapper, Frank noted, was just as dirty as Myrtle and smelled like a dead rat.

"Now tell us what you saw that night," Frank suggested.

Trapper looked to be about a hundred years old. He turned his rheumy gaze to Gino and then to Frank as if trying to judge their determination. Apparently, he decided it was too strong to resist. "I been sleeping in the lobby of that building for a couple months."

"Billy told us," Gino said, stretching the truth a bit. "Billy Funhouser. You don't have to worry about getting him in trouble, though. He already got fired over the girl getting killed."

"He was doing a kindness to me. Them boys—devils, they are—they wouldn't leave me be, so Billy let me come in of a night."

"And did he let you come in on the night Louisa Rodgers was killed?" Frank asked.

"Is that her name?" Trapper asked with a frown.

"Yes. So did Billy let you sleep in the lobby or not?"

"He would've, I guess, but I didn't get the chance."

"Why not?" Gino asked impatiently. Frank raised a hand to indicate he should slow down.

"When I got there, I saw a carriage pull up out front."

"A carriage?" Frank asked. "What kind of carriage?"

"Like one of them cabs you see all over."

"A hansom cab?" Gino asked.

"No, the bigger kind."

"A brougham," Frank guessed.

Trapper shrugged. The proper names for horse-drawn vehicles were of no importance to him.

"Tell him the rest," Myrtle said.

Trapper sighed in resignation. "Somebody got out and went inside."

"Did you recognize him?" Frank asked.

"I didn't. And it wasn't a *him*. It was a *she*."

"You saw a woman get out of the cab? Are you sure?" Frank asked.

"I can tell a woman from a man," Trapper declared, obviously offended. "Women wear skirts."

"Can you tell us what she looked like?" Gino asked.

"It was too dark. I just knowed it was a female because of the skirts and the hat."

"Tell them the rest," Myrtle urged.

Trapper sighed. "She went inside, and the cab just stayed there, so I figured she wouldn't be in there long. I decided to wait until she left and then I could go in."

"How long was she inside?" Frank asked, thinking Louisa must have been planning ahead to have come in a cab.

"Only a few minutes. Then she came out again and got back in the cab and left."

So it wasn't Louisa at all. "Did you hear what she said to the driver?"

"No, I was too far away, and she was moving fast. Didn't even wait for the driver to help her inside."

"And you're sure it was a woman," Gino repeated.

"I told you, yes," Trapper said, annoyed now. "She got there, went inside, then came back out and left."

"And then you went inside," Gino prompted.

Trapper looked down and grunted.

"Tell them all of it," Myrtle said.

Trapper sighed. "When they was gone, I went inside and then I saw her."

"You saw Louisa?" Frank asked sharply.

"I saw a woman laying on the floor. I don't know who it was. I yelped in surprise, but she didn't move. I didn't know what was wrong with her, but I knew I'd get blamed, so I ran off quick as I could."

He probably would have been blamed, so he'd been right to run away.

"What time was this?" Frank asked.

Trapper gave him a sly look. "I don't know. I think somebody must've stole my gold watch."

"You numbskull," Myrtle said. "What was the last time you heard the clocks sound?"

Clocks all over the city struck the hour and some rang the half and quarter hours, too. Even the poor who owned no timepieces at all could tell the approximate time if they just paid attention.

"It was after eight o'clock," Trapper said grudgingly. "I had to wait until Billy came on for his shift. Then I always waited a bit longer to make sure all the daytime guards had went home. Billy would have to turn me away if any of them saw me."

"How long would you wait?" Frank asked.

"Thirty minutes or so. Just to make sure."

"It was probably around eight thirty, then," Gino said.

"I guess. Can I go now? I don't know nothing about that girl who died, I swear."

Gino looked to Frank, who nodded. Both men released Trapper, and he got up slowly, using the wall behind him for support. When he was on his feet, he said, "Didn't you say there was a reward or something?"

Frank fished a dollar out of his pocket and passed it to Trapper. Then he gave Myrtle one, too.

"Why does she get one?" Trapper protested. "I should get them both."

"You wouldn't have anything at all if it wasn't for me," Myrtle said. "Now come along, you old coot."

The two of them shuffled away.

When they were gone, Gino turned to Frank and said, "It's Nellie."

UNABLE TO SLEEP, SARAH HAD BEEN WAITING UP FOR Malloy to return. It was foolish, of course. He might be gone for hours and still not locate the elusive Trapper, but she would sit up as long as she could, just in case. She didn't have to wait long, though. It was just past eleven when she heard the back door open.

She hurried from the parlor to the now-dark kitchen, where she found Malloy alone, stealthily searching for a snack. He must have dropped Gino off before coming home.

"Did you find him?" she asked.

"Yes," he said, but he didn't sound as happy about it as she would have expected.

"Is he the killer?"

Malloy shook his head. "We don't think so. He told us he saw a cab pull up in front of the building and a woman got out and went inside."

"That must have been Louisa."

But Malloy shook his head again. "The woman only stayed inside for a short time and then left in the cab, and when Trapper snuck into the lobby, he found Louisa dead on the floor so he left in a big hurry."

"I don't understand," Sarah said, trying to make sense of it. "Who was the woman in the cab, then?"

Malloy didn't answer. He just set the loaf of bread he had been holding down on the table, giving her a chance to figure it out for herself.

"Oh dear, it must have been Nellie," she realized.

"That's what we thought," Malloy said. "We were just trying to work it all out."

"Did you?"

"Not quite, but I think we know enough that we can frighten her into confessing."

"I'll make you a sandwich while you tell me what you've

figured out so far," Sarah said, picking up the loaf of bread and carrying it to the cutting board.

"Let's see," Malloy said, pulling out a chair at the kitchen table and sinking wearily down into it. "We know Louisa went to the rooming house around five o'clock and stayed there for a period of time. Then she left and went to the office building."

"Presumably, she waited until the night guard came on duty at eight, although she could have gone in earlier and the other guard just didn't see her," Sarah said.

"We know she spent some time emptying her desk, but she left the box because it was too heavy to carry by herself."

"Would she have known ahead of time the box would be too heavy?" Sarah wondered aloud.

"I don't know. Would she?"

Sarah considered. "Women do tend to think about things like that in a way that men don't. Because we're not usually as strong as men, we have to figure out how to accomplish things. No matter the weight, though, she would have had to carry a box of some kind, maybe two boxes, because she had a lot of notes. Even if she could have lifted it all, would she want to carry a box through the streets for blocks? It doesn't sound practical."

"So she would have known she'd need help even before she left for the office," Malloy said.

"Probably, and a woman raised the way Louisa had been raised wouldn't be accustomed to carrying her own shopping bags, much less transporting heavy boxes around the city on foot."

"Then she would have realized she needed help, but would she have asked Nellie for it?" Malloy asked.

Sarah set the sandwich down in front of Malloy and went to pour him some beer. "If Nellie arrived in a cab, she must have known Louisa needed help, so Louisa must have asked her or at least let Nellie know what her problem was."

"And knowing Nellie, maybe she offered to help, because she was always trying to prove she and Louisa were friends."

"But would she have offered knowing Louisa had threatened to tell the police she had been stealing things? That seems unlikely," Sarah said.

"Maybe she thought she could win Louisa's forgiveness by doing her a favor."

Sarah set the glass of beer in front of Malloy and took a chair across from him. "Something like that must have happened because now we know Nellie arrived in a cab. What we don't know is whether Nellie killed Louisa."

Malloy gulped down the bite of sandwich he had just taken, nearly choking in the process. "But it had to be her. She was *there*. She went into the lobby and then she came back out without Louisa, who would most likely have been waiting for her near the front door. Nellie *must* have killed her."

"But why go to all the trouble of getting the cab—because the cabdriver might have remembered her—just to kill Louisa?"

"She probably didn't intend to kill her. Maybe it was an impulse thing," Malloy mused. "She had gone to all this trouble to help Louisa, and Louisa insulted her or belittled her or—"

"—or did one of the dozens of things rich girls do to show they are superior to poor girls," Sarah said.

"Yes, and Nellie strangled Louisa in anger and left her there."

"Or she went in the lobby and found Louisa already dead."

Malloy shook his head. "Why didn't she scream, then? Call for help? She wouldn't have known Louisa was dead, not at first. This was about eight thirty, so she probably wasn't even cold yet."

"Maybe she was also afraid she'd be blamed, just like Trapper," Sarah said logically.

Malloy took another bite of his sandwich and considered the possibilities. "I guess there's only one way to find out for sure."

"You'll have to question Nellie," Sarah agreed. "Will you take someone with you?"

"I thought about that on the way back from dropping Gino off. I want her to feel intimidated, so I'm going to do it myself, but I think I need a female with me, in case she tries any feminine tricks."

Sarah smiled at that. "Do you think she'd try to seduce you?"

He did choke this time, spitting his beer across the table. Sarah grabbed a towel to wipe it up, which Malloy had to do because she was laughing too hard.

When she had finally stopped laughing, he said, "No, I am not worried about seduction. I was thinking more about her playing the helpless female and crying and getting hysterical. Nellie seems like the kind of girl who would do something like that to get out of an unpleasant situation."

"Like being questioned about a murder," Sarah said. "I understand your concern. I would be happy to go along and protect you."

He glared at her but that only made her grin back at him.

"I'm going to take Maeve," he said finally. "She won't feel sorry for Nellie no matter what she does."

"And you think I will?" Sarah said in mock outrage.

"I know you will, and I'm going to have to be mean to Nellie to get her to confess. I know you don't want to see that."

He was right, of course. Maeve was the better choice. "Maeve will be happy to help, I'm sure."

"We'll have to wait until Nellie gets home from work tomorrow. It might be late if she goes out dancing with the other girls."

"From what Maeve said, I got the feeling she doesn't usually go out with them. She was at home the day Maeve first went to the house, but the other girls weren't. The other girls don't seem to like Nellie much either." Sarah frowned.

"See?" Malloy said. "You're already feeling sorry for her."

"I'm sure she's had a difficult life. A young woman living alone in the city always does. If she had a family, she would be living with them, if only because they'd want her to give them at least part of her salary to help out."

"That's true, but it doesn't give her license to kill anyone, no matter how rude Louisa might have been to her."

"If that is what really happened," Sarah said with a sigh.

"And that," Malloy said with resignation, "is why I'm taking Maeve."

XIV

FRANK TOLD MAEVE HIS PLANS FOR HER THE NEXT MORN-
ing at breakfast. They agreed she would come to the office
as usual after escorting Catherine to school, since she no
longer had a job at the magazine. Frank went straight to his
office, where he began organizing his notes on the case so
he and Maeve could discuss what to reveal to Nellie and
what to keep secret in their efforts to get her to confess.

When he heard the office door open about an hour later,
he thought it was probably Maeve or Gino arriving, but the
voice who called out was Oscar Rodgers's.

Frank went out to meet him. "Did you have some information for me?" he asked Oscar when they had exchanged
greetings.

"I was hoping you might have information for *me*, but I
forgot to ask you not to come to my home to deliver it. I've

decided not to tell my mother you are still trying to find Louisa's killer. The subject upsets her dreadfully."

"I'm sure it does," Frank said, "and seeing me would probably upset her even more after she fired me. Come in and I'll tell you what we know so far."

When they were seated in Frank's utilitarian office, Oscar said, "I hope you're close to solving the case. I'm getting rather tired of people avoiding me or whispering about me behind their hands."

"I'm sure that's hard," Frank said with false sympathy. It wasn't nearly as hard as getting murdered, but most people cared about only themselves. "And yes, we do have some information for you. We found a witness who saw a woman arrive at the office building around the time Louisa was killed. She only stayed a few minutes and then left. The witness found Louisa's body just a few minutes after this woman left."

"A woman? Are you sure?" Oscar looked far from elated by the news.

"The witness was positive. We believe we know who this woman is, too."

Oscar rubbed his chin as he absorbed this news. "Who do you think it is?" he asked as if he didn't want to know the answer.

"A young woman who lived in the rooming house with Louisa. You'll remember her from Louisa's funeral. She was the one wearing Louisa's scarf."

"Oh," Oscar said in surprise. "Yes, of course. I remember her well. Mother insisted she must have stolen the scarf from Louisa. And for her to come to Louisa's funeral after she . . . I can't believe she had the nerve."

"We aren't positive yet, but it certainly looks like she was there when Louisa was killed. She would have at least seen something. I'm going to question her this afternoon."

"Why are you waiting? She might try to get away," Oscar said, probably thinking he should assert his authority as Frank's client.

"She's at work now, and we don't know where she is employed. Besides, I'm not a police officer, so I don't have any right to barge into someone's place of business and demand to speak to an employee. She's not likely to run away, though, since she has no idea we suspect her."

"If you say so, I guess I must bow to your higher level of experience in these matters. I just want to get this settled as soon as possible. Aside from my own problems, Mother is a bundle of nerves."

"I'm sure it's very upsetting to lose two family members so close together," Frank said, although he was pretty sure Mrs. Rodgers had little love for either of them. "When is your father's funeral?" He would have expected it to be today or tomorrow since no one had even considered an autopsy on Mr. Rodgers because his cause of death was so obvious.

"We, uh, buried him yesterday," Oscar admitted reluctantly. "Mother couldn't bear the thought of another funeral so soon after Louisa's, and she couldn't face all the questions she knew people would ask. It was a private ceremony. We'll have an obituary in the newspapers in a day or two."

"I understand society people are already sharing the news," Frank said as tactfully as he could.

"How would you know that?" Oscar asked in a condescending tone.

Frank had to admit Oscar would have reason to doubt an Irish Catholic private investigator could have any knowledge of New York society, but he couldn't help being annoyed all the same. "Felix and Elizabeth Decker are my in-laws."

Oscar blinked in surprise. "Oh" was all he could manage for a moment and then he said, "They came to Louisa's funeral."

"They were very sorry to hear of Louisa's death. Mr. Decker was one of your father's clients."

Oscar obviously needed a few moments to digest this surprising information. "Were they there to *spy* for you?" he asked, a little outraged at the thought. "And is that how *society people* found out about my father's death? You told them!"

"Absolutely not. You don't think I employ the Deckers as my agents, do you?" And he didn't, of course. They worked for free. "And we told no one about your father's death. In fact, Mrs. Decker called my wife to inform *us*. She heard the news at a dinner party."

Oscar looked a bit chastened, or at least he sat in troubled silence for another long moment. "Mother was so impressed that they came to the funeral. Several of father's clients were there."

"Your father was held in high esteem. I'm sure his friends will be sorry they didn't have a chance to pay their respects."

Oscar's face hardened. "I didn't hold him in high esteem,

and he never gave me any reason to. In fact, I'm rather glad I didn't have to listen to people telling me what a fine man he was." He rose to his feet abruptly. "I wish you success in questioning this girl. Hopefully, we can put this all behind us soon. You'll keep me informed, I assume."

Frank rose, too. "If you don't want me to come to your house, can I telephone?"

"Just send word to my club. They'll give me the message."

Before Frank could even come from behind his desk, Oscar was out the door.

Frank sank back down into his chair with a sigh. Bernard Rodgers had a lot to answer for in the way he had treated his son, as did his wife for the way she had treated Louisa, but Oscar seemed to be damaged the most. With no profession and now a shadow on his reputation, his future looked bleak, even with his father's money. A man needed work and friends and family. Oscar had none of these except for a mother who suffered from nerves.

At least Frank might be able to remove the shadow of guilt from him.

Mr. Malloy drove Maeve and Gino in his gasoline-powered motorcar up to the Rose Hill neighborhood where Louisa had lived. Maeve couldn't help feeling a little cocky since Mr. Malloy had chosen her to go with him to question Nellie. Gino also had an important task, but not as important as questioning the possible killer.

Gino was assigned to knock on the doors of the neighboring houses to see if anyone remembered seeing Clyde

Hoffman loitering on the street the night Louisa was killed. Of course, it wouldn't matter if Nellie turned out to be the killer, but it was always a good idea to check people's alibis just in case.

"What are you going to do if Nellie confesses?" Gino asked as they removed the dusters and goggles they had worn to protect themselves during the ride uptown and stowed them in the motorcar's trunk.

"If she confesses, we'll take her to the police station, but someone who lies as well as Nellie does probably won't confess. We'll have to trick her or something," Mr. Malloy said.

"Which is why I'm going along," Maeve said with a grin.

Gino just rolled his eyes at that. Then he went off to talk to the neighbors.

Nellie was waiting for them when Maeve and Mr. Malloy reached the front door.

"I heard your motorcar. I couldn't imagine who it could be driving a motorcar down our street, and here you are, coming to visit us. I'm surprised to see you in that machine, Mr. Malloy. I thought you had an electric."

"I do,' Mr. Malloy said, somehow managing to get a word in edgewise.

Nellie didn't seem to notice. "The other girls aren't home. They always stop on the way home to get supper and then they go dancing. Unless they come by here to change their clothes, but then they only stay a few minutes and won't have time to see you. Come in, come in," she urged. "What about that young man who came with you? He's very handsome, isn't he?"

"He has an errand to run," Maeve said quickly. She

certainly didn't want Nellie paying too much attention to Gino.

"Did you want to see Mrs. Baker? She's resting right now, but I can get her if you like. She won't be too happy about it, though, so maybe you should come back tomorrow if you want to see her. In the morning is the best time. She—"

"We just wanted to see you, Nellie," Mr. Malloy said.

"Me?" she said, pretending to be surprised and a little humbled, although Maeve was not impressed with her acting abilities. "I can't imagine what you need to talk to me about. I thought you got all the information you needed from the *other girls*." The way she said *other girls* told Maeve she wasn't forgiven for neglecting to question Nellie at her last visit.

"It was remiss of me not to speak to you then," Maeve said, doing a better job of pretending to be humble than Nellie had. "Mr. Malloy took me to task and insisted on coming along while I ask you more questions."

"I should hope you will. I was Louisa's very best friend in all the world, you know. She told me everything."

"Would Mrs. Baker object if we take Mr. Malloy into the parlor so we can be comfortable?" Maeve tried.

"She won't even know," Nellie said with a sly grin. "We break her rules all the time, but she takes her medicine and never even notices."

Nellie turned to lead them into the parlor, and she didn't see the glance Maeve exchanged with Mr. Malloy. So, the girls often broke the rules and Mrs. Baker never knew.

When they were all seated on the mismatched chairs in the parlor, Nellie said, "I bet you still don't know who killed poor Louisa, and I bet the other girls didn't tell you anything that helped you figure it out either."

"Nellie," Maeve began as she and Mr. Malloy had agreed, "didn't you tell me that Louisa never came home after work on the day she died?"

Nellie had been perched eagerly on the edge of her chair, ready to give them whatever information they wanted, but she suddenly sat back, frowning. "I don't think I said that."

"I think you did. I know I asked you specifically, and that's what you said. But maybe you just didn't see her."

Nellie took her cue. "Yes, that's it. I didn't see her that night, and Mrs. Baker made such a big fuss the next day when she wasn't in her room and hadn't been all night, so naturally, I thought she hadn't come home at all."

"Except she did come home. Angie saw her," Maeve said.

"Angie," Nellie said with a dismissive wave of her hand. "She makes things up."

"What about you, Nellie?" Mr. Malloy asked suddenly. "Do you make things up, too?"

"Me? Never," she claimed, a little put out.

"But you told Miss Smith that you knew about Louisa's secret engagement to Mr. Hoffman."

"And Mr. Hoffman has admitted that he and Louisa were never engaged. They were never even keeping company," Maeve added.

Nellie's confidence evaporated. Her gaze darted back and forth between them for several seconds before she said, "I never said they were. You asked me if I knew about Louisa's secret engagement, so of course I said yes. I wanted to prove what good friends we were. I couldn't believe she didn't tell me, but I also knew she would have, so I said I already knew. But now you say it wasn't even true. That was a mean trick to play on me."

What a neat dodge, making it Maeve's fault, which also happened to be true.

Maeve felt the heat rising in her face. The curse of red hair was the blushing that came with it. She turned to Mr. Malloy. "I did ask her if she knew about the secret engagement," she confessed. It had been, she knew, a poorly phrased question that suggested the answer Maeve had wanted. Nellie had merely played along.

Maeve wouldn't make that mistake again.

"Then you did see Louisa come home that night," Mr. Malloy said, making the same mistake.

But it wasn't really a mistake, and it worked. "I didn't see her come in, but I did see her later," she admitted.

"Then why did you tell me she wasn't here?" Maeve asked, trying not to sound too irritated.

"She'd been murdered," Nellie reminded her with a huff. "I didn't want the police coming here and . . . and bothering us."

Because Louisa might have already told the police that Nellie had stolen from her. In any case, Nellie wouldn't have wanted the police nosing around the rooming house for anything at all.

"You said you saw her later that night," Mr. Malloy asked. "When was that?"

Nellie took a moment to pick a piece of lint off her skirt and she didn't look up when she said, "It was around seven thirty or maybe eight. I don't know for sure."

"And what was she doing?" Maeve asked, pleased to hear her voice sounded gentle.

"Leaving."

"She was leaving the house?" Malloy asked.

Nellie nodded.

"Are you saying you saw her go out the front door?" Maeve asked.

Nellie looked up in surprise. "No, not the front door. She went out the back door. We're not supposed to use it, but if you need to go out and you won't be back before Mrs. Baker locks the front door, you can use it and leave it unlocked so you can get back in."

"But doesn't Mrs. Baker check the back door when she locks up?" Maeve asked.

Nellie actually laughed at the very idea. "She doesn't like to go downstairs if she doesn't have to. Hurts her bunions, she says. More likely, she's too unsteady on her feet by that time of night. She takes her medicine, like I told you."

"And how did you happen to be downstairs yourself, Nellie?" Mr. Malloy asked. "Your room is upstairs, isn't it?"

Nellie shifted uneasily in her chair. "I don't remember."

"Were you going to visit your good friend Louisa?" Maeve asked blandly.

"Yes, that's it. I was going to visit Louisa," Nellie decided.

"But you said you didn't think she was home. You hadn't seen her arrive," Mr. Malloy reminded her.

"But you went downstairs, thinking Louisa wasn't home. Were you looking for something, Nellie?" Maeve asked. "Were you going to look through Louisa's things and see what you could take?"

Nellie's face had grown scarlet. "No, I was looking for something to eat."

Maeve and Mr. Malloy stared at her in surprise for a long moment. Finally, Maeve managed to say, "Something to eat?"

"Don't look so surprised. These other girls, they work in offices, but I work in a factory. I barely earn enough to pay my rent. I can't always afford to buy my supper, so I went downstairs to pinch some bread. The old lady won't notice if a heel is missing."

"Is that why you don't go out dancing with the other girls?" Maeve asked.

"Of course it is. It costs a nickel to get into a dance house. If you have a fella, he can treat you, but the only way to get a fella is to go dancing. If I have a nickel, I can eat dinner, take the trolley home, or go to a dance house. I didn't even have a nickel that night."

"And when you went downstairs, you saw Louisa leaving," Maeve said.

Nellie sighed in disgust. "Yes."

"And she saw you and asked for your help," Mr. Malloy said.

"What?" Nellie asked with a puzzled frown.

"She was going back to her office," Maeve said. "She had quit her job that day, and she was going back to get the things out of her desk. She knew she would need help, so she asked you to go with her."

"No, she didn't. She didn't even see me," Nellie said.

"Or," Mr. Malloy said, "she asked you to find a cab and bring it to the office building because she knew she wouldn't be able to carry all her belongings back to the rooming house."

"She didn't ask me anything," Nellie insisted. "I told you, she didn't see me."

"And when you brought the cab, you went inside the building to find her, and she was there in the lobby," Maeve said. "Was she wearing that pretty scarf you liked? Did she say something mean to remind you of how much better she was than you are, Nellie?"

"I don't know what you're talking about," Nellie cried. "I never hired a cab in my life, and I never went anywhere with Louisa that night. I never even left the house. I swear it!"

"I don't suppose anyone can vouch for that, what with Mrs. Baker and her medicine and the other girls going out dancing," Mr. Malloy said.

Nellie looked near tears, but she suddenly brightened. "Yes, someone *can* vouch for me."

"Who?" Maeve asked skeptically.

"That man, the one who came to see Louisa in the summer. He used to stand across the street and watch the house sometimes. We'd laugh about it and tease Louisa, but she never thought it was funny."

"How could he vouch for you?" Maeve scoffed, although the hairs on the back of her neck were standing tall because Hoffman had claimed to have done just that the night Louisa was killed. "Mrs. Baker wouldn't have let him in the house."

"He didn't come in the house. He was standing across the street, under the streetlamp like he always did. I noticed him after I saw Louisa sneak out. I went back upstairs right away and looked out the front window to see if I could catch her meeting somebody. If I could, Mrs. Baker would throw her out for sure."

"And you wanted her out, didn't you?" Mr. Malloy said.

"She accused me of stealing from her, but Mrs. Baker searched my room and didn't find anything. I wanted her out before she caused me real trouble."

"Did you catch her meeting somebody?" Maeve asked.

"No. I didn't see her at all, but that's when I saw him, that fella. He must've seen me watching him out the window, too. Maybe he thought I was Louisa. Anyway, I could tell he saw me looking at him."

"Did he leave then?" Mr. Malloy asked.

"No. That's when I got my idea, though."

"What idea was that?" Mr. Malloy asked.

"I figured out that I could bolt the back door so when Louisa came home, she wouldn't be able to sneak back in. She would have to come to the front door and knock and everyone would know she'd broken the rules."

"And Mrs. Baker would throw her out," Maeve guessed.

"That's right. So I went downstairs and locked the door. Then I ate some bread and went back upstairs. I checked to see if that man was still there, and he was. What an idiot. I sat down and looked at a magazine and then I checked again, and he was still there. It got to be a bit of a game. I started waiting for the clock to chime the quarter hours." She gestured to the clock on the mantel that chimed as if on cue, a lovely sound. "When it did, I would look out. He was still there every time."

"How long did this go on?" Mr. Malloy asked.

"A couple hours, I think."

"You're sure he was there the whole time from when Louisa left the house until . . . What time did you stop looking for him?" Mr. Malloy asked.

"Ten o'clock. I looked out at least every fifteen minutes and he was there every time."

"I suppose you went to bed at ten," Maeve said, thinking they just needed to confirm one more detail.

"I was tired of our little game, and I felt sorry for that poor man. He was a victim of Louisa's, same as me. Before I went to bed, I went outside on the porch and hollered at him."

"What did you say?" Malloy asked, feigning amazement.

"I just said Louisa wasn't here and he should go home." She shrugged. "I don't know if he did or not because I went to bed."

Maeve turned to Mr. Malloy, who looked as flummoxed as she felt. Without realizing it, Nellie had just given both herself and Clyde Hoffman a perfect alibi for Louisa's murder.

But if Nellie hadn't gone with Louisa that night, who was the woman in the cab? There was only one other woman who might have been angry at Louisa that night, and Maeve didn't even want to think about what Oscar Rodgers would say if they accused his mother.

THE NEIGHBORS WERE NO HELP AT ALL," GINO TOLD Sarah later, after they had returned to the Malloy house for supper and the children were in bed. They were gathered in the parlor and had just finished telling Sarah about their visit to the rooming house. "Some of the neighbors did remember seeing Hoffman lurking around the neighborhood on many nights, but they couldn't say for sure which nights or how long he was there. Maybe if we'd asked them the next day, someone might have noticed, but after more than a week, no one could recall."

"But Nellie and Hoffman can vouch for each other," Maeve said. "That's the important thing. Neither of them could have killed Louisa."

Sarah shook her head. "Then who is the woman in the cab?"

No one spoke for a long moment. Finally, Malloy said, "There's only one other woman we've considered a possible suspect."

"But how would Mrs. Rodgers have even known to go to the magazine's office that night? We already decided Louisa wouldn't have asked her mother for help," Sarah argued. "I think we agreed that she would certainly have asked her father, but never her mother or brother."

"And her father was out of town, so she couldn't ask him," Gino said.

"Did the girl *know* her father was out of town?" Mother Malloy asked from her corner.

Sarah had to cover her mouth to hide her rueful smile, and the others were having a little trouble, too.

"Ma, what would we do without you?" Malloy said.

"Nothing, probably," she replied tartly.

That did earn a laugh. When they settled down again, Maeve said, "Why didn't we think of that?"

"Because it's so obvious," Malloy said. "Mr. Rodgers himself told me he hadn't been in contact with Louisa for a while. She made a point of not visiting her family, probably because she wanted to avoid her mother."

"And if she didn't live in the same house with her parents, she wasn't likely to know where they were or what they were doing on any given day," Maeve said.

"So, Louisa went to the magazine offices to collect her notes and empty her desk," Sarah said. "She probably intended all along to telephone her father from the magazine office and ask him for help."

"Because the rooming house didn't have a telephone," Gino said.

"But when she did call, her father wasn't home, so . . ." Maeve let her voice trail off as they all considered what might have logically happened then.

"It's hard to believe her mother volunteered to take a cab all the way to Rose Hill alone at that hour of the night to help Louisa move her things back to the rooming house," Malloy said.

"Yes, respectable women don't walk around the city alone after dark, even if they're just looking for a cab," Maeve said. "It seems more likely she would have told Louisa she needed to solve her own problems if she was so intent on being independent."

"But she's Louisa's *mother*," Gino argued. "*My* mother is always complaining about her boys, but she would still walk through fire to help us if we needed it."

"And *my* mother pointed out the other day how Mrs. Rodgers had chastened Mr. Tibbot for the way he treated

Louisa," Sarah said. "That proves she had at least some tender feelings for her daughter and may have come to her aid if asked, even if she had to go out alone after dark."

"Wait," Maeve said, nearly jumping out of her seat. "Maybe Louisa didn't intend to go back to the rooming house at all, at least not to live. I just remembered, the first time I was at the rooming house, Nellie said Mrs. Baker had asked her to pack up Louisa's things so she could rent out the room again, but Nellie said someone else had already done it. Maybe that someone was Louisa."

"Which would explain why she returned to the rooming house," Sarah said. "We know she didn't go directly there after leaving the office, so maybe she spent that time considering her options and decided to go back home. If she wasn't working at the magazine, she didn't need to live in the rooming house anymore. She might have called her father to get her at the magazine and then fetch her things from the rooming house."

"And her mother might have agreed to come for her in his place," Maeve said. "She would have been delighted to have Louisa crawling back home after failing in her career."

"No matter what we think of Mrs. Rodgers," Malloy said, "the fact remains that we know a woman arrived at the magazine office at the time Louisa was killed. We need to find out who that woman was."

"We can start by finding out if Mrs. Rodgers even went out that night," Sarah said. "That should be easy enough."

"We should ask the servants," Maeve said, echoing Sarah's quintessential advice.

"But Mrs. Rodgers isn't going to let you in, and the servants aren't likely to believe you're returning more of Louisa's papers," Malloy told Sarah.

"They don't know me," Maeve said. "*I* could claim to be one of the other lodgers in her rooming house. I could be returning some of her things that we found."

"And I could go with you to check around and see if they keep a carriage," Gino said. "That's another thing we didn't consider. She might have used her own driver."

"I thought the old man said it was a cab," Maeve said.

"He could've been wrong. It was dark, after all," Malloy said.

"If they do keep a carriage, then it wouldn't have been quite as daring for Mrs. Rodgers to go out alone that night," Maeve said. "She would have just gone in her own vehicle."

"But what about her driver," Gino scoffed, "who would know she had gone into the building to meet Louisa, who ended up dead. Would she have taken a chance like that? What would stop the driver from figuring out what happened?"

"That does sound a bit risky," Sarah said, "but speculation is a waste of time at this point until we know if she even went out that night."

"Catherine's school is on the way to the Rodgerses' neighborhood," Maeve said. "If you let me have the electric tomorrow morning and Gino meets me here, we can get to the Rodgerses' house early, hopefully before they're up and about so I can talk to the servants without the family knowing."

"Good idea," Malloy said. "I wouldn't want either Oscar or his mother to realize we're gathering information about her, at least not until we know if it's even possible his mother had something to do with it."

"The real question," Gino said, "is, How are you going to explain it to Oscar if we do find out his mother is the killer?"

No one had an answer for that.

THE NEXT MORNING, BRIAN PROTESTED WHEN HE REAL-ized his sister was getting to ride to school with Gino. There wasn't room in the electric for Mrs. Malloy and Brian along with Maeve, Gino, and Catherine, but Gino was able to placate him with the promise of a trip to the zoo on the weekend.

"It will have to be on Saturday," Gino informed Maeve when they were on their way to drop Catherine at school, "because you and I are going to my mother's for Sunday dinner."

Gino knew Maeve would be glaring at him, but he had to ignore that and keep his eyes on the traffic. He couldn't help grinning, though.

"How do I even know I'm invited?" Maeve tried.

"Because I said so. Besides, Ma doesn't mind if I bring a friend. You'll get to see Baby Robert. He's really cute."

"*I* would like to see him," Catherine piped up. "We get to see the Ellsworth twins sometimes, but they're too little to play with us."

"Baby Robert is even younger than they are," Maeve said. "But it won't be long until they're all big enough to play with."

A lot of their friends had babies. Gino couldn't help wondering if that gave Maeve ideas about marriage and a family. Maybe he would work up his courage and ask her.

But not today.

They saw Catherine safely delivered to Miss Spence's School and then headed for Morningside Heights where the Rodgerses lived. Gino parked around the corner so Maeve could appear to have walked over from the El station and then Gino could stroll by to see what he could find in the mews.

He waited until Maeve had walked down the alley to the back of the Rodgerses' house and been admitted. Then he waited a bit longer and started down himself. The mews were on the opposite side of the alley, and Gino nodded to a couple of men working in the stables behind other houses. He was glad to see the one behind the Rodgerses' house had the doors open to the fall air, and as he got closer, he could hear and smell the horses inside.

He slowed his pace and casually glanced inside to see a middle-aged man in work clothes brushing down one of the horses. But then he noticed something else that stopped him in his tracks.

"You lost or something?" the man called.

Gino shook his head to clear it. Suddenly, he knew the answer to one of the many mysteries surrounding Louisa Rodgers's death.

MAEVE KNOCKED ON THE KITCHEN DOOR AND SMILED when a maid opened it.

"I'm sorry to bother you, but I'm a friend of Miss Louisa Rodgers . . . I mean, I *was* a friend of hers. We lived in the same rooming house, you see, and well . . ." She held up a canvas drawstring bag. It contained a few bits and bobs that

Maeve and Mrs. Frank had collected from their dressing tables to give some credence to Maeve's story, just in case someone looked inside. "When we packed up her belongings, we missed a few things. I thought I'd drop them off since I was passing by."

The maid had frowned at the mention of Louisa, but she tried to be polite. "That's kind of you. I'll see that Mrs. Rodgers gets it."

She reached for the bag, but Maeve said, "I don't suppose I could step in for a glass of water, could I? I'm parched."

"Let the poor girl in," a voice called. "She brought Miss Louisa's things. It's the least we can do."

Maeve knew a moment of guilt, since none of this stuff had belonged to Louisa, but she gratefully stepped into the fragrant kitchen. The cook was pulling two loaves of bread out of the oven, and Maeve inhaled appreciatively.

"Sit down and have some bread and jam. That's yesterday's bread on the table." It would be too soon to slice the new loaves.

Maeve set the unopened canvas bag on the table and did as instructed while the maid poured a glass of water for her.

"You knew Miss Louisa, did you?" the cook asked.

"We lived in the same house," Maeve lied. She was very good at it, unlike Nellie. "We didn't see much of her, though. She was always in her room, writing. I don't know how she found so much to write about."

"We've seen some sadness here lately," the cook said, sinking down into one of the chairs herself.

"I heard Mr. Rodgers died, too," Maeve said. "I was shocked."

"As well you might be. Too much trouble for one family."

"We keep trying to figure out what happened to poor Louisa," Maeve said. "The other girls at the house and me, I mean. We did decide that she probably went back to her office to work late. She did that sometimes."

"Is that what it was?" the cook asked.

"We wondered why she would've been there that late," the maid added. She was hovering by the door as if she knew she should be doing something else but didn't want to miss the conversation.

Maeve took the piece of bread the cook had sliced for her and began to spread it with jam. "The thing I can't figure out, though, is if she was in danger, why she didn't telephone someone for help. I'm sure the magazine must have a telephone line. She didn't call here that night by any chance, did she?"

"That's funny you should say," the cook said. "She did telephone one time. Was it that night, Flo?"

The maid nodded. "I think it was. She asked for her father, but he wasn't expected back until after midnight. I didn't know if Mrs. Rodgers would want to speak with her, so I asked, and she did."

Maeve felt little chills going up her arm. "Did you hear what she said?"

GINO TURNED TO LOOK AT THE MAN WHO HAD SPOKEN to him. "I'm waiting for a lady friend, but I just happened to notice the carriage. I've been thinking of buying one, but I can't decide on what style. That's a brougham, isn't it?"

The man came forward, picking up a rag on the way to wipe his hands. "It is. Just like the kind they use for cabs. Sturdy as they come and gives a comfortable ride. That's why they use them for cabs, you see. Mr. Rodgers, God rest his soul, chose it to use around the city."

"Does the family drive it themselves, then?"

"They could, although I don't think Mrs. Rodgers would even try. They always have me drive it for them, though. Or they did. Now it's just Mrs. Rodgers and her son, but he never uses the carriage."

Was it possible? "So," Gino said as nonchalantly as he could, "you would've been the one who drove Mrs. Rodgers to Rose Hill on Monday night, nearly two weeks ago."

XV

Maeve had directed her question about the telephone call to the maid, who was the most likely one to have overheard Mrs. Rodgers's conversation with Louisa, but she shook her head. "The mistress was mad. She doesn't like getting telephone calls in the evening. She says it upsets her so she can't sleep."

The cook made a rude noise. "She just has to take her medicine and she sleeps like a baby."

The maid winced a little, but she said, "She was saying mean things to Miss Louisa about calling so late, so I tried not to listen."

"How sad that the last time they spoke was an argument," Maeve said.

"Every time they spoke was an argument," the cook said.

"She wasn't quite so mad by the end, though," the maid

said as if trying to defend Mrs. Rodgers. "And in the end, I heard her say she'd tell Mr. Oscar."

"Tell him what?" Maeve said.

The maid shrugged. "I don't know. After she hung up, she asked me to find Mr. Oscar, but I reminded her he was out for the evening."

"She forgets things when she takes her medicine," the cook said.

Maeve was pretty sure Mrs. Rodgers must use her medicine much the same way Mrs. Baker did, with similar results.

"I don't suppose she went out after that, did she?" Maeve said, knowing it was an odd question that might get her a rebuke for being so nosy.

Indeed, both the cook and the maid gave her a disapproving look.

"You seem awful interested in Miss Louisa's family, miss," the cook said.

"We're all interested," Maeve said quickly. "All of us who knew her."

"Well, Flo here will give these things to Mrs. Rodgers, and I'm sure she'll appreciate that you brought them, but I think you'd best be on your way now."

H ow did you know I took Mrs. Rodgers out that night?" the driver asked Gino.

Luckily, he didn't sound offended, only curious.

"I'm investigating Miss Rodgers's death," Gino said. "A witness saw you arrive at the office building."

The man nodded, still not at all alarmed. Was it possible he didn't know what had happened?

"She wasn't in there long. Mrs. Rodgers, I mean. She went inside. Said I should wait with the horses. She said Miss Louisa would be waiting and they'd be right out again."

"And were they?"

"Mrs. Rodgers was, and she was mad as a wet hen. She and Miss Louisa didn't get along, you see. They hardly ever had a kind word to say to each other, so I wasn't surprised."

"Do you think they had a fight when Mrs. Rodgers went inside?"

"Oh no," the driver said quite confidently. "They couldn't've had a fight because Miss Louisa wasn't there."

Gino didn't have to pretend to be surprised. "She wasn't there?"

"No, Mrs. Rodgers said she must've went on home—not here, though. To the place where she was living—and she'd sent us all the way down there for nothing. No wonder Mrs. Rodgers was so mad. And I guess that's how Miss Louisa got herself killed."

"What do you mean?"

The driver shrugged. "Walking around the city alone at night. Mrs. Rodgers told me somebody strangled her, poor girl. If she'd just waited for us that night, she'd still be alive."

Gino was waiting at the electric when Maeve got there.

"Louisa did telephone her father for help that night," she said as soon as she reached him.

"And the Rodgerses own a brougham, which looks just like one of those cabs," Gino said, "especially in the dark. Their driver admitted he took Mrs. Rodgers to the office building that night, too."

"Is it really possible that Mrs. Rodgers killed her own daughter?" Maeve marveled.

"It's starting to look like the only explanation," Gino said. "I'm just glad I'm not the one who has to explain it to Oscar Rodgers."

FRANK WAS WAITING AT THE OFFICE FOR MAEVE AND Gino, and they needed only a few minutes to tell him what they had learned.

"Is it possible the driver really doesn't suspect a thing?" he asked Gino. They had gathered in Frank's office.

"I asked him if he'd read about Louisa's death in the newspapers, but he said he doesn't read newspapers. I gathered that he doesn't read at all, and he chose to believe what Mrs. Rodgers told him and not the gossip going around the neighborhood."

"She must be terrified that he'll figure it out, though," Maeve said. "If she's ever sober enough to think about it at all. The cook and the maid hinted that doesn't happen often."

"Do you suppose Louisa chose to write about patent medicine because of her mother and not Mrs. Baker, like we thought?" Gino asked.

"That does seem more likely," Frank agreed, wishing Sarah were here to give her perspective. "It also might be one of the things they were arguing about."

"From what the servants said, they argued about everything, but maybe Mrs. Rodgers was just trying to even things out since Mr. Rodgers favored Louisa and was so mean to Oscar."

"Neither of them were very good to their children," Frank said.

They all sat in silence for a few moments, mulling over what they now knew.

"Do you know what it means if Mrs. Rodgers really did kill Louisa?" Maeve asked suddenly.

"It means I have to tell my client that his beloved mother murdered his sister," Frank said with a sigh.

"And it also means that Mrs. Rodgers probably killed her husband, too."

"But all the evidence indicated suicide," Gino reminded her.

"Only because we were sure that no one else in that house had a reason to murder him because neither of them had killed Louisa."

"But if Mrs. Rodgers did kill Louisa . . ." Gino said.

". . . then she would have had a good reason to want us to stop our investigation," Frank said in dismay. "I told her myself that we were close to identifying the killer, even though we weren't. I was trying to reassure her. Then the first thing she did after her husband died was fire us."

"And what convinced us that Mr. Rodgers had taken his own life?" Maeve said.

"A pile of papers," Gino said in disgust. "Mrs. Rodgers could have put the sleeping powders in his cocoa and then snuck in later and scattered the papers to make it look like he had done it himself."

"So easy," Maeve murmured.

"And so convincing," Frank said, angry now and mostly with himself for not thinking of it before. How on earth was he going to explain all this to Oscar Rodgers?

They all heard the main office door open and groaned at the interruption. Maeve jumped up to do her duty and greet whoever had arrived.

But she had never met Oscar Rodgers, so he had to tell her who he was. By then Frank was on his feet, having recognized his voice.

"Is Mr. Malloy here by any chance?" Oscar was saying when Frank reached the front office.

He greeted Oscar and made introductions. Then he invited Oscar into his office.

Frank closed the door to give his client at least the illusion that what they discussed would be confidential. Oscar looked troubled today, his usual spirit subdued.

"I guess you're here for an update," Frank said, trying to decide how to begin.

"I hope you have one, yes, but I really came because I . . . I've been thinking about what you said about a witness seeing a woman arriving in a cab that night . . . the night Louisa was killed, I mean."

"Yes, that's true. The witness couldn't identify her because it was too dark, though."

"And you said you thought you knew who the woman was," Oscar said with a slight trace of hopefulness.

"We did think we knew. We thought it was one of the young women who lived in the rooming house with Louisa."

"But it wasn't, was it?" Oscar asked. "I can tell from your voice."

"No, it turned out that she couldn't have been there. We have proof she was at the rooming house all evening."

Oscar rubbed a hand across his mouth. "I was afraid of that."

"Mr. Rodgers—" Frank began, steeling himself for the revelation, but Oscar interrupted him.

"I think it was my mother."

Frank hesitated, not sure he'd heard Oscar correctly. "Why do you think it was your mother?"

"Because she said . . . Well, she said a lot of things after Louisa died. She's been even more disparaging than usual about my sister, continuously listing her faults, both real and imagined, as if she was trying to somehow justify the tragedy of her death. Mr. Malloy, my sister and I never got along, but I certainly never wished her dead. My mother, on the other hand, seems to be rejoicing that she is. I can't imagine what she would have been doing there that night, but . . ."

"Mr. Rodgers," Frank began again, "we have just learned today that your mother *was* the woman our witness saw that night."

"The one in the cab?" Oscar asked in dismay.

"Yes, but it appears it was actually your family's carriage, which would look very much like a cab in the dark. Your driver confirms that he took her to Rose Hill and she went inside the building."

"Did he see . . . ? I mean, did he see what happened?"

"No, and your mother told him Louisa wasn't there, and he took her home again. But our witness found Louisa's body in the lobby only a few minutes later. Your mother couldn't have missed seeing her."

"Then she could have been already dead when mother went in, couldn't she?" Oscar tried.

"It's possible," Frank allowed. Anything was possible, but why hadn't she called for help in that case? He wouldn't point that out to Oscar just yet, though. "There is only one way to know for sure. We need to ask her."

Oscar nodded. "She might lie, though. She . . . she hasn't been herself for a while."

"Is she ill? I remember you said something about her taking some medicine."

"We call it that, but . . . It's not something the doctor gave her."

"A patent medicine?" Frank guessed, certain he was right.

"I suppose you'd call it that."

"Watson's Blood Purifier?"

"Yes," Oscar confirmed in amazement. "How did you know?"

"Louisa was writing an article about it, revealing that it wasn't really medicine at all, but mostly alcohol."

"That's what they fought about most, at the end. Louisa kept saying it was killing her, but Mother insisted it was the only thing that helped her. And you say she was writing an article about it?"

"Yes. The magazine wouldn't publish it, though, which is why Louisa left her job that day."

"Dear heaven," Oscar muttered, rubbing a hand over his face again. "How could this happen?"

Frank had no answer for him. "I'll need to speak with your mother."

Oscar nodded numbly. "Should I be there?"

"You don't have to be, but maybe you could be close by, in case . . ."

"Yes, yes, of course. Are you going to do it now?"

"I'd like to bring my wife along. She's a trained nurse and . . . Well, your mother might get emotional." Frank didn't mention that Sarah would probably do a better job of getting Mrs. Rodgers to confess than he would, too. "I'll have to go home first and explain things to her. Then we'll be along this afternoon. Does that seem reasonable to you?"

"Yes, and if she did . . ." Oscar couldn't bring himself to say it. "What will you do then?"

"That's your decision. You—and your father—hired me to find Louisa's killer. What you do about it is up to you."

BEING A SOCIETY MATRON WAS RATHER BORING. ELIZA-beth Decker did enjoy seeing her friends and hearing the latest gossip, but it was just dinner party after luncheon after fancy dress ball and the same people misbehaving in the usual ways. Was it any wonder she enjoyed helping Frank and Sarah with their cases? Not that they often required help, but even hearing about them gave her something new to think about.

Bernard Rodgers's obituary had appeared in the newspaper this morning. Felix had left those pages and the Society section for her as usual. Sarah hadn't thought that visiting Mrs. Rodgers was a good idea, but the woman must be suffering terribly after losing both her daughter and her husband. She had seemed grateful that Elizabeth and Felix had come to Louisa's funeral, too. The obituary said Mr. Rodgers's funeral had been private, so they wouldn't have an opportunity to express their condolences in person if Elizabeth didn't pay a visit.

Which was the reason she had given herself and why she was standing on the Rodgerses' doorstep and ringing the bell.

The maid who answered glanced at the mourning wreath as if checking to make sure it was still there as a warning to would-be visitors. Elizabeth explained she was a close friend of the family coming to offer Mrs. Rodgers her support at this difficult time. She gave the girl her visiting card to present to her mistress so Mrs. Rodgers could decide if she was "at home" this afternoon.

The maid left her standing in the foyer, but she returned in a few moments to say Mrs. Rodgers would be glad to receive her in the parlor, as Elizabeth had expected. Not many women in the city would turn away Mrs. Felix Decker.

The parlor had been put to rights again after Louisa's funeral and it was tastefully furnished but a bit too formal for Elizabeth's liking. Mrs. Rodgers appeared after about fifteen minutes. Her cheeks were flushed and her eyes red, but she had probably changed her clothes and had her maid tidy her hair before she came down.

"Mrs. Decker, how kind of you to come." She didn't sound particularly grateful, but Elizabeth put that down to her having been disturbed unexpectedly. "May I offer you some tea?"

"That would be lovely." And would help prolong the visit.

Elizabeth waited until Mrs. Rodgers had rung for the maid and ordered the tea. When her hostess had seated herself in a chair opposite hers, Elizabeth said, "I was so sorry to see your husband's obituary this morning. Please accept my condolences."

"Yes, Bernard's death was a shock, but he adored Louisa, and he took her loss very hard."

"I was sorry to see you kept the funeral private. I know my husband would have wanted to pay his respects. He and Mr. Rodgers had been doing business for many years, I understand."

"I simply couldn't face another funeral so soon after Louisa's. My health is rather delicate, you see."

"I had no idea," Elizabeth said, ignoring the red-rimmed eyes and the slight tremor in the woman's hands. "One would never guess to look at you."

"You are too kind. At any rate, I must avoid upsetting situations, so I chose to bury Bernard privately."

"Yes, under the circumstances, I think that was the best choice," Elizabeth said.

But Mrs. Rodgers frowned. "What do you mean by that?" she asked sharply.

"By what?" Elizabeth asked in confusion.

"What *circumstances* are you talking about? What are people saying?"

Elizabeth knew what people were saying, of course, but she said, "Nothing. Nothing at all."

"You're lying," she said, shocking Elizabeth even more. Although people in society lied with great regularity, one did not ever accuse them of it to their faces.

"No, really—"

"What is it you've heard? That Bernard killed himself or that Oscar murdered him *and* Louisa?"

"How awful!" Elizabeth tried. "Why would anyone say such things?"

"Because they're evil and spiteful, but I know that's what they're saying. The men at Oscar's club told him. For his own good, they said."

"Then that's probably why he hired Frank to find out who really killed his sister," Elizabeth said in an effort to calm her.

But Mrs. Rodgers just scowled at her. "Oscar didn't hire anyone . . . Wait a minute. Are you talking about that private detective? What's his name? Malloy?"

Oh dear, she shouldn't have mentioned Frank's name. That was a stupid mistake. How did Sarah manage to remember what she should and shouldn't say to people when she was talking about a case? "Yes, but perhaps I was mistaken—"

"And you called him *Frank*. You know him, don't you? You are on intimate terms with him," she accused.

Elizabeth couldn't allow Mrs. Rodgers to think she and Frank were involved in something illicit. "He's my son-in-law, and I must have been confused about who hired him."

"They were at the funeral, he and his wife, and so were you," Mrs. Rodgers remembered. "But you never said you were related."

"It never came up. I assure you—"

"Are you here on his behalf? Did he tell you to question me?"

"Absolutely not. I told you the truth. I saw Mr. Rodgers's obituary and thought I should pay a condolence call. That's all."

Mrs. Rodgers stared at her for a long, unnerving moment, as if trying to judge her sincerity. Then she stood up. "What can be keeping that girl with our tea?" she said quite pleasantly. "I'll just go check. I won't be a moment." She left in a swish of skirts.

Oh dear. Elizabeth shook her head to clear it. What on earth was wrong with the woman? Grief could do strange things to a person, but she didn't seem particularly grief-stricken, just angry and strange. Elizabeth had made a terrible mistake in coming here. All she had accomplished was upsetting her hostess. She should make an excuse and leave, and she would just as soon as Mrs. Rodgers returned.

I THINK WE HAVE TO BELIEVE THAT MRS. RODGERS IS THE one who killed Louisa," Sarah said when Malloy had told her what Maeve and Gino had learned that morning.

"Yes, even Oscar believes it now," Malloy said. They were in their private parlor upstairs so their servants wouldn't hear. In Sarah's opinion, they were subjected to too much unpleasantness as it was.

"What are you planning to do now?"

"I need to confront her and see if she'll admit it. Oscar must be certain before he decides what to with her."

"Oh, Malloy, what a terrible decision for him. She is his mother, after all."

"It is, but I can't see him just allowing her to remain free. What if she decides she doesn't want to take the chance that *he* will tell someone and kills him, too?"

"She is obviously not thinking clearly, so he should be concerned. When are you going to confront her?"

"I was going to go right now, and I'm hoping you'll go with me. You know how to handle women like her."

"Murderers, you mean?" she asked with some amusement.

"*Society ladies,*" he clarified sternly. "And she also takes Watson's Blood Purifier in excess, according to her cook."

"Yes, I see. *Drunk* society ladies," Sarah said. "I will do my best."

E<small>LIZABETH HAD BEGUN TO THINK SHE SHOULD JUST</small> leave without even telling her hostess after Mrs. Rodgers was gone so long, but finally she returned. Oddly, she was carrying the tea tray herself.

"I'm terribly sorry," she said so sweetly that their previous conversation might never have happened. "That girl is hopeless. I'm going to have to replace her now that Bernard is gone. He would never let me properly discipline the servants, and I'm afraid they've become even more lax now that he's dead." She set the tray down on the sideboard, which was odd, but perhaps she didn't trust herself to put it on the lower table in front of where they were sitting without spilling something. "Do you take milk?"

"No, I, uh, I think I should—"

"Louisa always took milk in her tea," she said, pouring the tea. "Did you ever meet her, Mrs. Decker? She was an amazing young woman. So clever. We shall miss her."

This was a surprise, considering Mrs. Rodgers had never gotten along with her daughter. "I understand she was writing an article for the magazine she worked for."

"Yes, but she said they wouldn't publish it," Mrs. Rodgers

said. "That's why she walked out. She was coming home, you know. That's what she told me."

Mrs. Rodgers carried over their two cups. They rattled a bit in their saucers, but she managed not to spill them. She handed Elizabeth one of them. With milk, Elizabeth noticed in surprise. "I think you gave me yours."

But when she looked, the other cup had milk as well. Not that it mattered. She was going to make her excuses and leave.

"No, I gave you the right cup. I was very careful," Mrs. Rodgers said. Her hands were still trembling a bit. She must be inebriated, which explained the confusion about the milk and why Mrs. Rodgers was being so careful. "Did I tell you Louisa was coming home? They didn't appreciate her at the magazine. That's what she said."

"I remember at Louisa's funeral you chastened that man who owns the magazine," Elizabeth said to make conversation. But then she suddenly realized something she hadn't before. When had Louisa had an opportunity to speak with her mother about what had happened at the magazine that last day? Mrs. Rodgers had already known about it at the funeral, and she had said Louisa had told her, but when had this conversation happened? It would have had to take place between the time Louisa left the magazine office and when she died, and hardly anyone had seen her during that time period.

Except her killer.

Something must have shown on Elizabeth's face because Mrs. Rodgers nodded as if she'd spoken her thoughts aloud. "Drink your tea, Mrs. Decker, before it gets cold."

• • •

Malloy had reclaimed the electric from Gino and Maeve so he could drive Sarah to the Rodgerses' house. The neighborhood was peaceful in the early-afternoon hours. They had no sooner parked the motorcar than Oscar Rodgers appeared beside them.

"Did you just get here?" Malloy asked as he held the door open for Sarah.

"I've been here awhile, but I didn't go in. I decided I didn't want to have to talk to her until . . ."

"Until you know for sure," Sarah said. "I understand." And she did. No one wanted to believe such horrible things about their mother.

Oscar led them to the porch and up the steps. He opened the door with his key and escorted them inside.

"Oscar, is that you?" his mother called from the parlor.

Oscar sighed and gave Sarah and Malloy a look of dismay. "I thought she'd be in her rooms," he whispered before saying, "Yes, Mother, and I've brought some visitors."

He went ahead into the open parlor door with Sarah and Malloy close behind, but he stopped short.

"I see you already have a visitor," he said uncertainly. They couldn't miss her because Mrs. Decker had instantly risen to her feet at the sight of them.

"Yes, I do, and look who my son has brought. Quite a little family reunion, isn't it?" his mother said.

Sarah couldn't hide her consternation at finding her mother here after she had explicitly told her not to visit Mrs. Rodgers. Well, maybe not *explicitly*, but she'd certainly tried to warn her away. Then she realized what Mrs. Rodgers had said: *family reunion.* She knew about their relationship, too.

"We were just discussing poor Louisa's last disappointment," Mrs. Rodgers was saying. "Did you know she was writing a terrible piece about Watson's Blood Purifier? She said she was planning to put them out of business so I would never be able to use it again, but the man who owned the magazine wouldn't publish the article, thank heaven. That's why she left her position."

Sarah stepped around Oscar and moved closer to Mrs. Rodgers, smiling so the woman wouldn't be alarmed. "Perhaps you'd like to take some of your medicine now," she said, realizing from the tremor in her voice that the woman was teetering on the edge of hysteria.

"Mrs. Rodgers was just explaining that Louisa had told her all about the article *after she left the magazine office that last day,*" Sarah's mother said rather urgently.

"Yes," Sarah said, moving closer to where Mrs. Rodgers still sat. "I understand you spoke with Louisa shortly before she died." Hopefully, her mother would understand what they had discovered.

"Yes, I did speak with her," Mrs. Rodgers said, oddly proud.

"Mother," Oscar said in anguish, but Malloy grabbed his arm to silence him.

Mrs. Rodgers looked at Oscar with pity. "Poor boy. You tried so hard, but you could never be as smart as she was, could you?"

Oscar made a distressed sound, but he didn't move.

"Mrs. Rodgers," Sarah said gently, "we know you went to

help Louisa that night after she telephoned you. What happened when you went inside the building?"

"I told her I was glad to see she had finally come to her senses and realized that decent women are content to marry and stay at home, raising their children. That's what I thought she had chosen, you see, because she had wanted her father to bring the carriage to get her at the office and then take her to the rooming house to collect her things because she had decided to come home."

"But wasn't that what you wanted, Mother?" Oscar reminded her desperately.

His mother sighed. "Yes, but it wasn't what *she* wanted. She laughed and told me she had no intention of marrying or having children. She was going to find someone else to publish her article and she was going to make sure Watson's didn't poison anyone else again, and then she was going to keep writing and keep exposing other companies that did evil things."

"That must have made you angry," Sarah said, wanting to weep at the way this family had torn itself apart.

"I couldn't listen to her anymore. I wanted her to stop talking such nonsense, so I put my hands around her throat and—"

She stopped when Sarah's mother gasped in horror.

Mrs. Rodgers sighed again. "It's all over now, I suppose." She picked up her teacup and drank down the last of it.

Sarah saw the two teacups sitting on the low table and had an awful thought. "Mother, did you drink anything while you were here?"

"Just the tea, but not much because she put milk in it and

I never take milk, and when I took a sip, it tasted bitter, so I didn't drink any more and—"

"Oh dear," Mrs. Rodgers said lightly. "I guess I wasn't as careful as I thought." She picked up the other cup and before anyone could react, drained it as well.

"What on earth . . . ?" Oscar muttered, but Sarah guessed.

She hurried over, snatched the cup out of Mrs. Rodgers's hand, and peered inside. "What's this residue in the bottom? What did you put in it?"

Mrs. Rodgers just smiled. "Oscar, I never intended to make things hard for you. I know there's gossip now, but it will die down and people will forget."

"Mother, what have you done?" Oscar cried, watching Sarah sniff the cup, then dip her finger in the residue and touch it to her tongue.

"Your father went very peacefully, so I will, too," Mrs. Rodgers said. "I should have let Louisa ruin her life instead of trying to save her. No good ever comes of that, does it?"

"She must have taken sleeping powders," Sarah had determined from the taste. Arsenic had no taste and cyanide smelled like bitter almonds. "Someone send for a doctor."

"No, no doctors," Mrs. Rodgers said firmly. "This won't take long. I drank a whole bottle of my medicine just now, too, to help things along. Did you know I had to drink a whole bottle the night I . . . the night Louisa died, too? I couldn't stop shaking."

"I'll get a doctor," Malloy said, but Oscar caught his arm before he could move.

"No, that's not what she wants," he said.

"But you can't just let her die," Sarah said. "Perhaps an

emetic . . . I don't have my bag, but you could send someone—"

"*No!* She killed Louisa, and she must have killed Father, too," Oscar said. "What will become of her if she lives? Prison or even worse. I won't allow it."

"You're a good boy, Oscar. You always were," his mother said, but her words were slurring, and she had leaned back in her chair, her head lolling.

Oscar went to her, kneeling beside her chair, and he took her hand in both of his. "I'm here, Mother."

"Good boy," she murmured. Her eyes closed.

Oscar looked up at them looming over her chair. "Get out. All of you."

"But—" Malloy tried.

"Saving her now would be cruel," Oscar said. "I'll just say I found her like this. We'll say she died of grief, like Father did. No one will ever have to know the truth."

"Mr. Rodgers—" Sarah said.

"Just go. Don't make me throw you out bodily," Oscar cried.

Sarah's mother was already heading for the door.

"We can't just leave them," Malloy said.

But Sarah shook her head. "She's already unconscious, and she drank all that alcohol . . . I don't think even a doctor can help her now, no matter how quickly he could get here. And if we do save her, then what? You said yourself that Oscar might not be safe if he decides not to turn her over to the police, and if he does, she'd be locked away for the rest of her life or perhaps even executed."

"I'm showing her mercy, Malloy," Oscar told them. "I'm

letting her execute herself. It's the least I can do after the way she protected me from Father all those years."

"Wait until you're sure she's dead," Sarah told him. "Then send for the doctor. Tell him you thought she was just asleep after taking her medicine, but you couldn't wake her up."

"And wash out that cup," Malloy added as Sarah started hustling him out of the room.

Her mother was waiting in the hall, pulling on her gloves.

"What on earth were you doing here, Mother?" Sarah said.

Malloy opened the door for them, and they hurried out of the house.

"Paying a condolence call," her mother said meekly as they walked down the front steps. "Do you think she actually meant that poison for me?"

"I don't think we want to know the answer to that question. We will choose to believe she got the cups mixed up," Sarah said, finding herself in the awkward position of chastening her mother.

"You mustn't ever tell your father about this," her mother said. "He'll never let me out of the house again."

"Don't worry," Malloy assured her. "Your secret is perfectly safe."

"But did we do the right thing, do you think?" her mother asked.

Sarah looked at Malloy, silently asking his opinion.

"I don't think there is a right thing in this situation. We know it wouldn't have been safe to let her remain free, and her future would have been awful if we turned her over to the police," Malloy said. "Oscar decided to show her mercy, whether she deserved it or not. It was his choice to make, not ours."

"It would have been a terrible scandal if she had been arrested, too," Sarah's mother pointed out. "Oscar is the only one who would have suffered for that."

"And he is the only truly innocent one," Sarah said. "Gossip will be bad enough as it is, but if he just sticks to his story that his parents died of grief, it will eventually pass."

"Oh dear, I think my hands are shaking," her mother said.

"Don't even think of taking some patent medicine," Sarah said. "A glass of Father's brandy should do just as well. Now let's get you home."

Maeve had been to Mass often enough with Mrs. Malloy and Brian that she now knew when to sit and when to stand and when to kneel. Mrs. Malloy had taught her the prayers to say with the rosary, too, although she wasn't sure what that was supposed to accomplish. She hadn't had the courage to try to take Communion yet, though. You had to go to confession first, and she wasn't too sure how that would work since she hadn't done anything she was sorry for.

Still, she enjoyed the ritual and the beauty. The church was gorgeous and smelled lovely, unlike many parts of the city. Being here today with Gino was nice, too, even if it wasn't proper for them to hold hands in the sanctuary. The only bad part was that they had to go to the Donatellis' house for Sunday dinner afterward.

Gino offered his arm for the short walk to his parents' house.

"Do you ever go to confession?" Maeve asked.

"Sometimes."

"What do you confess?"

He grinned. "Well, let's see . . . I tell the priest that there's this pretty red-haired girl I lust after . . ."

She swatted him, making him laugh.

"You know what would make this day perfect?" he asked when he had stopped laughing.

"Yes, but sadly for you, I'm not that kind of girl," she replied cheekily.

He chuckled. "Well, that, too, but I was thinking more along the lines of announcing our engagement."

Heat prickled her face as a knot formed in her stomach. "Are you asking me to marry you?"

"Not until I know you'll say yes. I figure I only have one chance, and I don't want to waste it."

"Coward," she said.

"Guilty," he replied. "You're very scary, Miss Smith."

Actually, she was very scared, but she said, "Maybe you should just try your luck."

He stopped dead in his tracks, forcing her to stop, too, much to the annoyance of the other pedestrians crowding the sidewalk. "Right here?" he asked in surprise.

"Why not?" she challenged.

But he shook his head. "I want it to be nice. I'll surprise you."

A man walking by jostled Gino. "Do your mooning someplace else," he snapped.

Gino started walking again, taking Maeve along with him.

"When? When will you surprise me?" she demanded.

"It won't be a surprise if I tell you."

"And what if I say no?"

"You won't."

"You're awfully sure of yourself all of a sudden."

He didn't respond to that. He just kept walking, a smug look on his handsome face.

"Did your mother really say she'd like red-haired grandchildren?" she asked suddenly.

"No, but she will," Gino replied.

"If we get married, everything will change," she tried.

"Yes, but it will work out."

"How do you know?"

He stopped again and this time he pulled her into a nearby doorway so they wouldn't be blocking the sidewalk. "Maeve, I know your life has been a lot tougher than mine. You've lost a lot and your family is gone and you've been disappointed over and over, but you can trust me. I won't disappoint you, and whatever happens, we can figure it out together."

She thought that over for a minute. "Then maybe I will marry you," she said.

He grinned, his dark eyes gleaming with mischief. "But I haven't asked you yet."

"No," she said, echoing his own certainty, "but you will."

Author's Note

THE *NEW CENTURY* MAGAZINE IS A FICTIONAL INVENTION
of mine, based loosely on *McClure's Magazine*, which was
publishing at that time and whose offices were in the building where I placed the *New Century* magazine. This story is
set in September of 1901, when Ida Tarbell was just starting
to think about the famous series of articles she would publish the following year exposing the corruption behind the
rise of John D. Rockefeller and the Standard Oil Company.
Tarbell and others continued to write exposés of various
businesses, a type of journalism that was dubbed *muckraking*
by President Theodore Roosevelt in a speech he made in
1906, although he didn't mean it as a compliment.

Most muckraking was done as nonfiction, but fiction
proved a valuable tool as well. Upton Sinclair wrote *The
Jungle*—a book you probably read in high school—to arouse

sympathy for immigrants by exposing the horrible conditions in which they were forced to work in the meatpacking industry. Instead, it aroused outrage in consumers when they realized how unsanitary the food they were eating was. Sinclair lamented that he had aimed to hit America in the heart but hit them in the stomach instead.

The work of the muckrakers led to such legislation as the Pure Food and Drug Act and antitrust legislation, which Theodore Roosevelt happily signed and which changed the way America did business.

I loosely based Louisa Rodgers on the real Ida Tarbell, who was a teacher before getting a job at *McClure's Magazine.* She was first allowed to edit and then to write articles herself. She wrote a series on the life of Abraham Lincoln that was collected and published as a book, as were her articles on Standard Oil. Her father had been an oil distributor in Pennsylvania who was put out of business by John D. Rockefeller, which may have motivated her to write the exposé. Today we would call the muckrakers *investigative journalists.* They have uncovered a lot of evil through the decades and inspired a lot of change.

President McKinley was indeed assassinated as I described. Sadly, he received very poor medical care. This was partly because medical science was still not very advanced but also because the doctors who attended him were not experienced in treating wounds like his. Ironically, there was a primitive X-ray machine on display at the exposition where McKinley was shot, but no one considered using it to locate and remove the bullet the doctors had been unable to find and which ultimately killed him. The doctors did continue to insist the president would make a full recovery right up until he died.

Please let me know if you enjoyed this book, and if you send me an email through my website, www.Victoria Thompson.com, I will put you on my mailing list and send you a reminder when my next book comes out. Or follow me on Facebook at Victoria.Thompson.Author or Twitter @GaslightVT.